After leaving full-time education Terry Cade became an apprentice joiner. He then continued his studies at college and worked in a joiner's workshop, on many construction sites, in a builder's office, with an architectural practice, as a college lecturer, and has been self employed on three occasions.

He's built two wooden boats. The first was a dinghy, which he sailed mainly on the River Mersey. The second was an offshore cruising sloop in which he sailed the Irish Sea and beyond, with friends, and sometimes single handedly.

He likes cats, and dogs taking their owners for walks. He is married with children and grandchildren. He lives modestly in the beautiful county of Cheshire.

THE MAN WHOSE BOAT CAME IN

TERRY CADE

GALAXIA

Published in 2008 by
Galaxia
Cheshire

ISBN 978-0-9558424-0-5

Printed and bound by Highlight Print Ltd,
Warrington, Cheshire.

Cover illustration by Steve McGrail.

This book can be ordered direct from the publisher.
But try your bookshop first.

galaxia@btinternet.com

To my family.
Who prevent me from having dull moments.

N

Loch Riddon

Bute

Largs

Lochranza

ARRAN

Firth of Clyde

Mull of Kintyre

Ailsa Craig

Portpatrick

NORTH CHANNEL

Mull of Galloway

Solway Firth

NORTHERN IRELAND

ISLE OF MAN

Douglas

River Lune

Wyre Marina

Fleetwood

River Wyre

Clitheroe

Blackpool

Preston

River Ribble

IRISH SEA

Frampton Marina

Liverpool

ANGLESEY

Miles 0   10   20   30   40

Chapter 1

Mr and Mrs Bantry had run the Burnside guest house for 32 years. Mr Bantry was originally from Burnley, where he was a joiner in the construction industry. He applied for the position of woodwork teacher at a Blackpool secondary modern school, now a comprehensive, was offered the job and had been middle-class ever since.

Mrs Bantry was a nurse in Burnley, but on their arrival in Blackpool, recognising the potential for self employment and (hopefully) financial success, took out a mortgage on 12 Victoria Road – a three-storey Victorian terrace house, with a cellar, a small front garden and a large back yard. All the rooms were of a good size with the potential for splitting some into two, and they obtained planning permission for change of use.

As well as working as a woodwork teacher Mr Bantry had assisted in the running of the guest house, dealing with maintenance and fixing of wooden items such as wardrobes, bath panels, cupboards, bed heads, radiator shelves and doors. Most of these were made between the hours of four and six; on those evenings he was paid overtime for teaching woodwork to adults, whose lessons started at six.

All in all they now had a rather nice guest house, with a rear extension, six en-suite bedrooms, lounge, dining room and kitchen. Mr Bantry was a dab hand with a paint brush and roller. Each winter he'd delight in bringing all the rooms back to pristine order. He'd decorate the walls and ceilings in neutral shades, then add ornate paper borders to give them a splash of colour, then gloss paint the doors, architraves and skirting boards. The carpets had a floral design, with reds and greens intermingled; they'd be steam cleaned, along with the lounge sofas and chairs. Mrs Bantry liked frilly things. The cushion covers, chair backs and pillowcases were testimony to this fact. She also liked to place ornaments and vases on horizontal surfaces, especially on window bottoms and radiator shelves; also, all the lavatory cisterns in the en-suite bathrooms had a *Thank you for not Smoking* notice clearly displayed upon them. The property had been awarded three crowns in the Lancashire Good Guest House Guide. Mr & Mrs Bantry lived in the basement, which was a little damp and seldom decorated.

Mr Bantry never felt happy or fulfilled as a woodwork teacher; he often thought it would have been better had he remained in the construction industry where he felt comfortable. When he became a woodwork teacher he stepped out of his comfort zone. What with all the kids knowing more than him, knowing their rights … he considered them cheeky little gets, half the time they had no interest in the subject. Parents' evenings produced parents he considered wealthier and more successful than him. And he always felt inferior to his more academic and eloquent colleagues. But that was all behind him now. He'd recently retired with his index-linked pension, telling himself that he'd led a happy life. But deep down he felt neither happiness nor fulfilment.

Mrs Bantry was a big woman with a round red face, a huge personality, and a caring and friendly demeanour, well suited to the hospitality industry. Mr Bantry, on the other hand, was a thin, gaunt man, easily forgettable, lacking in personality. Mrs Bantry suggested he should get out more often. Some evenings he would walk to one of the many local pubs and have a couple of pints. Although he enjoyed a drink, he was racked with guilt at spending so much money on so little pleasure, and seldom spoke to anybody in the pub. But Mrs Bantry kept every Monday evening free to go out with the girls for a game of bingo and a 'good old-fashioned chin wag', as she put it.

The guest house had been busy over the past month. This July Saturday morning was like any other July Saturday morning as far as the Bantrys were concerned, with one set of guests vacating their rooms 'by 10.00 am', and another set of guests arriving 'not before 2.00 pm'. This provided the opportunity of cleaning the house from top to bottom and changing the bed linen. Full English breakfast was the norm and usually served between 8.00 and 9.00am. Mrs Bantry prided herself on ensuring guests enjoyed the very best Blackpool breakfast. Knives and forks were heavy, all china was plain white and thin, and napkins were contained in plastic rings. Bacon could be ordered well done or lightly grilled. Eggs could be ordered fried, poached or scrambled. Sausages were organic. Tomatoes were always fresh. 'None of that tinned muck', as she would say several times per week during the summer months, and her mushrooms were a delight to behold. Guests rarely asked for anything other than the standard cuisine, apart from the occasional boiled egg. These would be hard or soft, as preferred. Mrs Bantry had developed that unique ability to precisely time the egg boiling pan, and any recipient of a Bantry breakfast boiled egg knew, with the first strike of a spoon, that perfection was guaranteed.

It was a warm sunny day with a little high wispy cirrus cloud and light breeze. The dining room windows were open, traffic noise and squawking gulls could be heard, and most of the guests had by now left the premises. But by 10.00am the nice single gentleman, who for two nights had occupied room No. 3 on the first floor, had not come down for breakfast.

Mrs Bantry prided herself, after all these years in business, on her ability to judge people on their arrival. Some guests returned year after year whereas others were just passing through, staying just for the odd night or two. The bad ones seemed to have something to hide, gave false names and addresses, and paid in cash. Mrs Bantry knew the signs. And Mr Thompson, 4 Elm Road, Cirencester in room 3 was obviously a gentleman, with his neatly pressed trousers and cotton shirts. But where was he today? Mr Bantry was finishing off in the kitchen when his wife came in.

'Stanley, I wonder what's happened to Mr Thompson? I hope there's nothing wrong with him, he hasn't come down for breakfast.'

There had been regret in her voice as she thought she may have misjudged Mr Thompson. Mr Bantry was still busying himself with the final wiping down of the surfaces, with tea towel in hand.

'Ethel, he came in pissed last night, sorry, this morning, the front door slammed about one, he'll be sleeping it off, now go and wake the drunken bugger up.'

Ethel climbed the stairs and boldly knocked on the door of No. 3. No answer. She turned the handle and found the door was unlocked. She slowly poked her head around the door and, although the curtains were drawn closed, she could see Mr Thompson lying in bed beneath the sheets. She knocked several more times with the door ajar. No response. Unable to venture further into the room, she returned to the kitchen to explain things to Stanley.

'Good God, Ethel, can't you do a simple job like wake the bugger up, I'll sort him.'

Stanley went through the same routine as Ethel but to no avail. In spite of rapping firmly and continually on the door there was no response.

'Well,' said Stanley. 'He's either dead drunk or just plain dead.'

'Oh, you don't think so, do you, Stanley?'

'I bloody well do.'

With that, they both entered the room, opened the curtains and saw that Mr Thompson looked to be in a tranquil state, most certainly at peace with the world and was most certainly dead.

In all of their years in the hospitality industry they'd

never before had to deal with a situation like this and were unsure what to do. They knew, however, that room No. 3 had to be made ready before 2.00pm, for that was when their next guests, Mr and Mrs Jolly, from Rawtenstall, were due to arrive.

At Regent Road Police Station, Constable Johnny Johnston had been assigned the task of manning the desk this bright Saturday morning and was feeling 'bleeding rough', as he had just informed one of his fresh-faced colleagues. The reason for his discomfort was his general lack of discipline. He hated the 6 till 2 shift which meant he had to be up before 5.00am to prepare himself for the day ahead. But Johnny Johnston being Johnny Johnston tended to forget about such matters when he arrived at the pub in the evening. And last night being Friday he'd had a skinful. But not to worry, this was the last of 'the dead dog shifts', as he'd begun to call them, and after a few days off he would be returning to the far more civilised 2 till 10 shift.

He enjoyed the 2 till 10 shift, which provided him with an opportunity to have a lie-in each morning, take a leisurely breakfast, read the paper and, sometimes, have a spot of lunch from the chippy, before preparing himself for the tasks ahead. His favourite lunch was chips, steak pudding and peas. This always seemed to set him up for the day. Another advantage of that shift, which always proved to be compatible with his natural body clock, was the fact that he could often engineer an early dart in the evening, enabling him to be in attendance at his favourite watering hole by 10.00pm.

Here, he was a popular member of the last orders brigade.

Johnny had two sisters, each of them older than him. He'd been educated at the local primary and secondary schools, before attending catering college where he'd trained to become a chef. He'd always been overweight. As a child his mother would say he had big bones and a little puppy fat, which he would shed as he got older. His school friends, who were less kind, referred to it as whale blubber. But to be fair to Johnny, after applying at the age of 19 to join the police, he took to visiting a gymnasium and shed a considerable amount of weight. Johnny completed his police training at the Bruche Police Training Centre in Warrington, and returned to his native Blackpool as a fully fledged member of the Lancashire Constabulary. That was 20 years ago and much water had gone under the bridge since then. He had a wife Sarah and twin teenage boys John and Jim who, in spite of his many failings, simply adored him. He'd always been good fun and was the life and soul of any social gathering.

Johnny was still overweight; in fact, he was bordering on being clinically obese, and resembled many such policemen in many constabularies around the country who had become afflicted by a weight problem. But all this added to the character of the man whose friends and colleagues had come to like and respect.

It was 10.15 when the telephone rang. 'Good morning. This is the Regent Road Police Station, Constable Johnston speaking, how may I help?' This was the way desk personnel had been taught to answer the telephone, in a 'customer-friendly manner', before they were inspected for their Investors in People Award.

'Good morning, Constable, this is Mrs Bantry from the Burnside Guest House, we have a problem.'

'Is that B-A-N-T-R-Y?'

'Yes, it is.'

'And address?'

'12 Victoria Road.'

'And telephone number?'

'Blackpool 46789.'

'What seems to be the trouble, Mrs Bantry?'

'Well, we've had a gentleman staying with us for a couple of nights and we've found him dead in bed this morning.'

'Oh dear, you wouldn't know if the gentleman has been on medication, would you?'

'No.'

'Or if he has a local doctor?'

'No.'

'Do you have his name and address?'

'Yes, it's Mr Thompson, 4 Elm Road, Cirencester.'

'Very well, Mrs Bantry, we'll have someone pop round in about fifteen minutes.'

'Thank you, Constable.'

The man in charge of the morning shift was Sergeant Skinner, a wholesome, friendly character who looked as if he should have retired before now.

'Sarge, we've got another death in a hotel.'

'It's amazing, Johnny, you can't believe it, can you? That's five this week. It's this bloody hot weather, they're dropping like flies. Dr Cunningham will be over

16

the moon, you'd better tell him and meet him down there, you look as if you could do with some fresh air.'

Doctor Cunningham was the police doctor on duty to deal with occurrences of this type; he'd attended four such deaths this week, established by visual examination that the deaths were due to natural causes, and, in each case, following post-mortem examination, his prognosis had been proven correct.

'Thank God you've arrived, Constable, me and Stanley are beside ourselves with worry, aren't we, Stanley?'

'Please don't worry, Mrs Bantry, we've had a few similar cases this week, it's this hot weather. Dr Cunningham will be along shortly then we'll look at the body.'

'Cup of tea, Constable?'

'That would be very nice, Mrs Bantry.'

'Would you like to sit in the lounge?'

'Thank you.'

Johnny Johnston had found that when people offered him a cup of tea, the tea had normally been accompanied by a plate of biscuits of various flavours, and on this occasion he was not to be disappointed. Mrs Bantry provided him with tea and a plate containing many of his favourite plain chocolate digestives.

Mrs Bantry didn't think Dr Cunningham, the man standing in the glazed vestibule, looked much like a doctor, with his worn baggy corduroy trousers and open-neck shirt. But he did have a black bag with him. He was of medium height and build – in fact, a very ordinary looking chap.

'Good morning, I'm Doctor Cunningham, you must be Mrs Bantry?'

'I am. Please come in, Doctor.'

'What are you doing to me, Johnny? There's never any peace when you're on duty.'

'Nothing to do with me, Doc. I only take the messages.'

'Would you like to lead the way, Mrs Bantry?'

'This way, Doctor.'

Mrs Bantry showed them to room No. 3, Johnny and the doctor entered. They each inspected their surroundings. Johnny ensured that no disturbance had been caused which may suggest foul play. And Doctor Cunningham, concerning himself with the body, folded down the sheets and examined the chest, opening and closing the eyelids, and establishing the progress of rigor mortis. He decided that death had occurred through natural causes, possibly the heart, about seven hours earlier, and explained his findings to Johnny. He said goodbye to Mrs Bantry and left Johnny to arrange for the removal of the body to the mortuary, together with Mr Thompson's belongings, which were packed into his suitcase, and to arrange for relatives to be notified. The ambulance arrived at midday, and removed all evidence of Mr Thompson. Johnny returned to Regent Road Police Station, communicated with Gloucester Police, wrote up his report, and decided to sample the 'hair of the dog' on his way home.

By the time the body had been removed, the house had been thoroughly cleaned and linen changed, apart from room No. 3. So both Stanley and Ethel got stuck in and gave it a good going over. All was spick and span by 2.00pm.

Stanley was never happier than when the guest house was full, and full it was on that Saturday evening. He and Ethel discussed the day's events in their basement flat, decided they had done all that could be done, treated themselves to a sherry, and retired to bed.

Sunday was just as hot as Saturday. One of Stanley's delights at breakfast time was to count heads in the dining room and multiply the number by the B&B rate, then by seven, to try to establish weekly income. The little ritual always cheered him up at this time of year.

Chapter 2

'Good morning, this is the Regent Road Police Station, Constable Hughes speaking, how may I help?'

'Good morning, Constable, this is Sergeant Jenkins of the Gloucester Police, is Constable Johnston available?'

'Sorry, Sergeant, he's not in until Tuesday afternoon, can I help?'

'Well, maybe you can. He's provided us with an incorrect address for a deceased person who was holidaying in Blackpool and we need it checking out.'

'Is there a reference number?'

'J6832.'

'Okay. Yes, the files to hand and the address is … let me see, yes, it's 4 Elm Road, Cirencester.'

'Well, Constable, there appears to be a cock up. There is a 4 Elm Road in Cirencester, but nobody there knows of any friend or relative by the name of Mr Thompson. So we are assuming an incorrect address has been provided. Would you check it out with Constable Johnston and get back to me? Preferably today.'

'Very well, Sergeant, will do.'

Johnny was contemplating a leisurely Sunday liquid lunch, when the phone rang.

'Hello.'

'Johnny, it's Pat.'

'Hi, Pat. What's up, mate?'

'Gloucester have been on. The address you gave them yesterday was wrong.'

'Get away.'

'Nobody at that address knows a Mr Thompson.'

'Bloody hell. That's the address in the visitors' book!'

'Did you see the visitors' book yourself?'

'No. Mrs Bantry gave me the address.'

'Johnny. You're going to have to look at it yourself and if it is 4 Elm Road you'll have to go through his wallet and possessions at the mortuary, to find out exactly who he is. They want a reply today.'

'Alright, leave it with me.'

Johnny drove to the guest house, rang the bell and was greeted by Mrs Bantry.

'Hello, Constable, sorry about all the fuss yesterday, what can I do for you? You look younger out of uniform.'

'Mrs Bantry, the address you gave me for Mr Thompson, could you have made a mistake?'

'I don't think so, Constable, come and look for yourself.'

Sure enough, there was no doubting the address in the visitors' book. It read 4 Elm Road, Cirencester.

'Thank you very much, Mrs Bantry.'

'Lovely day again, Constable?'

'Yes, Mrs Bantry, it is. Goodbye.'

Johnny took himself down to the mortuary, where he knew the body and possessions would be. He introduced himself to the technician who quickly located the possessions, which were handed to Johnny for inspection. Every pocket of every coat was turned inside out. So was every pocket of every pair of trousers. All the compartments of Mr Thompson's luggage were opened and inspected. No driving licence, no credit or debit cards, no receipts, no club membership cards, £150-00 in an envelope in the inside pocket of his sports jacket, no watch, no rings. Nothing to identify the body.

He established that the post-mortem examination was scheduled for Monday afternoon, and set off for Regent Road Police Station. On arriving, he rang Sergeant Jenkins of Gloucester Police to explain what had happened.

'Okay, Constable, if you find he's from our patch let me know.'

'I will do, Sergeant, thank you very much, bye.'

Pat Hughes was still on the desk and he and Johnny discussed the strange details. After giving the matter due consideration they decided that Johnny should put Sergeant Skinner in the picture.

'Hello.'

'Hello, Mrs Skinner. Is Eric there? It's Johnny.'

'Oh. Hello, Johnny, love. I'll just get him.'

Johnny explained all he knew to Sergeant Skinner who'd decided that nothing had changed, other than the fact that they had no name and address, and the way they proceeded would depend on the outcome of the post-mortem examination. The results of the examination should be available on Tuesday.

'So, Johnny, don't you worry yourself about it, son, go and have a pint as you normally do.'

'Thanks, Eric, see you Tuesday.'

Johnny arrived on Tuesday for his favourite shift, as one

of his colleagues was leaving the station.

'Afternoon, Johnny, good weekend?'

'Yeah, great.'

Johnny was lying. It had been a dreadful few days. Since speaking with Eric Skinner on Sunday it had gone from bad to worse. He'd felt personally responsible for the cock up. Maybe if he hadn't got drunk on Friday night he would have felt fresh and alert on Saturday; maybe he would have looked to inspect Mr Thompson's possessions. Maybe, had the present information been available, Dr Cunningham would have been more cautious with his prognosis and maybe, if a crime had taken place, the scene of crime officers and forensic team would have found evidence. But with the room no doubt having been cleaned and new guests installed, any evidence would have been obliterated. He was desperate for the post-mortem examination to reveal that Mr Thompson had died from natural causes. Sergeant Skinner was at his desk when Johnny arrived.

'Afternoon, Sarge.'

'Afternoon, Johnny. We've got to go and see Superintendent Hird. Mr Thompson's cause of death … lethal injection.'

'Fucking hell.'

Chapter 3

Jeffrey Dewhurst had been born at the Preston Royal Infirmary to Marie and Robert Dewhurst, both aged 24. They were ordinary, hard-working people, who'd looked after the pennies. They lived in a natural stone cottage with a slated roof in Swinebeck, a small village in the Ribble Valley, about four miles from Ribchester, off the Clitheroe Road. The rear garden backed onto a field, in which sheep usually grazed. At the bottom of the field flowed the crystal clear waters of the River Ribble.

When Jeffrey was three, his sister Angela was born. Jeffrey and Angela proved to be healthy children, never sickly, only suffering the minor illnesses that all children suffer. They enjoyed their childhood with relatives, neighbours and friends, in the beautiful Ribble Valley.

In the cottage next door lived Jeffrey's Uncle Harold, his father's brother, the local cabinet maker and a confirmed bachelor. Next to Uncle Harold's cottage stood a stone stable, which he'd converted into a workshop when he became self employed, and in which he'd inserted extra windows to improve the light. Jeffrey was mesmerised by the many tools of Uncle Harold's craft. The saws, planes, chisels, gouges, squares, dividers and many more. The tools were hung from racks, specially designed and constructed to accommodate them, and fixed to the wall by the side of his workbench.

Jeffrey always remembered a particular occasion when he was eight years old. Uncle Harold was going to collect an item of furniture from the french polisher in the next village and deliver it to a customer. It wasn't possible to french polish items in his uncles' workshop as it was too dusty. Jeffrey accompanied his uncle to the french polishers, and while he'd seen lots of his uncles' work before polishing, he'd not seen a completed piece until now.

'Corr, Uncle Harold, have you made this?'

'I'm afraid so, Jeff.'

'Can I make one?'

'Well, you never know, one day perhaps.'

Jeffrey was never happier than when he was in the workshop helping his uncle. Harold encouraged him and taught him to use the various tools of the trade. Little by little, Jeffrey became more confident and was able to make small items of joinery. Uncle Harold taught him how to make dovetails. Though this task proved difficult, Jeffrey was tenacious and eventually succeeded. He and his uncle made a tool box for him and painted it black. Uncle Harold put some tools in it for Jeffrey's use.

Harold used to say to his friends that when Jeffrey came into his workshop it was like the sunlight streaming through a window and lighting a darkened room.

At school, Jeffrey was not particularly academic, though he'd been quite good at technical drawing, geometry and maths. These were the subjects that interested him most and while he'd never excelled in any one subject he'd managed to achieve good results in these subject areas.

During the summer months he would often go with his friends across the field, down to the river where they would fish, and sometimes swim in the deep pools. Because they lived close to the river, parents ensured their children could swim at an early age and that they were well aware of the dangers involved.

There was also Uncle Harry. He was really Jeffrey's mother's uncle who lived with his wife Amy in Warrington. Their two children were grown up now and had left home. Harry and Amy lived in a small modern house on the outskirts of the town, about 500 metres from the River Mersey. Since being a teenager Uncle Harry had kept a boat on the river. He'd spent the war years between 1939 and 1944 in the Royal Navy, patrolling the North Atlantic in a minesweeper and the sea was in his blood. He'd often regaled his friends with tales of his exploits, suitably embellished to turn Harry into the hero who had saved the nation from Mr Hitler.

As Harry had recently retired and had spare time on his hands, he'd suggested to Marie, Jeffery's mother, that Jeffrey might like to spend a few weeks in the summer with him and Amy. Marie would never agree to such a suggestion as she knew what Harry was like.

She said to Robert, 'Before you could say boo to a goose he'd have him on that bloody boat of his, how Aunt Amy puts up with him, I'll never know.'

Robert, on the other hand, couldn't see anything wrong with the suggestion. 'After all, Amy and Harry have always been very nice and they've brought up their own children, who've turned out to be decent people. There's not much wrong with Harry. And Jeff's thirteen and very sensible.'

'Don't you be fooled by Harry.'

But Jeffrey kept prompting his dad, who'd spent many days convincing Marie of the benefits it would have on Jeffrey to spend time with an older couple who had lived through the war and knew about life.

Against her better judgment, Marie finally agreed that Jeffrey could go, but only for two weeks.

'But if I hear you've been on that bloody boat, you're coming home.'

That Saturday afternoon Marie and Robert took Jeffrey and Angela to Uncle Harry's and Aunt Amy's. Jeffrey was delighted to find that Uncle Harry had a dog, a border collie whose name was Dan. Dan was slightly overweight, unlike the border collies Jeffrey had been used to seeing in the field behind their house. Dan had probably never seen a sheep.

It proved to be a pleasant afternoon. Aunt Amy provided tea and a cold meat salad followed by homemade cake and trifle. At about five o' clock, with hugs and kisses all round, Marie, Robert and Angela prepared to return to Swinebeck; Angela was on the back seat of the car. As they were leaving, she pulled her tongue out at Jeffrey and crossed her eyes by looking at the tip of her nose. Jeffrey was left with Uncle Harry and Aunt Amy. The house seemed quiet when they'd gone.

Jeffrey was escorted to his room; he put his clothes in

the wardrobe. He was told to treat the house as if it were his own and to have a shower or a bath whenever he chose. He then returned to the living room and joined Uncle Harry who'd been reading.

'Jeff, do you fancy a pint?'

Jeffrey thought he was hearing things.

'Pardon, Uncle Harry?'

'You heard. Do you fancy coming for a pint?'

'Well, if you like.'

Harry shouted, 'Dan!' The dog seemed to know exactly where he was going, wagging his tail as he came towards them.

'Amy, I'm just going to show Jeffrey the river.'

'Alright, love, don't be late.'

Jeffrey thought this was a strange thing to say as it was mid-summer and not yet six o' clock.

They walked down towards the river. Harry threw a stick for Dan then the dog brought it back to Jeffrey who in turn threw the stick, which was returned to him over and over again.

'This is fun.'

Standing at the waters edge, Harry looked longingly at the river as if he wanted to submerge himself in its beauty.

'Jeff, see that boat over there, the one with the white hull and red sails bent on the boom, that's my boat, I built her thirty years ago, she knows the river better than any other boat.'

Jeff thought it was a strange thing to say about a boat, and was sure Uncle Harry's voice faltered with emotion when he said the last few words.

'Right, let's have that pint!'

They walked down to the Jolly Sailor, a pub dating back about 200 years. It had a small lawn that sloped towards the river.

'What are you having to drink, Jeff?'

'Lemonade, please.'

Jeffrey was convinced that had he said a pint of bitter, Uncle Harry would have bought him one. But he'd never know for sure as he came back with a lemonade and a pint for himself. He chose to sit at a table on the lawn in a position that enabled him to look at his boat, and did so constantly, even when he was deep in conversation. Dan sat next to Jeff with his chin resting on Jeff's knee.

Some of Harry's friends came to join them. Jeff was introduced to them, and they to him, all by their Christian names, even though some of them were ancient and he was Jeff, Harry's nephew.

'Same again, Jeff?'

'Please, Uncle Harry.'

Jeff felt comfortable amongst these men. Some wore sailing smocks, some wore blue Guernsey sweaters, some had bare arms with tattoos showing, some had beards, some smoked pipes and all had red faces. Harry returned with the round of drinks.

'Thank you, Uncle Harry.'

Harry whispered in Jeff's ear.

'Jeff, cut the crap. Call me Harry.'

They had two more rounds of drinks. All the men were cheerful and happy and there was lots of laughter. But Harry kept his eyes on his boat. 'That knows the river better than any other'.

As dusk closed in, Jeff, with his new found friends Harry and Dan, walked home and went straight to bed. 'If only my mother knew,' he thought.

At six the following morning Jeff heard Harry and Aunt Amy talking. He could smell bacon. He got up, washed and dressed, and went into the kitchen just as Aunt Amy was putting out his breakfast. Dan greeted him with a wagging tail.

'Jeff, we're going down river today with some friends, you'll enjoy it.'

'Harry, you be careful with Jeff. Do you hear? You know what Marie said.'

'He'll be fine.'

They set off for the river. Jeff didn't know border collies could sail.

Harry went to a shed and produced some oars and a large carrier bag, which had *Sailors Den* written on it. Harry said, 'You'll need these, put the buoyancy aid and wellies on, and bring the other gear to the boat.' The bag contained a buoyancy aid, sailing wellingtons, sailing jacket and trousers, a woollen bob hat and sailing smock. All brand new.

Then he turned over a small dinghy, which had been placed upside down. He called it a 'tender'. He put Dan in then told Jeff to climb in, before pushing off and climbing in with them. At that moment, in this tender, watching the bank get smaller in the distance, Jeff felt something he'd not felt before. Freedom.

They came alongside Harry's boat, which bore her name on the side, Amy. Jeff thought he'd entered a strange new world. Dan was thrown on board followed by Jeff and Harry. Harry had done something with some ropes and let the tender go and it was attached to the mooring buoy.

He'd done some more things with ropes, hoisted the mainsail, dropped the mooring and soon they were off. Jeff had been watching Harry while holding onto Dan, and generally keeping out of his way as much as possible. He hadn't noticed what the others were doing. But as they got underway Jeff looked astern towards the east and saw the coloured sails of eight other boats, set against the rising sun. And at that moment he knew he was hooked.

They began to sail down river towards Liverpool. Harry said they were only able to do it at this state of tide because it had been raining heavily during the week, and there was a lot of fresh water in the river. They passed under the Runcorn Widnes Bridge, rounded Hale Head Lighthouse, passed Dungeon Banks and Oglet Banks then entered the Garston Channel. Harry said he'd point these places out on a chart later. Sometimes you couldn't see over the exposed sand banks, they were so high.

Harry showed Jeff what happened when the helm was moved from side to side and how the boat reacts then he said, 'You take over and I'll hoist the headsail.' Jeff took over with all nine vessels sailing in close proximity. If anything went wrong, Harry would take the helm. Some of Harry's friends were shouting, 'Well done, Jeff!' or 'Don't give the tiller back to that old bugger!'

When they were well into the Garston Channel, Harry said, 'We're going to beat over to Tranmere. You continue to sail. I'll guide you and adjust the sails.'

Jeff's Uncle Harry began to pull in on some ropes and the sails were brought in closer to the centre line of the boat. Amy came alive and began to heel and pick up speed. Jeff looked astern and all vessels were heeled and going like trains, with spray bouncing over their foredecks. By the time they'd picked up moorings at Tranmere, Jeff was saturated with salt water; he'd been able to taste the salt, and felt as if his face was as red as everyone else's. 'My mother would blow a fuse!' he thought.

They had lunch; each boat had a bucket and if they needed to go to the toilet they would use the bucket and throw it over the side. Jeff found out later that this was called 'bucket and chuck it'.

Harry had said something about going upriver with the young flood and they'd set off back up river, taking a channel on the Cheshire side. He'd also pointed out Eastham Locks and said that this was where ships enter the Manchester Ship Canal. Everyone seemed to know where they were going and ended up at Hale Head Lighthouse. Then continued upriver, the way they'd sailed down, and picked up their moorings. Then they stowed sails and other gear, got into their tenders, rowed ashore, turned the tenders upside down, stowed their oars in the shed before finally going to the Jolly Sailor. Harry got the round of drinks in and sat where he could keep an eye on Amy. Everyone had a cheerful evening with Dan seemingly unfazed and sitting with his chin on

Jeff's knee. Jeff didn't think the border collies at home could do this.

They went home and then straight off to bed. Every time Jeff closed his eyes he saw the sun rising behind the many-coloured sails, before eventually drifting off to sleep.

For the next two weeks, each day was spent on the river doing what the tidal conditions allowed them to do. There were only a few boats on the river during the week but at weekends there were many more. Harry taught Jeff nautical terminology, and Jeff was quick to pick up the terms. He taught him how to set sails and steer, how to tie various knots, and gave him a piece of rope to practise on. Jeff was shown how to anchor and told about spring and neap tides, and how to easily calculate the next high water times. All in all he learnt a lot during that fortnight and felt comfortable in a boat from that moment on. After each day's adventure Harry pointed out where they'd been, using a framed chart of the river which he'd hung on his dining room wall.

Jeff often had this two-week adventure over the next two years while he was aged fourteen and fifteen. Marie was pleased he enjoyed Harry's company so much. But when Jeff was sixteen he began attending a full-time college course which required him to spend the summer months on work placement. He hadn't seen much of Harry and Aunt Amy since, but continued to maintain an interest in all things nautical.

Jeff continued to study at college. Then he went on to Lancaster University where he completed a degree course in architecture. He became a junior architect in a Preston-based practice and continued to live at home with Marie and Robert. Architectural work was something he enjoyed but he couldn't see himself doing it for the rest of his life. At the age of twenty-five he developed a burning desire to have his own boat. Indeed, he decided to build a yacht as he was confident he possessed the necessary skills.

Many designers advertised in yachting magazines. Jeff obtained details of their stock designs and decided on a particular design he thought most suitable for use in the north-west, with its drying harbours and fast-flowing rivers. He chose the design for a twenty-five foot sloop, with a dagger board operating through a cast iron ballast keel, and fitted with a pivoted rudder blade, suitable for taking the ground, with four berths, galley, heads and chart table. Auxiliary power would be provided by a diesel engine. Uncle Harold ordered the timber at trade prices and the boat was built on land next to his workshop using the available facilities.

First, a temporary shelter was erected with a waterproof roof and polythene sides to provide as much light as possible. A level base was constructed and the boat was built upside-down on it. After about twelve months the joinery to the hull had been completed. The hull was then turned over and placed onto a cast iron ballast keel, which was bolted into position. The remainder of the joinery to the decks, cockpit and coach roof continued along with internal woodwork. A diesel engine was purchased and installed by Jeff, albeit with a little help from a friend who was a mechanic and knew about engine electrics. The vessel was fully painted and stanchions, guard rails, winches, and cleats were fitted. The mast, boom and rigging were purchased and delivered.

Jeff continued to work as a junior architect. All his spare money was ploughed into the project. His mother would sometimes say, 'Are you going to name her after me, love?' Or, if she was with Jeff and other people were present, she would say, 'He's going to call her after his mother,' not thinking for one moment that he would.

When Jeff was twenty-eight, a crane and lorry arrived. The nearly completed vessel was loaded onto the lorry and taken to the Wyre Marina for finishing off the electrical installation, rigging, and fitting the spray hood and spray dodgers.

On the day of the launch, Jeff's mother, father, Uncle Harold, Harry and Aunt Amy, and lots of friends attended the launch. His mother was overcome with emotion when she saw the large white letters on the blue spray dodgers. He'd named his boat *Marie*. The launch went well and Marie was tied alongside a pontoon. Family and friends climbed on board, but not all at once.

Jeff left the architectural practice at twenty-nine and joined his current profession. He remained a bachelor and spent his spare time sailing Marie around the Irish Sea, normally from the Solway Firth down to Anglesey and across to the Isle of Man and Ireland. In common with other sailors he seldom had enough time to do the things he would have liked. When he had the time he sailed north up the Clyde, through the Crinan Canal and visited the Western Isles. Or he'd go south to the Scillies and the south coast. But passages of this type would take up a lot of time and organisation. He always felt privileged to have been able to do the things he'd done, and particularly so when he'd sailed to Anglesey and beyond. Especially when passing Llandudno and the Great Orme, and looking up the Conway River and Menai Straits. And also seeing the Snowdonia Mountain Range with Mount Snowdon capped in snow. Jeff was comfortable at sea, thanks to Harry. He lived in a modest semi-detached house in Cleveleys, a few miles from the Wyre Marina where Marie was berthed.

When Jeff was in his early twenties he went on holidays abroad, with friends, but he'd been disappointed in the places he'd visited; the usual holiday destinations were not, to him, as attractive as the beautiful Ribble, Lune or Wyre Valleys. He'd been on a flotilla sailing holiday to Greece and found the sailing tame compared to the excitement of sailing the Mersey and surrounding areas. Jeff no longer needed holidays abroad. The North West was his playground and he felt as if he was on a permanent holiday.

He was forty-two years of age and exactly where he liked to be – twelve miles offshore, beating hard to windward in the Irish Sea, in a pleasant force 5, with a wind-over-tide situation, surrounded by white horses, and Marie providing him with a roller coaster ride. ETA Douglas, Isle of Man, two hours. After arriving he'd report his arrival to Liverpool Coastguard then visit the yacht club for a shower and a light meal.

36

One of the things about sailing in good conditions is that once you've established a course to steer, set or reefed sails and set the auto helm, there's not much else to do. Other than feed yourself, keep a look out and just relax and enjoy the passage. This provides ample time for reflection and problem solving. Jeff solved many a problem just sitting in the cockpit attached by his harness to Marie.

Jeff enjoyed cruising with friends but it was not always possible to arrange a passage with friends at short notice as people often need time to prepare, and if you plan too far in advance it's impossible to predict the weather; therefore, when good weather and a few days off coincided, Jeff went sailing, and this was one such occasion.

ETA fifteen minutes.

When you're sailing single-handedly there's a need to provide extra time to deal with the tasks that have to be completed, such as reducing and stowing sails, preparing fenders, and lines for coming alongside.

Select VHF channel 12.

'Douglas Harbour, Douglas Harbour, this is Marie, Marie, over.'

'Marie this is Douglas Harbour, go ahead, over.'

'Douglas Harbour, this is Marie requesting permission to enter the harbour in ten minutes, over.'

'Yes, Marie, that's fine, come in when you're ready.'

'Thank you, Douglas Harbour, Marie, out.'

Select VHF channel 16.

'Liverpool Coastguard, Liverpool Coastguard, this is Marie, Marie, I have channel 86, over.'

'Marie, Liverpool Coastguard, go to channel 86.'
'86.'

Select VHF channel 86

'Liverpool Coastguard, this is Marie. We reported our departure from Fleetwood to you this morning, and can now advise you of our safe arrival in Douglas, over.'

'Marie, Liverpool Coastguard, thank you, sir, that's all recorded, Liverpool Coastguard, out.'

'Thank you, Coastguard, Marie, out.'

Jeff brought Marie into the harbour, under engine, and came alongside the pontoon. He then cast his aft line onto the pontoon so that it caught over a bollard and pulled in the stern; using engine and rudder he brought in the bow, stepped onto the pontoon with bow line in hand and secured the bow before finally fitting his springs. Marie was snug and safe for the night.

When tying a boat alongside a pontoon the bow and stern lines stop the vessel moving away from the pontoon, but to properly control the position of the vessel, springs are used, which are lines. One line is fastened to the bow of the vessel and led aft, and fastened to a bollard on the pontoon near the stern of the vessel, and another line is fastened to the stern of the vessel and led forward, and fastened to a bollard on the pontoon near the bow of the vessel.

It was 1200 hours and Jeff was feeling tired. He was ready for a shower and meal and an early night when his mobile phone rang.

'Jeff, I'm sorry to trouble you, it's Jean. I know you've got a few days off, but the boss wants a word.'

'Okay.'

'Detective Inspector Dewhurst.'

'Yes, sir.'

'Where are you? You're not on that bloody boat, are you?'

'I'm afraid I am, sir. I'm in Douglas.'

'Which Douglas? River Douglas or Isle of Man?'

'Isle of Man, sir.'

'How is it, that whenever I want you you're bloody miles away, when can you get back?'

'Well, sir, I can fly back and be with you in a couple of hours, or I can sail back and given the tidal predictions will be with you this time tomorrow.'

'God give me strength. See you tomorrow, oh, and Jeff…'

'Yes sir?'

'Be bloody careful in that boat.'

'Yes, sir, thank you, sir, goodbye, sir.'

'Bye, Jeff.'

Jeff continued as planned, strolled to the sailing club and signed in. He took a shower, had a meal and a pint of the guest bitter. He spoke with a couple of fellow yachtsmen, returned to Marie and planned his passage for the following day. Finally, he read his book in the cockpit for a while and turned in at 1700 hours.

Jeff was up at 0015 hours feeling refreshed and ready to go. He obtained permission to leave Douglas Harbour, reported his departure and ETA Fleetwood to Liverpool Coastguard and set off. He motored out of the harbour, set sails and autopilot, set course to steer, before preparing a mug of tea and a cereal. He never carried coffee on board as he'd been told years ago that it could contribute to sea sickness, and though he'd never suffered from this condition he wasn't prepared to take any chances. The dark sky brightened to the east. It was always a delight to see the sun burst over the horizon, around 0500 hours, lifting his spirits even higher. 'What a lovely life I have,' he thought. He entered the Lune Deep at 0800 hours and Marie was settled in her pontoon berth by 1000 hours. He reported his safe arrival to Liverpool Coastguard, closed the sea cocks and then isolated the battery, before taking his sailing holdall and locking Marie, finally walking up the sloping ramp to the car park.

Jeff had never been interested in cars, he'd always had a decent car, suited to his needs, which he'd have serviced regularly. It would normally be second hand. He'd had a Nissan X Trail for a couple of years and it was in this that he drove to his Cleveleys home.

He was five foot eleven inches tall, not thin, and not well built, he was best described as slim. He'd inherited a good head of black hair, which was greying slightly at the temples, and excellent eyesight from his mother. From his father, he'd inherited good strong teeth and a prominent nose. As for the latter, his father always said that a prominent nose on a man is a sign of character, but Jeff did not believe this to be the case. He wasn't given to outbursts of anger when things went badly or to expressions of great joy when things went well. He could be described as placid or easy going, but these attributes didn't detract from his ability to perform his work well. He was always determined and tenacious.

Living in a modest semi-detached house in a quiet close, he always considered the house to be more than adequate for his needs. He wasn't a gardener. But the house had a small garden, which he kept tidy. The rear garden backed onto a park with a good deal of open space and trees. The accommodation was typical: hall, lounge, dining room, kitchen, three bedrooms and a bathroom.

Harold, Harry and Amy had died. Marie and Robert, who had recently retired, were in good health and lived at the same address. His sister Angela was married and lived with her husband Tom, in a Cheshire village. They had two children, Alexandria and James. They always kept in touch. Jeff sometimes visited them and they often stayed with him for a few days. He'd furnished both spare bedrooms to accommodate them when they decide to stay. Alexandria and James enjoyed sailing and fishing with Jeff, and particularly so when they slept on the boat.

He showered, shaved and changed into one of his working suits. Next he made a sandwich and a cup of coffee, which he often drank at home, and went into his dining room. On the wall was Harry's chart of the River Mersey, which Aunt Amy passed on to him when Harry died. Next to the chart there was a photograph of Jeff, on Amy, with Dan on the foredeck and Jeff standing in the cockpit with his arms around Dan's neck, pressing ear to ear. Jeff was smiling broadly and Dan appeared to be grinning. Harry was leaning against the boom with an open-necked shirt and rolled-up sleeves. The photograph had been taken by one of Harry's friends one time when they had sailed beyond Liverpool and anchored in the Rock Channel off New Brighton. They had then caught the young flood, which carried them all the way up river, and had finished the day, as usual, at the Jolly Sailor.

It was often the way with sailing communities that when a person died, his boat might well be passed onto a deserving member of the sailing fraternity, with no money changing hands. Jeff had sailed into the River Mersey on many occasions with Marie. On one such occasion he'd seen Amy under full sail running up river before a moderate breeze, with what appeared to be a father and young teenage lad on board. He'd found the experience humbling.

Jeff set off for his meeting with Detective Superintendent Charles Hird.

Chapter 4

Superintendent Hird lived in a four-bedroom detached house in St. Annes. He was not a man to use foul language; he did swear but used only minor swear words, usually in jest when dealing with people he liked. He was 52 years of age with a thickening waist and was developing jowls. He had been married to Emma for 30 years. They had three daughters; the eldest, Ann, was a teacher aged 28, followed by Veronica, a nurse aged 27, and Catherine, a social worker aged 25. Ann and Veronica had been model daughters throughout their lives. Catherine, on the other hand, when she was sixteen and seventeen, was more likely to be found on Blackpool beach getting sloshed on wine and smoking cigarettes. Superintendent Hird only found out about his youngest daughter when on one occasion he'd attended a parents' evening, and one of the tutors claimed never to have clapped eyes on his daughter, even though her name was on the register. But that was in the past and all three daughters had turned out to be sensible and hard working and were employed in professions which provide an essential contribution to society. The problem was that they all still lived at home and seemed intent on continuing to do so. And Superintendent Hird was henpecked. Some said that was the reason he arrived at his office early and left late, but that was not the case. The reason was that Superintendent Hird believed in leading by example. He also believed that to gain the respect of others you must first treat others with respect and he'd developed a reputation as being a fair, reasonable and approachable man.

When Sergeant Skinner and Constable Johnston attended his office on Tuesday afternoon, Jean, his secretary, advised him of their arrival and they were shown through. He congratulated Constable Johnston on his thorough report, which was resting on his desk, but advised that not to have gone through Mr Thompson's personal possessions was a dreadful omission. Nevertheless, it was understandable given the circumstances of the other four deaths in the town that week. 'That will be all, Constable,' he said, dismissing Johnny.

'Thank you, sir.'

As he was closing the door behind him, Johnny heard Superintendent Hird say, 'Is your department very busy, Eric?'

He didn't hear the reply.

Sergeant Skinner returned to his office and continued to attend to his responsibilities. Johnny had been allocated a beat to patrol on foot in the centre of the resort, so off he went.

Johnny liked to know what was happening and though he knew he'd got off lightly, he also knew that Superintendent Hird had a reputation as having 'an iron fist in a velvet glove.' This troubled Johnny, his mind went into overdrive.

There was only one thing Johnny hated more than the 6 till 2 dead dog shift. That was to be seconded to CID, which had happened to him on four previous occasions in his career. And he'd hated it with a passion. They'd all been stupid bastards in CID, especially that mad dog Dewhurst. They never knew when to bleeding stop. 'I was knackered the last time I went with them,' he thought. He recalled starting at the crack of dawn and finishing after midnight. And when they went for a pint they don't have any bleeding fun. It was all bloody work. Johnny managed to convince himself that Superintendent Hird would like to make his life as bleeding uncomfortable and miserable as was possible. And for the first time in his career, Police Constable Jonathan Benjamin Johnston was not wrong.

On the occasions Johnny had been seconded to CID, his wife Sarah enjoyed the respite from constant care and was able to concentrate on looking after their twin sons, John and Jim. Because, after all, and even though she loved Johnny, he was a mess. A room with him in it was always untidy. In fact, any room he walked out of was left in a mess, and she found it easy to cope on those occasions when he at least returned home in a sober state rather than arriving from the pub soaked in booze. Also, the boys could watch their own TV programmes without him interfering and wanting his own way.

On the previous occasion he'd been seconded to CID, the boys had been watching Pink Panther films on a DVD their mother had bought and began to call their dad Inspector Clouseau and said things to him like, 'There was a man on the corner with a minkey.'

Or they would act out a little play in front of Johnny, with Jim saying to John in a French accent, 'Does your dog bite?'

'No.'

Jim would pretend to stroke a dog and be bitten, and would say, 'I thought you said your dog does not bite.'

'That is not my dog.'

They would fall about laughing, but Johnny was never amused.

Superintendent Hird was a man who liked protocol. He would never dream of addressing colleagues by their Christian names when others were present, and such was the case when Jeff arrived at 3.00pm on Wednesday and was shown in by Jean.

'Good afternoon, Detective Inspector.'

'Good afternoon, sir.'

'Jean, would you ask Sergeant Skinner to pop in?'

'Yes, sir.'

'Come in, Sergeant Skinner, you know Detective Inspector Dewhurst?'

'Yes, sir, good afternoon, Inspector.'

'Good afternoon, Sergeant Skinner.'

They discussed the events of the past few days. Sergeant Skinner explained that after having received the post-mortem report he had telephoned Mrs Bantry. She had informed him that room No. 3 had been thoroughly cleaned and disinfected by her and Mr Bantry immediately after the body had been removed. New guests, she added, had been checked-in on the Saturday afternoon. Superintendent Hird had discussed their options with forensics. They'd decided that in the unlikely event that they were to find evidence, it would be contaminated. And given the expense of setting up a scene of crime investigation and forensic analysis, and a positive result being unlikely, they'd decided the expense could not be justified.

They had agreed the way forward was to take fingerprints and DNA samples then record Mr Thompson's dental information and to take photographs of the face, so an artist could produce a sketch for identification purposes should it later prove necessary. They had also taken his clothes for forensic examination.

'So, Detective Inspector, it's over to you. As you will require some assistance, Sergeant Skinner advises he is able to release one of his men, for the duration of the investigation, and we have decided that Constable Johnston will be seconded to CID and assigned to the case as your assistant. Should you require further assistance please let me know, but we are very much overstretched.'

'Thank you, sir.'

Jeff and Sergeant Skinner left Superintendent Hird's office and agreed that Constable Johnston would join the investigation at 8.00am the next day.

Jeff decided he would visit the mortuary to view the body then go through Mr Thompson's possessions – such as they were – in the forensics department, so that he could try to envisage the type of man Mr Thompson had been. Then he would return home, read through the reports, have an early night and start afresh in the morning.

Sergeant Skinner located Constable Johnston and requested he return to the station at 7.00pm for a discussion, which he did; there he was advised of his secondment to CID. It was suggested he should tidy his desk, return home and take advantage of an early night.

When he arrived home he informed Sarah of his secondment – she was delighted. He then sank a few early pints at the pub.

Chapter 5

Jeff arrived at his desk at 7.30 on Thursday morning, contemplating how the day should be approached, thumbing through the reports. The only evidence forensics had found on the clothes confirmed they'd belonged to Mr Thompson and fingerprints had not found a match.

Johnny arrived just before 8.00 and knocked on the door.

'Come in.'

'Good morning, sir.'

'Good morning, Constable, would you like a coffee?'

'Yes please, sir.'

'Milk and sugar?'

'Please.'

Jeff walked to the coffee machine located in the corridor and returned with two coffees.

'I've been going through these reports, Constable, the only solid evidence we have is associated with Mr Thompson's teeth and the dentistry carried out over the years. Also, the reports suggest Mr Thompson, if that's his real name, was about 55 years of age. The post-mortem examination reveals he had drunk a moderate amount of alcohol, and traces of a drug were found, we are still awaiting toxicology results, and, of course, the morphine poison … not much to go on, Constable?'

'No, sir.'

'I'll leave you to browse through the reports for a few

moments, back shortly.'

Jeff nipped to the toilet.

In his absence, Johnny read only the conclusions of the various reports, and thought that DI Dewhurst was, perhaps, not all that bad after all. He'd never worked with him before and really only thought of him as being particularly mad, as he had a reputation for sailing the Irish Sea, and Johnny didn't like deep water.

Moments later, Jeff returned.

'Well, what do you think?'

'I'm not really sure, sir.'

'We've got to start somewhere, Constable. Where do you think we should start?'

'I think, sir, there's only one place to start, and that's at the Burnside Guest House, where we need to interview Mr and Mrs Bantry. We need to find out if they can recall anything that will enable us to make progress and obtain a list of guests who were staying on Friday night.'

'Constable, you've confirmed my thoughts precisely. Would you kindly telephone Mrs Bantry and ask if it would be convenient to visit her and Mr Bantry at, say, ten o' clock, when they've finished dealing with the breakfasts, and we'll meet back here at nine thirty.'

'Will do, sir.'

Johnny rang Mrs Bantry.

'Burnside Guest House.'

'Hello, Mrs Bantry. It's Constable Johnston.'

'Oh, hello, Constable.'

'Mrs Bantry, we'd like to come and interview you and Mr Bantry at ten o' clock, if that's convenient.'

'Whatever for?'

'Well, we've not been able to properly identify Mr Thompson and we think you may be able to help.'

'Oh, alright, Constable. I'll have the kettle on, but I don't know what I can do.'

'Thank you, Mrs Bantry.'

Johnny returned to Jeff's office a little before 9.30, knocked and walked in to find him at his desk making notes.

'Please sit down, Constable.'

Johnny had always been terrified of wasps, and crawling on the top of Jeff's desk was the most threatening piece of waspery he'd ever seen. It immediately horrified him. He tried to ignore it, but couldn't. He tried to control himself, but couldn't. When it turned through ninety degrees and started to walk towards him, he leapt out of the chair, which fell on the floor behind him.

'What on earth is the matter, Constable?'

'There's a wasp.'

'Good heavens, it won't harm you.'

Jeff was quite amused by Johnny's antics and took a glass beaker and carefully placed it over the wasp. Then he slid a piece of paper under the beaker and wasp, lifted the whole assembly, wasp in beaker, and released it through an open window.

Jeff never killed a thing, not even a fly or a spider. If one were to annoy him he'd capture it and release it into the fresh air. He believed all creatures on the planet had a right to life and he didn't see why, just because man is able to, he should kill unnecessarily. He did fish and sometimes caught a mackerel, as he enjoyed fresh mackerel and felt that when he was sailing and close to nature, it was the natural thing to do. 'To feast on the seas rich harvest' as he put it.

Johnny hated everything that walked on more than two legs. Spiders, flies or wasps that entered his house did so at their peril. As soon as he saw one, he'd not be content until he'd knocked the shit out of it, with a rolled-up newspaper or some other weapon, much to the annoyance of Sarah and the boys, who loved nature.

'Are we ready then?'

'Yes, sir.'

'We'll go in my car.'

When they arrived at the car park and got into Jeff's car, Johnny noticed that when the ignition was switched on the radio started automatically and was tuned to Classic FM. However, it was barely audible, just playing in the background, enabling conversation to take place. Johnny thought, 'Fancy listening to rubbish like that.' He also noticed that Jeff kept within the speed limit, something Johnny had never done since passing his driving test. Jeff was courteous to other road users. He allowed pedestrians to cross in front of him and flashed his lights to people wishing to join the main road from side roads and allowed them out in front of him. When two lanes merged into one, he held back and allowed cars to enter the single lane ahead of him. Johnny never did any of these things.

There were four parking spaces at the front of the Burnside Guest House. They parked in one of them, got out and rang the bell.

'Hello, Constable.'

'Good morning, Mrs Bantry, this is Detective Inspector Dewhurst.'

'Hello, Inspector.'

'Good morning, Mrs Bantry, Mr Bantry.'

'Now what's all this about, Inspector?'

'Well, Mr Bantry, since Saturday morning we've been trying to identify where Mr Thompson lived, he did not live at the address in your visitors' book. Furthermore, we have established that Mr Thompson was murdered.'

'Oh, Stanley!'

'Don't go upsetting yourself, Ethel.'

'And we were wondering that if we sat down and discussed the matter you may be able to remember something that will be helpful to our investigation.'

'Come and sit in the lounge, I'll bring some tea.'

'Thank you, Mrs Bantry.'

'Things never seem so bad over a cup of tea, don't you think, Inspector?'

'I'm sure you're right, Mrs Bantry.'

'I've brought some of those nice chocolate biscuits you like, Constable.'

'Thank you, Mrs Bantry.'

'Sit down, Stanley.'

'Yes, Ethel.'

'May I continue, Mrs Bantry?'

'Please do.'

'You see, as far as we know, you and Mr Bantry are the only persons to have communicated with Mr Thompson, and we thought that if we had a chat, and you could provide us with the names and addresses of the guests who stayed with you on Friday night, then we may have something to start with.'

'How did Mr Thompson die?'

'Lethal injection.'

'Oh dear, and you think one of our guests murdered him?'

'We don't know, Mrs Bantry.'

'Well, I know Mr Thompson was not from Cirencester.'

'Don't start that, Ethel.'

'Now you let me have my say, Stanley. You see, Inspector … That's a nice suit you're wearing, Constable.'

'Thank you, Mrs Bantry.'

'Now, where was I? Oh yes. You know, Inspector, I've been interested in dialects since Stanley and I were married. Forty years ago now, isn't it, Stanley, luv? When we got married we had no money and we needed to save for a deposit for a house. So my Stanley found out they were building a big hospital in Liverpool. We lived in Burnley and Stanley, being a joiner, got a job at this hospital. As it was so far away he only came home for two days each month and he was sharing a caravan with some other men to cut down on expenses, see? Now. What I noticed about my Stanley, who was working all hours God sends on this hospital, was that his voice had changed, and he had started to talk Liverpudlian. Not much at first, but after twelve months I thought I'd married a scouser. His mother used to say he sounded a right daft bugger talking like that. And since then I've listened carefully to dialects. You see, when the nice constable came on Saturday I knew he was Blackpool born and bred. Am I right, Constable?'

'You are, Mrs Bantry.'

'Stanley, get some more biscuits for Constable Johnston.'

'Now, Inspector, luv, I've been listening to your accent, and I know you're an educated, cultured gentleman. I also know that you don't live where you lived as a boy. I call it rolling "r" s. You don't roll your "r" s the way you would have done had you stayed where you were brought up. Now then, I know you're not from Blackpool. I also know you're not from this side of Preston, and you're not from Preston, but I think – in fact I know – you're from Ribble Valley. But not as far as Clitheroe. Probably somewhere up river from Ribchester. Am I right, Inspector?'

'You are perfectly right, Mrs Bantry.'

'You see, Inspector, we get people from all over the country in the guest house, and we get an awful lot of guests staying every year who come from the area where you were brought up. And because we've been in business for thirty-two years, and I've heard a lot of dialects during that time, I knew Mr Thompson was not from Cirencester, by his dialect. He could well live in Cirencester, but if he did, he moved there recently, because he still rolled his "r" s, and I think he lived all his life in the same area.'

'And where do you think that would be, Mrs Bantry?'

'Well, he had an accent something like yours, or more like yours would have been had you not moved from the Ribble Valley. He was an educated man, but I don't think he came from as far out as Ribchester, though there's not much difference in the accents. I'd say he came from Upridge.'

'You're marvellous, Mrs. Bantry.'

'You should tell that to my Stanley.'

'May I see room number three? And do you think Constable Johnston could make a list of names and addresses of the guests who stayed with you on Friday night?'

'Stanley, show the visitors' book to Constable Johnston, and I'll take the nice Inspector to room three, and Stanley, don't forget that bang.'

'What bloody bang?'

'The one you heard on Saturday morning. He'll tell you when we come down, Inspector.'

Jeff looked at the room and took in the view from the window, he felt he needed to see where the crime had been committed.

'Thank you, Mrs Bantry. Shall we go down?'

'Mr & Mrs Jolley are staying here at the moment, a lovely couple from Rawtenstall.'

'You've created a very pleasant environment for your guests, Mrs Bantry.'

'Me and Stanley have done our best, Inspector.'

'I'm sure you have, Mrs Bantry.'

'Now, Stanley, tell the inspector about that bang.'

'Well, Inspector, at about one on Saturday morning the front door slammed shut, which is most unusual as our guests are normally in bed before midnight, and when Mr Thompson didn't come down for breakfast I

56

thought he'd arrived back drunk.'

'Could you tell whether the person closing the door was entering or leaving the house?'

'I'm afraid not, Inspector. I was in bed and not fully awake.'

'Well, Mr and Mrs Bantry, you've been very helpful, Constable Johnston and I are most grateful to you, we'll bid you good day.'

'Good day, Inspector, Constable.'

'Goodbye, Mrs Bantry.'

'Oh, Stanley, aren't they nice policemen? I've never met an Inspector before.'

'Ethel, I'll just have to nip to Tesco. We're out of chocolate biscuits.'

Chapter 6

Jeff and Constable Johnston returned to the police station pleased with the progress that had been made. In fact, they thought they'd had a really lucky break. With Mrs Bantry being such a keen and accurate judge of dialects, they now had something to focus upon. They decided to set up Jeff's office to become a more functional incident room and moved in a small desk for Constable Johnston. They also brought in a wall map of Lancashire and the Fylde Coast. On one wall was a white board which was cleaned and ready for use.

Jeff brought in the coffees. 'Well, Constable, let's consider our next move, what do you think?'

'Well, sir. If Mrs Bantry is correct, and we're confident she is, then we need to communicate Mr Thompson's dental treatment to the various dentists in the area, and we should get a positive ID.'

'So ... Yellow Pages?'

'I think so, sir.'

'Let's get on with it.'

They browsed through the Yellow Pages and made a list of all the dentists from the outskirts of Preston, taking in Grimsagh, Upridge, down to Ribchester, and arrived at a figure of twelve. They obtained photostat copies of that part of the post-mortem report referring to dental treatment and decided that they would each visit six dental practices, expressing upon each dentist the need for expediency.

Working away from Preston, Constable Johnston would visit dentists numbered one to six and Jeff would visit dentists numbered seven to twelve; they'd exchanged mobile telephone numbers so they could keep in contact. They also agreed that the task would take up the remainder of the working day, and decided to meet back at base at eight in the morning.

Johnny decided to start at dentist number six and work back to number one, as there'd be less distance to drive home when he'd finished. He set off in his Ford Escort.

All went very well indeed. The final dentist on Johnny's list was Mr Higginbottom. Johnny arrived at about four thirty. As he entered reception he thought he heard a dog growl behind him, but couldn't be sure as one of the patients was coughing. The receptionist was on the telephone. Johnny looked around and saw there were four patients in the small waiting area, and one was a blind elderly lady with a guide dog. The dog was lying on its stomach with its front paws sticking out and its head resting on its front legs.

Johnny never trusted anything on four legs and he'd very good reason not to. The problem was he always seemed to have an adverse effect upon their behaviour. Many times, for no apparent reason, a passing cat had lashed out at him inflicting painful wealds, and if he had a pound for each time he'd heard dog owners say 'That's strange, he's never done that before', he'd be a wealthy man. When he was in the countryside with his family, or if he was on holiday, he'd always avoid walking through fields of cows for fear of having the same effect on them that he'd had on cats and dogs. He even avoided walking through fields containing sheep, in case an aggressive ram was lurking amongst them.

When the receptionist had finished on the telephone, Johnny explained his business. She said that Mr Higginbottom was completing a scrape and polish and she would let him know immediately he'd finished. 'Would you care to sit down?' she asked.

Johnny turned around and noticed the dog was looking at him, now sitting up with its front legs vertical and front paws resting on the carpet. He also noticed the only vacant chair was next to the blind lady. He reluctantly proceeded towards it and sat down. He kept himself to himself, ignoring the dog, but the dog kept turning its head, looking up and staring at Johnny.

The receptionist said, 'Mrs Jones, the hygienist will see you now,' and the blind lady got up and started to walk away. The dog saw his opportunity and snapped at Johnny, breaking the skin on the little finger of his left hand.

Mrs Jones said, 'That's strange, he's never done that before,' not realising the damage that had been inflicted. The receptionist cleaned and dressed the wound. Mr Higginbottom completed his scrape and polish and was advised that Johnny was waiting.

When he came to reception, the receptionist explained what the dog had done to Johnny and Mr Higginbottom recommended a tetanus injection at the hospital as Johnny couldn't remember having had one recently.

Johnny acquainted Mr Higginbottom with the reason

for his visit then set off for the hospital. He was sitting in the Casualty Department when his mobile rang.

'Constable, I thought I'd let you know I've visited my six dentists, how are things with you?'

'Okay, sir, all done.'

'Very good, where are you?'

'In the Casualty Department at the hospital.'

'Good heavens, what on earth has happened?'

Johnny explained about the guide dog.

'What breed of dog was it, Constable?'

'A black Labrador.'

'I never knew Labradors could be vicious.'

'Well you know now, sir.'

'Yes I do, Constable, see you in the morning.'

'Bye, sir.'

As Jeff was in the vicinity of Swinebeck and his parents' home, he decided to drop in and see them as he always did if he was close by. His mother, being naturally industrious, was busy baking cakes for a Women's Institute gathering planned for the weekend. His father, who'd recently retired, was sitting in the back garden reading a book. His mother let him in and they entered the kitchen, where she'd been stationed at a table surrounded by organised clutter. She put the kettle on, as was her way whenever anyone visited, opened the kitchen window and shouted, 'Robert, Jeffrey's here!' Robert waved a hand in acknowledgement and continued reading.

'Are you alright, Jeffrey, love?'

'I'm fine, Mum.'

'You know, Jeffrey, your dad doesn't like

retirement.'

'Most men look forward to retirement, Mum, there are times when I would like to retire.'

'Well, your dad thought he would, but it's surprising how work fills the day. Then when it's not there, you have to find something to replace it.'

'So what does he do?'

'What does he do? Well, he gets up at his usual time, he'll do the garden, go for a bike ride or a walk, then come home and read.'

'Sounds like a pretty good life to me.'

'Good life? It is. But he has all day to do the things he used to do in the evening after work.'

'He'll have to find a hobby.'

'That's what I said. But he's not interested in much. Doesn't like television or watching sport. Not interested in taking up bowls. And he can't stand golf. But he does like his walks.'

'Is she talking about me again, Jeff?' said Robert as he walked into the kitchen.

'I'm just telling Jeffrey about your retirement.'

'You know, Jeff, your mother doesn't think I'm happy unless I'm busy running around doing things. I'm perfectly happy and content walking and reading. I feel much fitter than when I was working. And you know what, Jeff? I'm planning to walk the Pennine Way.'

'That's good, Dad. When are you doing that?'

'In a few weeks when the children's school holidays have finished and it's quieter.'

'What will you do, camp?'

'No. I've been planning it for some time. I can split

the route into several easy walks and book into bed and breakfast in advance.'

'Is Mum going with you?'

'Don't involve me with your dad's daft ideas,' said Marie, 'I'm too busy. What with all my Women's Institute work, and the Older People's Forum, and the Older People's Engagement Group, I'm too busy going to meetings.'

'And don't forget the bingo on Mondays and Thursdays,' said Robert.

'You know, Jeffrey, your father begrudges me my little pleasures. I keep telling him it's a therapy for me. It's important to socialise. It keeps my mind alert. Would you like a piece of fruit cake with your tea, Jeffrey?'

'Please, Mum.'

'Now then, Jeffrey. You know Angela and the children are coming up the second week in August. And they're staying with you?'

'She's told me, and I'm trying to see them at the weekend.'

'And another thing, Jeffrey. Have you read the children's school reports?'

'No.'

'Well Angela's sent copies for your dad and me to read. You can take them home with you and read them. But make sure you let me have them back. You know I like saving things.'

'Okay, I will.'

'I've never seen such long school reports. The children are doing ever so well. They're a credit to

Angela and Tom. It's about time you started thinking about getting married.'

'Yes, Mother.'

Jeff finished his tea and cake. Whenever he visited his parents, he liked to walk through the field behind the house down to the river bank and stroll along it and today was no exception. He always felt drawn to water, rivers, lakes, harbours, beaches. They each held a fascination for him. As there'd not been much rain recently there was little water covering the river bed, and what there was tumbled and gurgled over rocks and stones, sparkling and shiny, on its way to the estuary. Much of the river bed was exposed. He could easily have walked across without wetting his shoes. He returned to the house, told his parents that if he didn't see them before, he'd see them in a few weeks, when Angela and the children came to stay. Then left his parents and headed home.

Over the years Jeff had learnt that solving a murder was like completing a jigsaw puzzle, where you'd first find the corners, then complete the sides and fill in the pieces, until eventually all becomes clear. He knew that within twenty-four hours the corners would be firmly established. The day had gone well.

As was Jeff's way when he finished work early, he'd go home, change his clothes, drive to the marina and check on Marie; there's always something to do when you have a boat. Then he'd have a cup of tea while sitting in the cockpit and ruminate. And that's what he did this evening.

Jeff found Constable Johnston an amusing sort of

64

chap. What Jeff had found over the years was that people who put effort into being funny usually aren't. There are also people who never try to be funny and are never funny. And there are people who don't try to be funny but usually are. He decided that Constable Johnston was in the latter category. It was part of his nature. Throughout his life he'd met men like this and he'd always found them to be non-pretentious, generous of spirit, caring, decent people, and decided that in spite of his failings – and we all have them – Constable Johnston's bad points paled into insignificance when compared to his good ones. 'Tomorrow, I'll call him Johnny.'

Having waited in Casualty, Johnny had received his tetanus injection and then had his dog-bitten finger dressed by the nurse. It was getting late. By the time he had got home he had a throbbing finger, a sore upper arm, and was feeling knackered. Jim and John played their Clouseau dog joke on him. So he pissed off to bed early. When Sarah went up to join him he was fast asleep.

Chapter 7

Jeff was up at six, showered, shaved and dressed. He went downstairs and consumed his usual breakfast – half a grapefruit and a mug of tea – while standing by the kitchen work surface, looking out of the window over the park. There was a clear blue sky on this July morning, and the park was bathed in sunlight and casting long shadows; it was full of shades of green, with its conifers and deciduous trees laden with leaves. He enjoyed observing the changing shades of greens and browns as the seasons rolled by. For him, all seasons were beautiful, even heavy rain was one of nature's delights; it made the park and other landscapes so beautiful. There were squirrels which he could see on the grass beyond his fence, and many birds, the more common ones he knew the names of, but there were some very small ones that he had often seen, while not knowing what they were. He'd been meaning to find out. He decided he must ask his mother, she'd know.

Jeff was at his desk, when Johnny arrived.

'Good morning, sir.'

'Good morning, Johnny, how's that finger of yours?'

'It's okay, that dog's probably died from alcohol poisoning by now.'

'If he has, you'll be blamed. I hope you're well insured.'

'So. What are we doing?'

'Well, I feel confident, today, we'll know where Mr

Thompson lived. But for the moment it's a waiting game. Each of the dentists I spoke to advised they would attend to the matter with the utmost urgency. So let's ring around nine or after to see if progress is being made. Fancy a coffee?'

'Please, sir.'

Jeff had just returned with the coffees when the phone rang.

'Dewhurst.'

'Good morning, Inspector. Charles Parker here, you came to see me yesterday regarding dental records, I've got a match.'

'Excellent, Mr Parker, would you like to give me the details?'

'Yes, Inspector. His name is Harry Taylor, date of birth 20/5/50, address is 8 Field View, Upridge.'

'No doubt about this?'

'None whatsoever. One of our regulars who comes for a check-up every six months … his wife's one of our clients too.'

'Mr Parker, as we'll be in Upridge in about an hour, will it be convenient to collect a copy of the dental records, for our file?'

'They'll be waiting for you, Inspector.'

'Thank you, Mr Parker, we'll be along in due course.'

Mr Parker was number five on Jeff's list from the previous day and had his practice in the centre of Upridge.

'Bingo, Johnny, are you ready?'

'Certainly am.'

'Let's go.'

They parked in a side street and had to walk about two hundred metres to the dental practice, passing a small shopping precinct and some houses along the way. As Upridge was a hilly area, buildings often had several steps in front, which made access difficult. A young woman with a small child in a pram was struggling up the steps of one of the houses and Jeff paused.

'May I help you, madam?'

He then proceeded to assist them by lifting the front of the pram, as the young woman held onto the handle and lifted the rear; they did this until the pram was securely positioned on the higher level.

'Thank you.'

'You're welcome, madam.'

Jeff and Johnny continued towards the dental practice but Johnny had noticed that the young woman had the word 'punished' written all over her face and looked as if she had never before been spoken to respectfully. He wondered if DI Dewhurst had noticed this. Nothing like Sarah who was always laughing and fresh faced.

The dental records were collected from reception. They returned to the car and continued onto 8 Field View – a close of about twenty detached bungalows, facing a field occupied by sheep, with views of the hills beyond. They parked the car, walked up the path and rang the front doorbell.

The next door neighbour was tending his front garden and advised them that there was nobody at home at the moment.

'Good morning, sir, I'm Detective Inspector

Dewhurst. This is my colleague, Detective Constable Johnston.'

'Good morning, gentlemen.'

'Will Mrs Taylor be home later?'

'I'm afraid not, they've gone away.'

'And you are?'

'Harris, Ted Harris, there's nothing wrong, is there?'

'Do you know where they've gone?'

'Well, Harry, he's gone sailing with friends, and Joyce, she's gone somewhere down south to her sisters.'

'You say Mr Taylor's gone sailing?'

'Yes. Every year, Mr Taylor, Harry, he goes off for a couple of weeks with friends. He has a small boat himself at Frampton Marina, but he has a friend with a bigger boat, and several of them go off sailing in that.'

'When did he go?'

'Last Wednesday morning. They left together. Joyce drops him off at the marina, then gets on the motorway and drives to her sisters.'

'Did you see them go?'

'Yes. They brought me the key.'

'What time was that?'

'About nine.'

'What was Mr Taylor wearing?'

'Just the usual, jeans and tee shirt, and those brown shoes sailors wear.'

'Did he have any luggage with him?'

'He did, I noticed the car boot was full of Joyce's stuff, so Harry put his holdall on the back seat.'

'What colour was the holdall?'

'Red. He takes it with him whenever he goes sailing.'

'Do you know where Mrs Taylor's gone?'

'You know, she tells me every year, but I forget. It's a place with an old stone breakwater, so she tells me, and they made a film there – the French Lieutenant's something or other – and it's near what they call a Jurassic Coast, where they dig for fossils.'

'Do you mean Lyme Regis?'

'That's the place.'

'Mr Harris. You say you have a key?'

'Yes. I take in the post from the hall, and look after Gerald.'

'Gerald?'

'Yes. I feed him every day, he's the cat.'

'Oh, shit.'

'I beg your pardon, Constable, did you say something?'

'No, sir, I was just thinking out loud … how big is he?'

'He's about five-eight, five-nine, about my size, Constable.'

'No, sir, Gerald. Is he a big cat?'

'He's just an ordinary, mature cat; he looks biggish I suppose, but only because he's fluffy.'

'Has he been fed this morning?'

'Yes, I fed him at about eight-thirty.'

'What does he look like?'

'Mr Taylor?'

'No. Gerald.'

'Well, he's black, with white paws, and a white patch around his left eye, and a white bit at the end of his tail.'

'When did you last see him?'

'Just before you arrived, he chased a bird off the lawn, and climbed that tree.'

Jeff was not one to interject whilst a colleague was in full flow, but surely this line of questioning could not be helpful; after all, this was a murder investigation.

'Mr Harris. Do you think we can look inside the house?'

'Well, I don't think Harry and Joyce would want me to let people into their house, Inspector.'

'Mr Harris, this is my warrant card. Constable, show Mr Harris your warrant card. The thing is, we are conducting a serious investigation, so serious that I could obtain a warrant to enter the premises within the hour, but it would be helpful if you allowed us access.'

'Oh, very well.'

Mr and Mrs Taylor had a neat and tidy bungalow, decorated in neutral colours, not cluttered, not too much furniture, with laminated flooring in the hall, lounge and dining room, clay tile floors in the kitchen and bathroom, and carpets in the three bedrooms. Johnny noticed the cat flap in the external kitchen door, and the two stainless steel bowls on the kitchen floor. When Jeff opened the door to the main bedroom, there, on the bed, was Mr Taylor's red holdall.

'Johnny, I'm just going to the car to get some gloves.'

On his return from the car he gave Johnny a pair of latex gloves, put on a pair himself, then unzipped the holdall.

He opened the holdall to find that all items of clothing had been tightly rolled into something about the size of a kitchen roll and stacked neatly, so that each item could be removed individually, without causing too much disturbance to other clothes in the holdall. All the clothes were removed and placed on the bed. The usual fairly worn jeans, tee shirts, rugby shirts, pullovers etc. The only items absent were toiletries and a towel.

Jeff was well aware that when a group of pals go sailing for a couple of weeks, they're not interested in sartorial elegance and tend to wear clothes they would not think of wearing for a hotel holiday.

In a small pocket inside the holdall was a padlock key hung from a key ring which had a short cord and piece of cork hanging from it. 'Obviously Mr Taylor's boat key,' he thought, as he put it in his pocket.

The wardrobe contents were inspected and at the bottom of what was obviously Mr Taylor's wardrobe were two pairs of brown deck shoes, an old pair and one pair fairly new. All the items were replaced in the holdall. Jeff and Johnny returned to Mr Harris who was waiting in the kitchen.

'Do you have a contact number for Mrs Taylor?'

'I'm sorry, I don't.'

'When will Mrs Taylor be home?'

'They're normally away for two weeks. Should be about next Wednesday.'

'What's Mr Taylor's job?'

'He's a design engineer for British Aerospace. He says that when he retires at sixty, with his lump sum, he's going to get a bigger boat as they'll have more time to go sailing.'

'So, Mrs Taylor sails?'

'Sometimes, on nice days only, she's not as keen as

Harry.'

'Does Mrs Taylor work?'

'She's a teacher at a primary school in Preston.'

'Do you know which one?'

'It's St. Wilfred's.'

'What sort of car does Mrs Taylor drive?'

'Well, she has a Nissan Micra, but that's in the garage. She's taken Harry's car to her sister's, that's a BMW.'

'You've been most helpful, Mr Harris, thank you.'

'Has anything happened, Inspector?'

'I'm not able to say at the moment, sir.'

When they opened the front door to leave the bungalow Gerald was sitting on the step. As they passed him, first Mr Harris then Jeff, he was most placid. But as Johnny walked past he must have forgotten his manners and thought Johnny's left leg was a scratching post, as he leapt at it and stuck all claws in Johnny's trousers. Johnny yelped. Gerald quickly realised his mistake and ran up a tree.

Johnny raised his trouser leg to reveal four trickles of blood.

'That's strange, he's never done that before, Constable. I've got some antiseptic cream, you can't be too careful with cats, you'd better come in the house.'

Johnny returned to the car, smelling of antiseptic cream.

'Well. What do you think, Johnny?'

'That cat's a bleeding menace.'

'Johnny. I'm one hundred per cent confident the dental records are correct and we've got our man. But it would be remiss of us not to double check. We'll go and see the post-mortem examiner, Dr Hughes, and ask if he can confirm that Mr Thompson and Mr Taylor were one and the same.'

They met with Dr Hughes, a bespectacled, studious-looking, thin man, with a pale complexion. Dr Hughes confirmed that the post-mortem examination results and the dental records belonged to the same person. Then they returned to Regent Road for coffee and a little deliberation.

Jeff and Johnny discussed the progress that had been made and decided that developments to date should be properly recorded in the case file, which Johnny agreed to bring up to date. He began to make notes.

They decided the best way to continue with the investigation would be to contact DVLA and obtain the registration number and description of Mr Taylor's car, then pass on the information to Dorset Police, requesting they find Mrs Taylor and inform her of Mr Taylor's death. Then, if Mrs Taylor preferred, Jeff would drive down to Lyme Regis to interview her. They'd need to visit Frampton Marina, go aboard Mr Taylor's boat, and find out who he planned to go sailing with. They'd have to find out if the boat left without Mr Taylor, or if the trip had been cancelled. Then they'd have to interview Mr Taylor's sailing friends.

The information quickly came through from DVLA which, together with all other relevant information, was passed on to Dorset Police.

They set off for Frampton. On the way Johnny said he thought things were going really well. After all, it was only the day before yesterday when they'd started the investigation. Jeff advised that things always went well when you were dealing with people who had nothing to hide and were intent on being helpful. The real fun and intrigue started when you were dealing with those who had things to hide, and seek at all times to misdirect the police. That's when the investigation can come to a grinding halt and become frustrating.

Frampton Marina was sited within a small dock complex that had been built in Victorian times as a commercial port. A decline in shipping had resulted in its closure. It had since been redeveloped to become a modern facility and was located about ten miles upriver from where the Ribble estuary enters the Irish Sea. The old dock had been dredged, and its stone walls repaired. The original decrepit, dysfunctional, rotting lock gates had been removed and new purpose-made gates fitted. The sunken, mud-filled barges, which had, for so long, been a feature of the basin, and had passed their possible restoration state, had been removed. The dock bottom had been cleared of prams, bicycles, metal bed frames and supermarket trolleys. The original Victorian lock keepers cottage, with its smooth, red, ornate brickwork, its sliding sash windows and slate roof, had been restored to become the nerve centre of the complex. The old stone warehouse had been converted to a cafe and chandlers at ground floor level, and the upper levels had been turned into luxury apartments. Additional houses had been built, set back from the basin, with views across the river to one of Lancashire's fertile agricultural farming districts, where all manner of vegetables were grown.

The marina was crowded this last day of the working week. It was the holiday season and with fair weather forecast for the weekend, many people were going off boating, some in power cruisers and others in sailboats. For some, it would have been the start of their summer holiday, they would be away for two weeks; some would be sailing down to Cornwall, to Padstow, Falmouth and Fowey, or the Scillies; some to Ireland, to Cork and Waterford, or to the Channel Isles and on to Brittany. Others would be going to Scotland and the Western Isles. Those away for the weekend only would be heading along the coast or across to the Isle of Man.

They managed to find a parking space in the nearly full marina car park, and walked across to the office, which was manned by the manager, Chris Jones, and his assistant Tracy Dempster. Chris Jones was short and slightly overweight, he looked a jolly sort of chap, designed for comfort, dressed in casual blue, seldom-ironed, well-worn leisurewear, with creased and ill-fitting trousers, tightly belted and drawn in at the waist. He had a round and healthy sun-tanned face and brown hair, in need of cutting, hanging over his forehead. Tracy Dempster, on the other hand, was tall and slim. She'd made an effort to be smart and casual, wearing well-ironed, well-fitting blue jeans, a pink and white horizontal-striped short-sleeved top, and polished brown deck shoes. Any form of make-up would have detracted from her healthy outdoor complexion, which contrasted with her blonde hair and white teeth. Jeff introduced himself as Detective Inspector Dewhurst and Johnny as

Detective Constable Johnston. He advised they were conducting an investigation and required information about Mr Taylor's boat and the boat he'd planned to sail on last week, together with details of the owner and the crew.

Computer records quickly revealed Mr Taylor's boat to be named *Curlew*, a twenty-two foot sloop, which he'd kept berthed at the marina for over five years, but Mr Jones hadn't known which vessel Mr Taylor planned to sail on last week.

They were given access to the marina and proceeded down the pontoon to Curlew's berth. Johnny noticed that Jeff seemed to develop a spring in his step and became more agile when walking along the pontoon, which moved slightly underfoot. Johnny, on the other hand, despite himself being quite agile, felt wooden and slightly unnerved as he walked along the floating platform. Curlew was found to be of fibreglass construction, with a green hull, grey decks and cabin sides. She had been securely tied alongside the pontoon.

Jeff stepped onboard, the boat rolling slightly under his weight. He opened the padlock with the key he'd taken from Mr Taylor's holdall. He slid the main hatch forward, removed the washboards and went below. Johnny stepped onboard into the cockpit and stayed there looking into the cabin from that position. Jeff observed the tidy cabin. A place for everything and everything in its place. Brass clock and barometer. Navigation table and instruments, including GPS and VHF. There was a small locker to starboard containing books on sailing, weather, seabirds and a nautical almanac. Fire extinguishers were in date, as were flares. A sleeping bag and pillow rested on a forward berth. Mr Taylor's sailing jacket and trousers occupied another berth. Safety harnesses and lifejackets were hanging in a locker behind a small louvred door. The galley had been fitted with a gimballed spirit cooker, which had been designed to remain in a horizontal position when the boat heeled over in the wind, enabling cooking to take place in normal sailing conditions.

Jeff's observations suggested that Harry Taylor had been an exacting man, not given to taking chances by carrying duff equipment. All equipment had been in good order, the boat well maintained, the cabin fresh and dry. The most significant thing as far as the investigation was concerned was the sleeping bag, the pillow, the sailing jacket and the trousers. These items would have been transferred to the other vessel if he'd intended to sail on her. Jeff and Johnny sat in the cockpit and discussed the questions posed by the investigation so far. At what stage had Harry Taylor decided not to sail on the other vessel? What circumstances had developed on that Wednesday to influence his decision? Had he gone on the other vessel? Who had he seen? When had he returned home to change his clothes and pack a suitcase? Why had he gone to Blackpool? Had his death anything to do with his sailing pals? Or were they barking up the wrong tree, and did the answers lie back in Blackpool with Mrs Bantry's guests?

Jeff explained to Johnny that a sailor would never let his pals down and leave them short handed for a two week cruise; there would be a planned rota with people on watch while others slept, who would feel fresh for the next watch. This would never happen unless someone broke a leg, or something serious occurred. They decided, at least for the time being, that the answers lay here and not in Blackpool.

'Have you noticed the CCTV cameras, sir?'

'No. I've been so engrossed in Curlew, but they'd obviously have them in a place like this, with all this expensive equipment around.'

'Let's hope they have them switched on.'

'We must be able to identify the other vessel, Johnny. Surely these people at the marina should know. And Mrs Taylor will know.'

Curlew was locked. They returned to the marina office. Chris Jones and Tracy Dempster were still in the office.

'Sorry to trouble you again, Mr Jones, we noticed you have CCTV cameras, I'm presuming they're operable?'

'Oh yes, we have a monitor on the desk if you'd like to come and see?'

'Thank you. Do you record the images on tape?'

'We record the information onto DVDs, in sequence. The information is stored for about a month then the oldest disc is recorded over.'

'Who looks at the DVDs?'

'Well, nobody. There's always someone on site, twenty-four seven, the monitors are always on, as we often have to direct visitors who don't know the marina to a berth, sometimes at night, and we can direct them more easily using VHF if we can see them. We don't suffer from theft but if we did, hopefully we'd have some images to help identify the culprits.'

'And the discs from, say, 8.00am last Wednesday to 4.00pm Thursday … would they be available?'

'Well, yes.'

Mr Jones opened a drawer under the desk to reveal a number of DVDs, numbered in sequence, and selected a couple. 'I think it should be amongst these.' He quickly established which discs covered the times referred to. The images were displayed on the screen and he pointed out the location of Curlew. The time and date were displayed in the top left-hand corner. The screen was split into four quarters and Curlew was in the top right quarter.

'Would you like to view it here or take it with you?'

'Could we take it with us? We'll return it to you when we've seen it.'

'There you go, keep it, I can always replace it, and I know where it is if I need it. Anything else we can do, Inspector?'

'Not at the moment, but if we find what I hope we'll find we'll need to return shortly.'

'No probs. See you soon.'

They returned to the car park and set off back to Regent Road.

'Well, Johnny, one of us has to look at this DVD and not miss a thing. We have to focus on Curlew and any movement between Curlew and any other vessel. With a bit of luck we should see Mr Taylor arrive at about 10.00am then observe what happens.'

'I can do that, sir.'

'You'll have to develop eagle eyes and not miss a thing. Do you have a DVD player at home or will you use the one at the station?'

'We have one at home, sir.'

'Okay, I'll drop you at the station and leave you to it, but I don't envy your task.'

'Thank you very much.'

'You're welcome.'

Chapter 8

It was 5.00pm when Johnny got home with an improving finger, a pain-free upper arm and a scratched leg. Sarah and the boys had planned to go to see the latest film at the cinema and would be leaving shortly. Johnny realised he'd not eaten all day, not like him, and was feeling ravenous. Sarah had put a ham salad in the fridge for him as she always tried to provide him with healthy food. He preferred chips but settled for the salad with wholemeal bread and butter, and a mug of tea.

'Bloody hell,' thought Johnny. 'Friday night. My favourite night in the pub and I've got to watch this bleeding DVD. Still, had I not gone to the pub last Friday and cocked up on Saturday I could have been on the 2 till 10 shift. But this isn't that bad really. I mustn't cock this up. This has got to be done carefully and properly, no matter how long it takes.'

Johnny showered and freshened himself up, brewed a mug of coffee and settled in for the night and morning, he'd no intention of letting DI Dewhurst down.

He switched on the DVD player and inserted the disc. The screen was split into four quarters, one from each of the four cameras positioned around the marina. Johnny was able to identify Curlew in the top right quarter as pointed out by Mr Jones. He set the DVD to run from 0800 hours Wednesday and watched.

At around 1000 hours two figures arrived at Curlew,

a man and woman, Mr and Mrs Taylor. They sat in the cockpit talking, looking as though they were drinking tea. At about 1030 hours they climbed out of the cockpit and walked along the pontoon. Johnny saw them enter the bottom right quarter on the screen. He'd now got his bearings. They walked up the sloping ramp to the marina entrance, kissed, and Mr Taylor walked back. Johnny rewound and started to write up a log, with times, that he could refer to when he reported to DI Dewhurst.

10.05 Two people arrive – Mr and Mrs Taylor.
10.33 Mrs Taylor leaves.
10.37 Mr Taylor returns and goes into the cabin.
11.16 Man arrives. Mr Taylor comes out and talks to him.
11.21 Man walks away.
11.22 Man enters top left quarter and walks through it.
11.23 Man climbs on boat in bottom left quarter.

Johnny was getting the hang of this and while it required concentration, he'd now got two quarters to focus upon … it was becoming interesting.

Sarah and the boys arrived back from the cinema at 9.30. The boys went to bed. Johnny paused and explained to Sarah what he'd been doing, saying that he could be up all night, but it was vitally important it was done properly. She understood the importance of the task and as there was no sound from the television she wasn't bothered by it. She put the percolator on in the kitchen, so he could drink plenty of coffee, made some sandwiches, and brought him coffee and a sandwich. She told him there was more coffee and sandwiches in the kitchen and retired to bed. Johnny pressed play.

12.44 Two men arrive at other boat. Johnny rewound and started again.

12.39 Two men enter marina bottom right.
12.44 They arrive at other boat and climb on board.
13.05 One of other men visits Curlew and climbs on board.
13.15 Mr Taylor and a man leave Curlew and walk to the other boat. Mr Taylor is carrying a holdall, sleeping bag, and a pillow. The other man is carrying a sailing jacket and trousers.

Johnny looked at the screen all night but there was no activity on either vessel.

Sarah got up and went down at 8.30 followed by the boys, who'd stayed in the kitchen and dining room, leaving Johnny undisturbed in the lounge.

23.45 Mr Taylor returns to Curlew, with holdall, sleeping bag, pillow, sailing jacket and trousers.

Sarah made Johnny some breakfast and went shopping with the boys, saying they'd be back about four.

23.55 Man leaves other boat and walks through other quarters of screen and leaves marina.
02.34 The other boat motors out of sight of camera and

leaves the marina.

05.31 Mr Taylor leaves Curlew, carrying holdall, and exits marina at dawn.

Johnny continued to watch the screen until Sarah and the boys returned.

06.35 Time on screen. No further action at Curlew. Johnny stopped watching.

It was getting towards 5.00pm, Saturday. Johnny had not slept. He went to bed and slept like a log. Sarah and the boys had a peaceful evening.

Jeff was up early on the Saturday morning. Though he planned to visit his sister Angela and family, he first went to Regent Road. He made a list of the local taxi companies and rang each of them to check if they had a record of having collected Mr Taylor at Frampton Marina on the Wednesday or Thursday. If so, perhaps they'd taken him to Upridge and then possibly on to Blackpool? He didn't have to wait long before the Silver Wheels Cab Company rang back to say they'd dealt with the call from Mr Taylor. Jeff arranged to meet with the driver at their office, in Preston, on his way to Cheshire, and find out more.

The driver explained that he'd collected Mr Taylor at 05.50. Mr Taylor had sat at the back of the cab, unusually quietly; the driver added that he'd taken him to Upridge. On arriving there, Mr Taylor had asked the driver to wait as he wanted to be taken on to Blackpool.

It was company policy to call the taxi control centre when a customer had been delivered to an address, and to receive instructions for the next collection. The driver had done this, but advised that the customer had requested a further trip to Blackpool. The driver said that after about ten minutes Mr Taylor returned to the cab carrying a suitcase. He noticed that his passenger had changed his clothes. 'The company's procedure,' explained the driver, 'is to record time of departure and the departure address, followed by the time of arrival and the arrival address.' The arrival address was an 'outside tower'. The driver hadn't noticed anyone following, or anything unusual, from Frampton to Upridge or from Upridge to Blackpool. But Mr Taylor had remained quiet throughout.

Jeff left the Silver Wheels Cab Company and headed for the motorway. The motorway was very busy with people heading for their holiday destinations and others making the return journey home. The amount of effort people put into planning and enjoying a holiday was amazing. Caravans were snaking along, towed by cars, obviously burdened by the task. There were cars towing camping trailers stuffed with tents and equipment, often with bicycles supported on racks over the boots or roofs. Cars were often stuffed with blankets and pillows, overloaded with children, and sometimes pet dogs on the back seat with the kids. Occasionally, passengers were asleep, with their faces distorted where their heads rested against the glass windows. Some mothers sat on the front passenger seats, with their shoes removed and their feet resting on the dashboard. Many passengers were telephoning or texting friends and relatives, keeping them up to date with their present location, the traffic and weather conditions, possible time of arrival, and the well-being of the children, dogs and grandparents. Jeff decided he'd have a coffee at the services.

Families spilled out of cars with stiff limbs. Mothers handed out prepared sandwiches and drinks to husbands, children, and grandparents, who were sitting on the grass with blankets used as tablecloths. People armed with plastic bags in their hands and pockets walked dogs along the dog walking section. Small children walked along holding hands with their parents, siblings and grandparents. Older and taller children linked arms with parents and grandparents. Everyone was intent on having a lovely time. A casual observer might easily have thought the world was filled with love.

Jeff continued his motorway journey and left at the usual junction. He then proceeded for a further five miles along the winding leafy Cheshire lanes. He arrived at Angela and Tom's house to find Alex and James in the middle of an argument. James had hidden one of Alex's earrings and refused to admit any knowledge of its whereabouts, telling her she'd misplaced it herself. Angela explained to Jeff, while making a pot of tea, that since Alex had had her ears pierced and started to wear earrings, this had become quite normal Saturday behaviour, and that when James became fed up he'd return it. It wasn't long before James pretended to find the earring under a chair cushion and innocently presented it to Alex. She'd snatched it from him, knowing full well he'd had it all the time.

Jeff had a close relationship with Angela, Tom and the children. They'd normally meet up at least once every month. Alex, who was fourteen, and James, who was nine, enjoyed having Jeff come to stay as he was kind and considerate and always saying and doing funny things. Jeff and the children had much in common, not least sailing and fishing. The children also liked to play computer games. Jeff often bought the latest game for them and he'd bring it along. James had loaded the game.

There was no special reason for visiting Angela and the family, there was no need for a reason, it was just what they did – they were a family and that's what families do. Spend time together. It was the same when Angela and the family visited Jeff; there was no particular reason, other than just being together and sharing time. Or when visiting parents and grandparents … it seemed the natural thing to do. Just keeping in touch. It was never thought of or mentioned, as there was no need to think of it or mention it when they were in contact with each other. But it would be noticed if it wasn't there or if it suddenly disappeared. The close, caring family links provided the children and all the family members with a greater sense of belonging, a stronger sense of identity, knowing and being at ease with each other, having a background, a sense of history. It was reassuring for the children to know there are many who cared for their well being, to feel they were surrounded by people who were beacons of kindness and understanding, and were always there should need be. But, of course, this was never mentioned or thought of. It was just understood. It was what they did.

Angela and the family lived close to a canal and within a few minutes walk of the Trans-Pennine Trail. This started at Southport in the west and meandered through mostly rural areas, along canals and rivers, through open countryside, sometimes along roads, along disused railways and finished at Hornsea on the east coast. This provided the family with ample opportunity to walk along the canal towpath or cycle part of the Trans-Pennine Trail. Walking and cycling the Trail had become a popular pastime among local residents. Having had a meal, prepared by Angela, Jeff washed the dishes, ably assisted by Alex, as was the custom.

Tom, Angela's husband, had been brought up in a rural farming environment. He'd become self-employed as a landscape gardener, and as a person who'd assist local farmers with their milking. This he'd done as and when it was needed and he would find himself quite busy, as farmers found it useful to be able to call upon a reliable helping hand. Angela taught at the local primary school.

They decided to take advantage of the pleasant weather and walk along the canal towpath. During Georgian, Regency, Victorian and Edwardian times, the canal had been one of the arteries of the industrial revolution, and, until about 1950, had been used commercially. But it was now used solely for pleasure pursuits, by people in narrow boats, and was often so busy that boats seemed to be in convoy, in both directions. There were fishermen dotted along the towpath, some with long poles that reached to the other side, which they'd constantly slide back and forth in order to avoid passing boats. As they walked along, James got up to his usual tricks, pretending he was about to fall into the water. Alex feigned disgust at his appalling and silly behaviour. They walked for about an hour, heading towards a locking system, and paused to watch the boats falling and rising in the locks. Then they returned to a pub about half a mile from Angela's house, where they had a couple of drinks in the beer garden. They then went home, watched a little television, chatted and retired to bed. Whenever Jeff visited, James was made to sleep on a small camp bed in his parents' room, and Jeff used James's bed. James never objected, in fact he quite liked it.

As usual, James was first up on Sunday morning and went downstairs to play with the game Jeff had bought. Other family members came downstairs washed and cleaned. By nine the only person not to have washed, cleaned his teeth and changed into his day clothes was James. Alex had made his breakfast, which he'd eaten sat on the floor, whilst still engrossed in his game play. Angela turned the television off and sent him upstairs to sort himself out.

They decided the Sunday would be spent taking a bicycle ride along the Trans-Pennine Trail before visiting a stately home, about fifteen miles away. Angela had prepared a packed lunch, and as there were a couple of spare bikes in the garage, Jeff pumped the tyres up on one and prepared it for his use. They set off at nine forty-five for a pleasant, stress-free day, with spanners, pump, puncture repair outfit and picnic.

At ten, Johnny rang Jeff's mobile.

'Hello, Johnny.'

'Hello, sir. I've looked at the DVD and logged the activity. There's this other boat. And Mr Taylor leaves the marina at 05.31. I stopped looking at 06.35, the time on screen.'

'Johnny. He signed in with Mrs Bantry at four forty-five. We need to know if he returned to Curlew before then. Could you continue to look at it until 16.15, Thursday? And we'll meet in the morning.'

'Will do.'

'Thanks, Johnny, see you in the morning.'

'Are you feeling alright, sir?'

'Yes, Johnny. Why?'

'You sound out of breath.'

'I'm riding a bike.'

'That's alright, sir. I thought you were doing something else.'

'Not at the moment, Johnny. See you tomorrow.'

'Bye, sir.'

Apart from the final mile, the whole of the journey followed the route of a disused railway. James spent some time weaving from one side of the Trail to the other, not allowing Alex to pass, until Angela chastised him and he began to behave himself. Cyclists were allowed into the grounds of the stately home without charge. They could either cycle through the grounds or leave their bicycles at the entrance and walk, which is what they decided to do. The grounds were extensive with herds of deer roaming freely. The deer had become so used to humans that they allowed people to get quite close, before moving away. But never close enough to be touched. People were not allowed to feed the deer. They picnicked in the open while sitting on the grass, surrounded by meadow flowers and ancient deciduous trees. There were grazing deer and a clear blue sky, with vapour trails, and a procession of low-flying aircraft, heading towards Manchester Airport.

They'd taken the same route home. And, having enjoyed a puncture-free day, Jeff had a cup of tea with the family and prepared to leave for Blackpool. Angela and Alex always kissed Jeff when he left for home. But James didn't 'do' kissing, apart from, and very reluctantly, when his nan and granddad visited, and his nan insisted on smothering him with a big kiss of her own. As Jeff was driving away, he looked through his rear view mirror to see Angela and Alex waving. Tom had already gone into the house and James was upside down, with his hands on the ground and his shoes resting against the house wall.

Johnny spent the whole of Sunday looking at the screen; there was no activity around Curlew.

He felt he'd really achieved something and that he had produced a comprehensive log of activities within the marina. He'd been surprised that so much general activity had taken place, with lots of people coming and going, and many boats leaving and entering. He was starting to enjoy working with DI Dewhurst – the investigation was proving interesting. In fact, he stayed in on Sunday night and, instead of going to the pub, had an early night. Sarah was surprised he was up early and arrived in the office five minutes before Jeff.

'Good morning, Johnny.'

'Good morning, sir.'

'Well, how'd you get on?'

Johnny explained the sequence, over a cup of coffee, as they went through the log he'd prepared.

'Excellent, Johnny. On Saturday I contacted various taxi companies. One collected Mr Taylor at five-fifty on Thursday morning outside the marina, took him home and waited. Then he brought him to Blackpool, dropping him off outside the tower at seven thirty-five. I've spoken to the taxi driver. He didn't notice anyone following.'

'So where do we go from here?'

'It's back to the marina with the DVD. Mr Jones and Miss Dempster will be able to identify the other boat and its owner. And with a bit of luck, also, the other men, particularly the one who left the marina before Mr Taylor.'

At the marina Mr Jones quickly confirmed the other boat to be *Duet*, a thirty-four foot ketch, owned by Mr Hargreaves, who lived at High View in Skidmore, a small village between the M6 river crossing and Ribchester. Mr Hargreaves was identified as the first person to visit Curlew at 11.16 on Wednesday. The other men could not be identified. Mr Hargreaves had kept his boat at the marina for nine months, paid his fees, but nothing more was known of him.

Mr Jones explained that a lock system was in operation, and vessels could lock in and out of the marina at half tide. But they had to call Marina Control on VHF to arrange arrival or departure.

When sailors plan passages they always try to make best use of the tides. Tidal height, direction and speed are predictable; the information is contained in tide tables and on charts which are used in passage planning. Sailors also sail boats to the best of their abilities, which means having the correct amount of sail compatible with the prevailing wind conditions, reefed down to reduce sail area if necessary, and not to over press a boat. These things are part of the skills associated with boats and sailing.

When sailors leave ports, marinas, or anchorages, they usually time their departure to enable them to take best advantage of the ebb or flood tide. If a boat travels at five knots through the water with a favourable two-knot tide, it will travel at seven knots over the ground. But if the tide is setting in the opposite direction to their destination, at two knots, a boat will travel at three knots over the ground, which can make a considerable difference to the passage time. A boat will have to 'punch the tide' until more favourable conditions are experienced. Where headlands stick out into the sea, the tide picks up in speed around the headland. This is often referred to as a tidal race. It is particularly important to time the passing of headlands so that conditions are favourable. Depending upon the information contained on charts, it may prove necessary, for safety reasons, to stay well away from a headland when passing it (to stand well off).

'Mr Jones. You say Mr Hargreaves has had his boat here for nine months only?'

'Yes, Inspector. But Duet has been here for about six years now. Mr Hargreaves bought her from her previous owner.'

'Do you know Duet's destination?'

'I'm afraid not. It's not something we would ask, with all the boats coming and going.'

'Will you telephone Constable Johnston or me if Duet returns?'

'Certainly will. No probs.'

'Thank you.'

Jeff and Johnny were walking back towards the car park.

'Would you like a coffee, Johnny?'

'Certainly would, sir.'

They decided to call at the cafe within the marina complex. Jeff bought the coffees and they sat at a table overlooking the river.

'We need to telephone the station, Johnny, to find out if Dorset have contacted Mrs Taylor.'

'I'll do that.'

'Okay. We also have to contact the coastguard to see if he knows where Duet is.'

'How would he know that?'

'It's usual to report your departure to the coastguard when you set off, together with your destination and ETA, then report when you arrive safely. If you don't report your arrival, after a while the coastguard will try to contact you then ask all other vessels if they've seen you, before implementing a search.'

'Those bacon rolls look nice, sir.'

'You have a bacon roll. I'll go back to the marina office and contact the coastguard and then you could find out if Mrs Taylor's been found.'

'Will do.'

Jeff returned to the marina office. Chris Jones gave him the telephone number of Liverpool Coastguard, which he promptly rang.

'Liverpool Coastguard.'

'Good morning, Coastguard. I'm Detective Inspector Dewhurst, from the Lancashire Police, I wonder if you could help me?'

'We will if we can, sir.'

'A boat named Duet left Preston Marina at about 0300 hours last Thursday. I need to know her destination and where she is now.'

'It'll be on our computer, I'll be about a minute, would you like to hold or shall I call you back?'

'I'll hold.'

'Detective Inspector?'

'Yes, sir.'

'Duet reported her departure when she'd cleared the buoyed channel at 0510 hours with two persons on board. Gave ETA Holyhead 2200 hours. If you need me to track her, I'll have to contact Holyhead Coastguard and if she's gone south, probably Milford Haven and Falmouth Coastguards, and ring you back in about fifteen minutes.'

'I'd be grateful if you would.'

'Give me your number and I'll ring back.'

Jeff was sitting on a bench in front of the marina office, looking out over the yacht basin, across the river to the flat farmland and small creeks beyond and watching geese in V formation set against the blue sky. His phone rang.

'DI Dewhurst.'

'Detective Inspector, it's Liverpool Coastguard.'

'Yes, sir.'

'Duet reported her arrival to Holyhead Coastguard at 2230 hours; as far as we're aware, she's still in the area and hasn't reported leaving.'

'Would you ask Holyhead to let me know immediately she reports in? But please don't call her.'

'Will do.'

'Thank you.'

For safety reasons the coastguards preferred that all passages, even if they were just a few miles, should be reported to them. But sailors tend to go off for a few miles around the coast and not report in as they can always make contact within a few seconds should they have a problem. So, a boat can be anywhere around Anglesey in its many coves and harbours, or in the Menai Straits, with its exact location unknown.

Johnny was waiting when Jeff had finished his call.

'Okay, Johnny?'

'Yes. I've been onto the station. Dorset Police contacted Mrs Taylor at about ten this morning, her sister's driving her back today. They'll ring us when they arrive.'

'Duet went to Holyhead and is still in the area.'

Jeff bought a chart of the Irish Sea from the chandlers

located in the marina development. When they returned to Regent Road the chart was fixed onto the wallboard next to the map of Lancashire and the Fylde Coast. Coloured pins were pressed into the wallboard through the chart and map, and notes stuck alongside indicating the following:

1. Burnside Guest House
2. Mr Taylor's address in Upridge
3. Mr Hargreaves address in Skidmore
4. Frampton Marina
5. The time Mr Taylor left the marina
6. The time the other man left the marina
7. The time Duet left the marina
8. The position of Duet and the time she reported her departure to Liverpool Coastguard
9. The position of Duet and the time she reported her arrival to Holyhead Coastguard

'Johnny, we need that boat. I believe there's something sinister going on.'

'How sinister?'

'I don't know. But Mr Taylor left that vessel because he didn't like what was happening or what was planned.'

'How do you know?'

'I don't. But I think that having found out what they intended to do, whatever it was, and not being prepared to compromise himself, he became dangerous and had to be removed.'

'You think so?'

'I do. I believe the man who left the marina before Mr Taylor is the murderer but, as yet, we don't know who he is.'

'We could always see if there's a Mrs Hargreaves. She'd know.'

'I don't think we should go poking around Mr Hargreaves' house just yet, what do you think?'

'Mr Hargreaves is going to find out soon enough, and we may learn much more if he's not there. I think we should visit the house.'

'Very well, that's what we'll do.'

Chapter 9

Detective Superintendent Hird's daughters, Anne and Veronica, spent most of their working days at school or in the hospital, and didn't torment their father during the working day. But Catherine, as a social worker, often found herself in the middle of Blackpool around lunchtime and sometimes visited her father at his office to have lunch with him.

'Hello, Jean. Is the old pates around?'

'Oh, hello, Catherine. He's in his office, I'll let him know you're here.'

'Sir, Catherine's here to see you.'

'Tell her to bugger off.'

'I'll tell her you'll be free in a few moments, sir.'

'He'll be with you shortly, Catherine.'

'How are you, Jean?'

'I'm very well, thanks.'

'And how's your Eddie?'

'He's fine.'

'Is he still watching those Father Ted videos?'

'Yes, but he's got them all on DVDs now, he's always watching them.'

'Men never seem to grow up, do they?'

'They never do, Catherine. Still, I suppose it's one of the few attractive things about them. Are you courting?'

'Not likely. I've got enough men around me acting daft, what with the old pates next door, and my boss at work. I don't want any more men in my life, thank you very much. Living with pates has put me and my sisters off getting married forever. I don't know how mother copes. Mother bought him a full set of Laurel and Hardy DVDs at Christmas. When he comes home at night, he puts them on in his study. How anyone can laugh at the same thing over and over again I'll never know. He has tears rolling down his cheeks he laughs so much, I'm sure they can hear him from the top of the tower.'

'My Eddie's the same, they're all stupid.'

'Pates sometimes starts laughing in bed and mother can't get to sleep, 'cos the bed's shaking, then she tells him to stop being so silly. One morning he was still laughing as he was leaving for work.'

'It's amazing, Catherine, how they can hold down responsible jobs and be serious at work. I just think it's useful to have one around the house, if only to observe his antics. We've been living in the same house for twenty-five years now, and Eddie still doesn't know where anything's kept. If I move the kettle or toaster to a different part of the kitchen he's completely flummoxed.'

'They don't improve with age, do they?'

'If anything, they get worse.'

'What do you want?'

'Father, you should feel privileged that your daughter has decided to spend her lunch break with you. I've brought you a sandwich and a cream cake.'

'You'd better come in then. Jean, could we have a couple of coffees, please?'

'Certainly, sir.'

Chapter 10

Mr Hargreaves had a substantial two-storey house with rough-dressed local stone walls, smooth stone windows and door reveals, sills, lintels and mullions. It had gable ends, with a slated roof and ornate chimney stack. It was set back from the road and had gardens to the front, sides and rear. The drive had been stone paved and there were two entrances to the lane so that vehicles could enter and exit without the need to reverse. A detached garage was positioned to the right-hand side, on which the house details had been replicated.

Jeff drove into the property and parked in front of the house. He and Johnny walked up to the oak-panelled double entrance doors and pressed the polished brass doorbell, which matched the door knob and letter plate. No answer.

The up-and-over garage door was open revealing a silver Range Rover and a small silver Mercedes coupe. It seemed obvious someone must be at home. They walked around the rear of the property, which had been generally laid to lawn, with a paved area directly behind the house. Islands of planting, with conifers and other species, were located in the lawn. A low dry stone wall formed the boundary to the rear and sides, with views of the open countryside beyond. A Scandinavian style, small log cabin was located to the rear of the garage, housing a changing room and hot tub from which music was playing. The door to the cabin was closed so they knocked.

The door was opened by a slightly bewildered middle-aged woman, wearing too much make-up, with dyed blonde hair, and pink and white checked top with blue denim jeans. A little too tight for her once slim but now slightly bulging figure.

'What do you want? You frightened the bloody life out of me.'

'Sorry to have startled you. I'm Detective Inspector Dewhurst. And this is Detective Constable Johnston.'

'Is anything the matter?'

'Are you Mrs Hargreaves?'

'Oh dear. I am, has something happened?'

'Nothing for you to worry about, Mrs Hargreaves. One of your husband's sailing companions has died under mysterious circumstances and we wondered if he could assist us with our enquiries.'

'You'd better come in the house. John's away, sailing, at the moment.'

'Thank you.'

Some of the walls inside the house were plastered and painted, others were finished in natural, rough-dressed stone with smooth stone detailing around doors and windows. All internal woodwork was of polished oak, with oak-boarded floors. Some rugs had been scattered around. All the fixtures and furniture were expensive and highly polished. Both Jeff and Johnny immediately noticed the absence of family photographs, suggesting that neither parents nor children existed. There were several limited edition abstract prints on the walls.

'You say one of John's friends has died?'

'Yes. A Mr Taylor, Harry Taylor. Did you know him?'

'No. I don't know any of John's sailing friends. I never go to the marina, we go to the golf club together and I play in the week, but I've never fancied sailing.'

'Has Mr Hargreaves been sailing long?'

'About two years, he did those navigation courses at college in the evenings then he bought his boat.'

'Do you keep in touch when he's away?'

'No. He takes his mobile with him but he never rings. He said he'd be home before Wednesday and if he was going to be longer he'd let me know.'

'What does Mr Hargreaves do?'

'For a living?'

'Yes.'

'He imports shoes, we have a warehouse and two retail outlets, one in Preston and one in Blackpool, you've probably heard of Hargreaves' Discount Shoes, that's us.'

'Yes, I have. Do you know where Mr Hargreaves has sailed to?'

'No. I don't think John knows until just before he sets off and gets the weather forecast.'

'Well thank you, Mrs Hargreaves, we'll probably speak with Mr Hargreaves when he returns.'

'If he rings I'll let him know you called.'

Mrs Hargreaves watched them drive into the lane and wondered how much they knew. She started to think about John who sailed close to the wind in his business dealings and always, especially at the golf club, pretended to be the forever honest, tax-paying businessman. Good God, if the Inland Revenue or Customs ever caught up with him and really scrutinised his business dealings. Everything would have to go, the house included.

Bloody hell, she thought, if they went back over the years. He'd always been a lying, cheating bastard, twenty-three years being married to a man you despise and can't trust – unbelievable, isn't it? Still, his dishonesty had provided a cracking lifestyle, lovely house, cars, holidays, pots of money. All that was needed was to keep up the pretence, to be the dutiful, loving wife, to keep up appearances. What a load of crap. But she was good at saying the right things, and smiling at the right people at the right times. Even though he was a lying bastard, she had to concede they were a good pair together. She was a lady of leisure. Walking around the golf club in all her expensive clothes. Monday was one of the evenings when that councillor on the Planning Committee came along. John would say butter the bugger up, get him on our side, let him buy you a drink, buy him one back, arrange a couple of dinner parties, invite him and his wife along together with a few respectable friends. No expense should be spared, give him a good time, find out his address, send them a card and presents at Christmas. Not too expensive mind, but expensive enough to make them feel obligated. She was bloody good at it. John knew this was where she excelled and said it was always nice to be able to call in favours. You know, you scratch my back and I'll scratch yours.

Planning Committee members were always good

friends to have, they could come in useful, especially when they lived beyond their income, with an ordinary job, and had a liking for the good life. But they weren't all bent, most were too honest for their own good, daft buggers. The Monday night piss-head, he'd be bent at the right price. Get the bugger on board, that's what she was preparing to do when them coppers arrived. A pair of no hopers. Lie in the spa bath for half an hour, bubbling away, music playing, come out smelling like a bunch of roses, get her hair done, get her make-up on, and put on her designer clothes. She might be forty-eight but she'd look like thirty-eight when she was finished. Get in her fifty-seven thousand pounds Mercedes. Nice day, open top, see the bastards green with envy at the golf club when she drove in; close the open top in the car park so they could all have a good gawp. That councillor wouldn't stand a chance, he'd be as bent as a nine bob note when they'd finished with him, as her dad used to say. Good old John, they both dropped lucky when they met each other. But if it all went pear shaped he'd be on his own. She was as white as white can be and knew nothing of any business dealings; notice she didn't sign for anything or have a business cheque book. What she did have was a little pot of gold. John knew nothing about it. Just in case the bubble burst, it wasn't in her name. But it was there for when she needed it, just enough to keep her comfortable. Thank God for bent accountants. Now she must sort that councillor out. She'd have him eating out of her hand and jumping through hoops before you could say Jack Robinson.

On returning to Blackpool they received a message that Mrs Taylor had arrived back in Upridge, but on seeing Mr Taylor's red holdall on the bed, had broken down. Her sister had spoken with the police and requested that the meeting with DI Dewhurst be postponed until the next day as Mrs Taylor was really too upset and tired at the moment and in no fit condition to see anyone.

As it was the school holidays, Sarah had taken the boys to visit her parents for a few days and had used Johnny's car. Jeff dropped Johnny off at his Bispham home and agreed to collect him at about eight in the morning when they'd go to Upridge to visit Mrs Taylor. Jeff then continued to his house, changed into his boating clothes and went to see Marie at the marina.

He bought some sandwiches on the way to the marina, climbed aboard Marie, made a mug of tea, and decided to settle down and consider the case. But he found it strange when he wanted his mind to focus upon a subject; something else kept entering it, he'd constantly think about something else. Jeff knew the problem, it had been the radio programme he'd been listening to when driving there. They'd been playing the music from his favourite musical and he couldn't get it out of his mind.

Jeff was sitting in the cockpit relaxed by the quiet atmosphere, the only sounds being the frapping of halyards on masts and occasional squawking gulls. He noticed a blue-hulled ketch entering the marina and wondered whether he was dreaming or hallucinating, unable to believe his eyes. The name of the ketch, *Duet*, with three people on board. One man was on the foredeck with a bow line in hand, ready to tie alongside and two were standing in the cockpit. Duet motored to a berth about ten boats along from Marie and tied alongside.

Chapter 11

When Jeff dropped off Johnny at home, he read the note Sarah had left for him, advising him to eat the salad she'd put in the fridge, and make sure he remembered to put the bin out on Tuesday evening for the Wednesday morning collection. She and the boys would be back on Thursday evening, the message continued, and that he be careful, not do anything silly, or drink too much. Johnny decided he'd ignore most of the note, especially the last bit. After all, it had been nearly a week since he'd had a pint, what with dogs, injections, cats, boats and DVDs. While the cat's away the mice will play, and tonight this little mouse was going to play like there was no tomorrow. He binned the fresh, colourful green salad and went to the chippy for his favourite meal, which he ate with bread and butter, swilled down with two mugs of tea. He settled down to watch the news at six before dozing off for half an hour. His natural body clock kicked in at seven. He woke in the chair and turned off the television just as the introductory music to a television soap was playing. He went upstairs, showered, shaved, changed, came down and decided to leave the few dishes until morning. Then the phone rang. It was Sarah letting him know they'd arrived safely at her parents' house and was making sure her own house was still in one piece. He assured Sarah that everything was fine and he'd be having an early night. It was eight fifteen when Johnny left the house to visit his first watering hole. He'd decided to visit three pubs, have two pints in each and finish at his favourite last orders pub and return home about midnight. Thank God for normality.

Johnny was in sight of his first watering hole, and could feel the pleasure and satisfaction as he closed in on his comfort zone, when his mobile phone rang.

'Hello.'

'Johnny.'

'Oh, hello, sir.'

'Guess what.'

'You're taking early retirement?'

'No. I'm at the Wyre Marina, and Duet has just come in, with three people on board. Can you come down here? We need to keep an eye on them.'

'I suppose so, sir.'

'Cheer up, Johnny. It'll give you something to do while Sarah's away.'

'I know.'

'And Johnny. Make sure you're wearing something casual and warm, and bring a waterproof jacket. If you ring me when you arrive, I'll open the security gate from the inside.'

Well, thought Johnny, that's pissed on the chips, no beer again, bleeding marvellous. What's he talking about, bring a waterproof jacket. The sun's been cracking the flags all day. I hope he doesn't think he's going to get me on that bloody boat of his. What a bleeding life.

Johnny returned home and thought he'd try to look like the people he'd seen at Frampton Marina. So he put on jeans, blue rugby shirt, thick blue sweater, trainers and his waterproof jacket with zip front and hood. He thought he would blend in quite nicely. He called a taxi and arrived at the marina at about eight forty-five. He rang Jeff on his mobile and was let in. They walked along the wobbly pontoon and climbed aboard Marie. Johnny had never been on a sailboat before. Jeff pointed out Duet. She could be clearly seen. He said they'd just need to observe to see if there was any activity, adding that he didn't think she'd come from Holyhead, and that he guessed she'd been north; otherwise, why would she drop into the Wyre Marina when, given the time of high water, Frampton would have been easier to enter from Holyhead? And she wouldn't be able to leave the marina until the morning. At nine fifteen, the three men, one with a holdall, stepped from Duet onto the pontoon and headed towards the exit. Jeff and Johnny followed at a distance.

They entered the first pub they came to on the corner of two roads, a couple of minutes walk from the marina. Mr Hargreaves was recognisable – as were the other two men – as being those on the DVD Johnny had seen. They took a pint each from the bar. Mr Hargreaves paid then they sat at a table. The pub was about half full, and most of the customers, judging by their complexions and clothes, were trawler men, fishermen or sailors. Jeff and Johnny sat down at a table close by, with a pint each that Jeff had bought. The man with the holdall kept looking at his watch, and after about twenty minutes downed the remains of his pint, got up, bid farewell to his friends and left.

'Off you go, Johnny. Follow him, stay with him if you can, see where he goes, and if you can, find out who he is. I'll watch these two.'

'Okay.'

Johnny left half a pint, something he'd never done before.

The man walked towards the town centre. He came across a taxi rank and took the first taxi. Johnny took the second. 'Follow that cab.' The taxis set off towards Preston Station.

On reaching the station, Johnny paid the driver then climbed the steps just behind the other man. They went to the ticket office and the man took his ticket. Johnny said, 'Same again, please,' and paid by card. He looked at his ticket to find he was going to Glasgow. 'Bloody hell!' After fifteen minutes the train arrived and they got on. Johnny kept a good distance behind and tried to look as inconspicuous as possible. From the position of the man's head, Johnny decided he must be sleeping and thought he'd close his eyes for a little while as he could be up all night, and, he thought, little cat naps tend to help. Johnny wasn't sleeping and opened his eyes every so often to find the man still in the same position. The train arrived at Glasgow Central. Johnny followed the man out of the station and on to the taxi rank. The man got into the first taxi, Johnny the second. 'Follow that cab,' he said.

They arrived at a house in a leafy Glasgow suburb. The man got out, walked up the drive, and entered the house. Johnny made a note of the name and number of the house, and the road name. He asked the taxi driver

112

what the suburb was called then asked to be taken to the local police station. On arriving there Johnny paid, got out of the taxi and walked into the station. He showed his warrant card to the desk sergeant and explained his business. The desk sergeant arranged for a driver and unmarked police car to be made available. They returned to the address Johnny had given and observed it. It proved to be a long night but eventually, at about seven forty-five, the man and a woman came out of the house. The man opened the garage door. The woman got into the driver's seat and drove a Volvo out of the garage. The man closed the garage door, got into the passenger's seat and they set off towards Glasgow, with Johnny and the driver keeping close behind.

The car reached the centre of Glasgow, the driver stopped by a pavement. The man got out, took a set of keys from his pocket and opened a shop door. Over the top of the door was a sign, which read *Brown's Chemist*. Johnny made a note of the address and decided to wait until after nine. Then he would go in and buy some lozenges. A lady arrived at eight forty-five and knocked on the shop door. The man opened the door and the lady walked in. At ten past nine Johnny entered the chemist shop. The lady was standing behind the counter near the till while the man, wearing a white coat, was at the rear in the dispensary. Johnny looked around the shop, slowly and deliberately, and took a tube of lozenges. He went to the till.

'That will be eighty pence, sir.'

Johnny produced a pound coin. 'Thank you. Excuse me, would that be Mr Brown?'

'Aye, it would.'

'Thank you.' Johnny took his twenty pence change and returned to the car.

As Johnny was leaving the pub to follow the man with the holdall, Jeff was finishing his pint. And seeing the two men buy another round, he decided to buy another pint for himself. Then he took up a position on a bench behind the men. He chose to wear that tired and vacant look that people in pubs sometimes have, a look which says 'do not disturb.' At ten-thirty, Mr Hargreaves and his friend got up and walked out. Jeff followed and they entered the marina. The two men climbed aboard Duet while Jeff climbed aboard Marie. He was certain there would be no more activity until morning. Duet's interior light went on and after about fifteen minutes went off. Jeff left Marie's sliding main hatch open so he could hear any sounds, and climbed into his sleeping bag. He was fully dressed in case he had to get up because of any activity. But nothing happened overnight, and when dawn came Jeff decided to sleep for a couple of hours. Duet left the marina a little after high water, she was obviously going south and Jeff knew she would catch the next flood tide to take her up the Ribble, to enter Frampton Marina at about high water in the evening. He'd be there to watch and observe, but decided to leave them alone for the time being. Jeff tidied Marie, checked everything was ship shape, and locked up. He left the marina and returned home where he showered, shaved and had some breakfast. He then decided to contact Johnny before heading out to meet Mrs Taylor.

*

It was nine thirty when Johnny's phone rang.

'Good morning, sir.'

'Good morning, Johnny, how are things?'

'Things are very well, sir. I'm in Glasgow.'

'Glasgow?'

'Yes, bleeding Glasgow. The man I followed is Mr Brown. He lives in a Glasgow suburb and has a chemist's shop in the city centre.'

'A chemist. … That's interesting.'

'I'm just on my way to the railway station now. I've got a lift in a police car. I should be back this afternoon.'

'Johnny, you've done very well. I'm going to see Mrs Taylor this morning. Duet left the Wyre Marina about seven thirty, she should be entering Frampton Marina this evening and we need to be there. I don't think we should intervene at the moment, but we need to find out who the third member of the crew is. I'll collect you at home about six then we'll go to the marina.'

'Okay, see you later.'

'Bye, Johnny.'

Johnny was dropped off at the station by his Glasgow colleague. He was beginning to feel quite hungry. He checked the time of his train and found he'd have to wait about an hour so he decided to take a walk outside the station and pass the time by having a light meal. He came across a small cafe, with plastic chairs and laminate-covered tables. The menu displayed in the window offered a range of light bites, plus a full breakfast – including toast and marmalade and a pot of tea. If he thought he could resist the temptation to have a greasy breakfast, he was wrong. Standing on the pavement, checking on the menu, with the aroma of frying bacon wafting through the open door, he weakened and went inside. Half an hour later he left the cafe and walked back to the station, feeling full, satisfied and set for the day.

Chapter 12

Jeff arrived at Mrs Taylor's Upridge home. Mrs Taylor's sister opened the door and he introduced himself. She introduced herself as Mrs Reading and they walked into the lounge to meet Mrs Taylor. Jeff could see their likeness immediately; they were of similar age, about fifty, though he couldn't tell who was the elder of the two. They each had square shoulders and straight backs, with greying hair left natural. They were both about five foot eight inches tall, slim, dressed smartly and without make-up. Jeff had always thought women who chose not to wear make-up or colour their hair to be confident and comfortable in themselves. He believed they didn't feel the need to attempt to improve upon what nature had provided, not to feel the need to follow current trends and not to be influenced by advertisements promising to enhance their appearance.

Mrs Reading went into the kitchen to make a pot of tea and Jeff sat with Mrs Taylor.

'I'm very sorry we have to meet under these circumstances, Mrs Taylor. You are aware the post-mortem examination revealed that Mr Taylor was murdered?'

'I am, Inspector.'

'Can you think of any reason why anyone would have wanted to harm your husband?'

'No. I can't imagine anyone wanting to harm Harry, Inspector, he wouldn't hurt a fly, he's worked hard all his life, then this should happen. He didn't deserve this.'

'I'm sure he didn't, Mrs Taylor. I do need to get to the bottom of this and I have to ask you some questions. You'll have to formally identify the body, but there's no doubt that it is Mr Taylor.'

Mrs Taylor's sister came in with the tea and biscuits, sat down and poured the tea.

'Do you know Mr Hargreaves, the man Mr Taylor intended to sail with?'

'No. Harry sailed with Duet's previous owner, the one who sold her to Mr Hargreaves, but I don't think he's very experienced so he asked Harry to sail with him, with Harry knowing Duet and being experienced.'

'But Mr Taylor didn't sail on Duet and ended up in Blackpool. Have you any idea why that would be?'

'None at all. I would have thought that had the trip been cancelled Harry would have spent his time on Curlew – that's Harry's boat – and sailed locally, something he enjoyed doing.'

'Have you any idea why he would go to Blackpool?'

'Well, if he decided not to sail on Curlew, and if he decided to go away for a few days, then he would most likely have chosen Blackpool.'

'Why Blackpool?'

'He'd gone there since he was a boy and always liked being in Blackpool. He'd say it could be as bawdy and coarse as you wanted it to be, or as sophisticated and genteel as you wished, and everything in between. He used to say that two days in Blackpool was better than two weeks in Barbados. But I've no idea how he would know, as he'd never been to Barbados.'

118

'You are aware that Mr Harris allowed me to enter your house on Friday?'

'Yes. He told me.'

'It was something I had to do. I took the key to Curlew from Mr Taylor's holdall, and I've been on board. I can now return the key.'

'Thank you. Fancy, all those years living together, still having dreams for when we retire. I wonder if the people who committed this crime ever considered the consequences of their actions?'

'I don't think so, Mrs Taylor, they're too selfish, concerned only with themselves and usually financial gain.'

'But Harry wasn't wealthy.'

'No. This is one of the puzzles. There seems to be no obvious motive, but we're working on it.'

'I do hope you find whoever did this, Inspector.'

'I hope so too, Mrs Taylor. Thank you for your time, if you do think of anything that may be useful, you will let me know?'

'Of course.'

Jeff was shown out by Mrs Reading.

'Goodbye, Mrs Reading.'

'Goodbye, Inspector.'

Jeff was driving past the shops along the High Street in Upridge when he noticed the young woman he'd helped with the pram on Friday. She was struggling down the same steps with the same pram. Jeff didn't believe in coincidences. And sometimes in police work things just happen, for no apparent reason. Reasons that cannot be explained or ignored. This, he thought, was one of those occasions. Just seeing the young woman wouldn't have triggered his imagination, but there was something that did: further along the road, parked against the kerb, was a clean, shiny, very noticeable, silver Mercedes drop head coupe, with the top open. He'd made a note of the personalised registration number yesterday, and knew it belonged to Mrs Hargreaves. He turned his car around, parked a little further up the street and waited. After about ten minutes Mrs Hargreaves came out of the same terrace house the young women had come from, looked around and walked down the steps. Jeff noted she was wearing expensive clothes and designer sunglasses and carrying a small shoulder bag. Finally, she got into her car and drove off. On his way back to Blackpool, he took his time and passed the Hargreaves' house in Skidmore. The Range Rover and Mercedes were side by side in the double garage. He continued towards Blackpool.

Jeff took the coast road, through Fairhaven and St Annes to see if Duet could be seen offshore. She was there, slowly heading along the coast. There was no rush, she wouldn't be able to enter the marina until about seven. He then went to Regent Road and brought the case file up to date, entering all known information, including Mr Brown's details and the address in Upridge where he'd seen Mrs Hargreaves. Then he decided to pop out for some lunch and take a leisurely walk along the promenade. As he did so, he reflected on what Mr Taylor used to say about Blackpool being bawdy and coarse, or sophisticated and genteel, and anything between. And my God, he'd been right; when you looked around it was all here, it was for everyone: families with babies; young children and dogs; middle-aged couples whose children had left home; elderly couples who had come here all their lives; pensioners' outings; single persons; groups of girls and boys enjoying their first holiday without their parents. It had been the time of low water and lots of people were on the beach, some enjoying donkey rides, horse and carriage rides, tram rides. Some buying ice creams, or playing the fruit machines, bingo, lots of noise, hustle and bustle. Some would spend the afternoon ballroom dancing in the cool of the Tower Ballroom, with its massive Wurlitzer. Others would take in a show at the end of the pier theatre. All the big names in entertainment played here. And of course, there was the big dipper or the big wheel, and lots more. Jeff liked the peace and quiet of nature and the outdoor life, river valleys and estuaries and offshore sailing. But this was just as much part of nature, with people enjoying themselves. All these happy smiling faces around, not a miserable face to be seen. It's strange, he thought, how you're able to live in a place and not see what's on your doorstep, until someone points it out to you. Jeff thought he might take a holiday here one day. He'd have liked to have known Harry Taylor. He decided they would have had a lot in common. Such an unnecessary waste of life and a terrible loss for Mrs Taylor. Johnny rang to say he'd arrived home. Jeff said he'd collect him at about five thirty, and to dress casual as he'd done the night before.

Johnny freshened himself up with a shower and a shave; he looked in the wardrobe mirror, convinced he'd lost weight. He never bothered about his weight but everything seemed tighter and trimmer. He wondered whether Sarah had changed the mirror for one of those that make you look thin, and checked the screws to check they hadn't been disturbed. No, he was definitely thinner. Not surprising, he thought, I haven't had a bloody pint all week. Johnny put on his jeans and leather belt, the buckle easily located in a hole, one up from its usual notch, and this made Johnny feel good. He noticed he'd been feeling better in the mornings recently, not hung over, and didn't feel as tired during the day. He'd been sleeping better at night, and had been asleep on the train. He felt good and fresh and he thought he may be more disciplined in future, but couldn't be sure. He'd promised himself a meal from the chippy, but decided that common sense should prevail, and he settled for whatever Sarah had left in the fridge. He made himself a ham sandwich with wholemeal bread, a mug of tea, followed by a banana and an apple.

Jeff had been home to change and he arrived at Johnny's house at about five twenty. They set off for Frampton Marina. Johnny had forgotten to put the bin out for tomorrow's collection. The bin was full, and he put the fresh salad Sarah had prepared for him at the very top.

They entered Frampton Marina and parked away from the basin, but in a position that gave them a clear view of the whole of the pontoons. They arrived early giving them time to walk to the office, which was manned by Chris Jones. Tracy Dempster had finished for the day. They spoke with Mr Jones and advised him that they still had an interest in Duet, and impressed upon him the need for discretion and not to bring their interest to the attention of anyone. Also, to advise them the next time Duet arranged to leave the marina. While they'd been speaking with Mr Jones, Duet made contact with the marina on VHF to arrange for the lock gates to be opened. They returned to the car park and waited. A silver grey Range Rover arrived, driven by Mrs Hargreaves, who parked by the entrance to the pontoons.

Duet entered, and tied alongside her pontoon berth. After about ten minutes Mr Hargreaves and his friend stepped off, each carrying a holdall. They also had a life raft in a blue valise, which they carried between them.

Had they been asked, the two of them could have explained that a life raft is contained either in a canister, which is fixed externally on the deck or coachroof, in case of emergency, or contained in a valise, which resembles a holdall, and is kept in a locker, usually in the cockpit, for ease of access. It has a strap either side and is quite heavy and best carried by two people. They walked to the Range Rover, placed the valise and holdalls in the back and drove off.

Jeff and Johnny followed, staying well behind. They headed towards Blackpool and dropped the man off at a detached house in Fairhaven. Mr and Mrs Hargreaves turned around and headed back to Skidmore.

Johnny made a note of the address. Then they

returned to Regent Road, brought the case file up to date, adding information to the map of Lancashire and the chart of the Irish Sea. They agreed that since reporting her arrival in Holyhead, the whereabouts of Duet had been unknown for twelve days. Jeff explained that this had been very strange behaviour for yachtsmen. All sailors would have wanted the coastguards to be aware of their intentions, for safety reasons. Another thing that puzzled Jeff was the fact that they'd brought a life raft from Duet. It could have been hired for that cruise only – perhaps they'd intended returning it – but most unlikely. A boat like Duet would have had her own life raft on board. Alternatively, the life raft could have been going in for servicing. Again, this was unlikely, as servicing would have normally been carried out every two or three years during the winter months when boats would be laid up.

At nine o' clock they decided to call it a day. Jeff agreed to drop Johnny off at home and collect him at six thirty in the morning. They'd go to Fairhaven to the home of the third man and try to identify him and what he did. Johnny was home at nine thirty, intent on being disciplined. He had a glass of milk, set his alarm for five thirty and went to bed.

Chapter 13

Jeff collected Johnny at six thirty. Johnny was up early, showered and shaved. He enjoyed toast and tea for breakfast and was feeling as bright as a button. He was dressed in a suit and tie and shiny shoes. When he got into Jeff's car, and they had left the street, Johnny failed to notice all the black bins lining the pavements.

They parked on the road, a little distance from the third man's Fairhaven home. Part of the road and pavement had been covered in wind-swept sand, blown from the dunes. The house had been sited to take full advantage of the panoramic views overlooking the grassy dunes and the estuary beyond. Seagulls stood on the ridge of the red brick house, all facing in the same direction; droppings had discoloured the ridge and slate roof just below the ridge line. There had been some activity around some of the houses, with children in uniforms being taken to school early, and people leaving for their places of work in Preston, Blackpool, Liverpool and Manchester. These were the early risers. All was quiet and uneventful at the third man's house until eight forty-five. The automatic garage door opened and the man in a black Lexus drove out, the garage door closing as he left. They followed, but had not travelled very far, as the man only went a short distance into the centre of St. Annes and parked his car in a side street around the corner from a shopping precinct. He got out, well dressed in pin-striped suit, wearing collar and tie.

Johnny also got out of the car and followed while Jeff parked up. The man headed towards the precinct and stopped at a newsagents where he collected a copy of the Telegraph. Then he unlocked a door, from the street, next to the newsagents. Johnny saw it offered access to a small entrance hall and the bottom of a staircase. The man closed the door. Johnny imagined him climbing the stairs to his first floor office. A plaque had been fixed to the brickwork to the left-hand side of the external door, *J C Baker Solicitor*. Johnny went into the newsagents and said to the person on the counter, 'Excuse me, was that Mr Baker I saw going to his office?'

'It was,' said the newsagent.

Armed with this latest piece of information, they returned to Regent Road and ran a check to establish the backgrounds of each of the individuals. They wanted to know whether any of them had a criminal record.

There was no recent criminality but they established that Mr Hargreaves was aged 52. During his twenties he had been fined for GBH and stealing a car. Mr Brown, the chemist, was aged 50. At the age of 32 he'd been fined heavily for tax evasion and fraud; at the time he'd been a partner in another chemist shop.

There was no evidence that Mr Baker, aged 45, had been involved in anything unlawful. Jeff and Johnny discussed the case and wondered what the connection was between Mr Hargreaves and Mr Baker. Were they members of the same golf club? Jeff knew the area around Skidmore quite well and felt he knew which golf club they'd most likely be members of. He rang the golf club, requesting that they fax or email a copy of their membership list, which they quickly did. The information was there. Mr and Mrs Hargreaves and Mr and Mrs Baker had been members of the same golf club.

Jeff knew he had to get away to think. The police station environment was not always conducive to clarity of thought, with traffic noise from outside and people walking up and down corridors, talking and visiting the coffee machine.

'Johnny, I'm just nipping out for a couple of hours, get yourself some lunch. I'll see you later.'

'Okay, sir. See you later.'

It took about thirty minutes for Jeff to drive to the Wyre Marina, buy a sandwich and climb aboard Marie. He brewed a mug of tea, sat in the cockpit and drifted into ruminating mode.

Over the years, Jeff had learnt that people who'd been honest as children, honest as adolescents, honest as teenagers, usually remained honest throughout their lives. On the other hand, those who'd been dishonest during those stages of life, usually continued to remain dishonest. There would always be exceptions, but this was the general rule, which he believed to be correct. He sympathised with people who seemed unable to tell the truth, and had known some who, if they'd had a clear choice to tell the truth or tell a lie, would always lie, even though it would not benefit them. It was their nature to do so, and it often appeared to be hereditary, as in father and son being dishonest, or honest, as the case may be. It was the same with greed. He'd known people who had very little material wealth and craved for nothing more than they had. And there were those

127

who had all the material wealth anyone could wish for, yet were still hungry for more. To the point of dishonesty. Jeff thought it right to have spoken with Mrs Hargreaves, even though it would have alerted them to the investigation. Much had been learnt by doing so. Jeff was convinced the valise had not contained a life raft, but something highly valuable. Something that was worth killing for. Greedy, dishonest and dishonourable men would do anything for money. Mr Hargreaves and Mr Brown were known to have been involved in criminal acts, but not Mr Baker. He had a fine house and car, and an expensive lifestyle, and yet worked from a modest office. Jeff suspected he'd been manipulated by Mr Hargreaves and probably, until quite recently, had been honest, and would be feeling guilty about his actions. He may not have known that Mr Taylor had been murdered. If he were to be interviewed, he'd be the one who would find it difficult to tell lies. Whereas for the others, lying would be their natural response, in all forms of conversation, even among friends at the golf club or elsewhere.

Jeff rang DS Hird's direct line. Jean answered.

'Jean, it's Jeff.'

'Hello, Jeff.'

'Is Superintendent Hird in?'

'Well, he is, but he's otherwise engaged at the moment. His daughter Catherine has brought his other daughter Anne, you know, the schoolteacher. She's on holiday at the moment, and they've come to have lunch with their father. His daughters are doing a lot of laughing, but I can't hear him.'

'Will he be there in an hour?'

'He will. The girls will have gone by then.'

'Will you tell him I wish to see him?'

'Okay, Jeff, see you later.'

'Bye, Jean.'

Jeff arrived back at Regent Road and climbed the stairs to Superintendent Hird's office. Jean showed him through. Superintendent Hird was at his desk writing.

'Good afternoon, sir.'

'Hello, Jeff. Jean said you wanted a word.'

'Yes, sir. It's about the case you've assigned to me.'

Jeff explained how the investigation had developed. The criminal records of Mr Hargreaves and Mr Brown. How he'd witnessed Mrs Hargreaves in strange circumstances in Upridge. The young woman he'd helped with the pram who, judging by the vacancy of her facial expression, had probably been on drugs. The unknown whereabouts of Duet for twelve days. And when she should have been south of Frampton, was most certainly north. The valise which he'd thought was not a life raft and how he'd decided it had probably contained drugs. And that if they were only investigating the murder of Harry Taylor then they were now in a position to bring Duet's crew in for questioning. But, he thought that if they were to give them a rope long enough they would hang themselves and others with them. He was referring to the golf club and the relationship between Mr Hargreaves and Mr Baker, and how he felt that Mr Baker was probably living beyond his means. The carrot had been dangled in front of him so he'd taken it. And that they were likely to end up with a more satisfactory outcome if they were to step back and observe. And he thought that the greed of these men would be such that they'd soon be repeating the trip. Jeff explained that he thought Mr Hargreaves brought in the drugs and Mrs Hargreaves distributed them. As Mr Hargreaves had been an importer of shoes, he declared, they'd probably been doing this for some time using other routes. Even though Customs were very keen, it would be impossible to check every yacht, and a lot of drugs don't take up a lot of space, but are worth a lot of money. Mr Hargreaves had started his sailing fairly late in life, not unusual in itself, but sailing was a passion which normally gripped people when they were young. Somehow, Mr Hargreaves and his friends didn't sit comfortably with the stereotypical sailor type. Jeff explained that he believed Mr Hargreaves had taken up sailing to provide himself with an additional means of trafficking drugs, another way to hoodwink the Customs. Mr Hargreaves, Jeff went on, had thought he needed Mr Taylor, but as he'd become a more skilful sailor and knew he could handle things himself, he knew he'd soon be at it again and then we'd be on to him. And while Jeff believed the murderer to be Mr Brown, he'd no solid evidence to prove this. But if they nailed them for drugs trafficking, it should be easy to extract the truth from Mr Baker, who was acting out of character, as he'd been manipulated, and was prepared to compromise himself. Unlike Harry Taylor. Two men had left Frampton on Duet but three men returned. Where did Mr Brown rejoin them?

Superintendent Hird had been a lover of family values all his married life, and while he'd often wished his daughters would get married and leave home, he'd also developed absolute respect for the way they'd each conducted their lives and their commitment to sound social values. He'd never believed his girls had ever indulged in drugs; some alcohol, yes, especially Catherine, but never hard drugs, and his heart went out to those families whose lives had been wrecked through one of their easily influenced teenagers becoming addicted to drugs. He thought drug trafficking was a wicked crime, carried out by people with no moral conscience, and any steps that could be taken to put these people behind bars, where they belonged, should be taken.

Superintendent Hird agreed with Jeff. Mr Taylor's death had been low profile. It had hardly warranted a mention in the newspapers, and they were under no pressure to solve the crime. He was able to see from the way things were progressing that they'd end up with a result. Especially if drug trafficking and distribution could be proven. But they'd need to speak with Customs, let them know what was happening, as they may have some useful information about Mr Hargreaves.

Chapter 14

When Jeff had left to go to the Wyre Marina, Johnny decided to pop out for some lunch. He went into a top floor cafe of one of the popular departmental stores, and was sitting down enjoying a tuna salad when he felt a tap on his shoulder. When he looked around, a lady said, 'Hello, Constable, luv.'

'Oh. Hello, Mrs Bantry.'

'I'll sit with you and keep you company. I don't know where my Stanley's gone. We come out every Wednesday, it gets Stanley out of the house. They make a lovely cup of tea here. Is there no sugar on this table? Oh, it's hiding behind the menu.'

'Have you lost him?'

'No. He always wanders off. He knows I'll be up here having a nice cup of tea. What are you doing here?'

'I'm having some lunch, Mrs Bantry.'

'So you are. I didn't have you down as a salad man, I'd have said you were more of a steak and chips type.'

'Well, it just shows how wrong you can be.'

'Oh. I don't think so, Constable. Are you on a diet? You're looking a bit pasty.'

'I'm not on a diet, I'm just trying to eat a little more sensibly, that's all.'

'Same thing if you ask me. Are you married?'

'I am well and truly married, Mrs Bantry.'

'Any children?'

'Two teenage boys.'

'I always think people are fortunate to have children, me and Stanley never had any. I always regretted it, but Stanley never had it in him. Has your wife put you on this diet?'

'I'm not on a diet.'

'Yes, you are. You're looking distinctly peaky. You'll be anorexic before you can say Bob's your uncle. Shall I get you some chips to go with it?'

'No thank you.'

'Does Mrs Johnston work?'

'She's a school teacher.'

'Oh, that's a nice job, how old are your sons?'

'They're fourteen and twins.'

'What's their names?'

'Jim and John.'

'Do they get called JJ?'

'How do you mean?'

'You know. Jim Johnston and John Johnston.'

'I don't think so.'

'I bet they do. Ask them when you see them.'

'I will do.'

'What's your wife's name?'

'It's Sarah.'

'That's a nice name. Have you booked any holidays?'

'No, Mrs Bantry. Sarah's taken the boys away for a few days.'

'Where've they gone?'

'She's taken them to see her parents. They'll be home tomorrow.'

'Where do they live?'

'Carlisle.'

'Carlisle? That's a long way. Have they gone on the train?'

'In the car.'

'You know, I've never driven a car. Stanley drives everywhere. And you know, we've never been on an aeroplane. When we go on holiday it's in the winter and we normally go to Devon or Cornwall, but it's very quiet, not like here. You can't beat Blackpool, Constable.'

'I know.'

'Are you going away?'

'I'm not sure at the moment.'

'Oh. Here's my Stanley now. Just look at him, talk about death warmed up, he can't see me. I'll have to go to him. Come around for some tea and biscuits. Bring that nice Inspector with you. Tell Sarah and the twins I was asking after them. Goodbye, Constable.'

'Goodbye, Mrs Bantry.'

Johnny strolled back to Regent Road feeling tired.

Chapter 15

Jeff went to Fleetwood where he knew there was a Customs office. He'd spoken with a Customs officer who'd run checks to see if they'd had any interest in Mr Hargreaves but so far nothing had turned up. However, the officer said they would keep a discreet eye on Duet's movements. Johnny was at his desk in Regent Road, thinking about Mrs Bantry and the case in general, when Jeff returned. He shared his thoughts and suspicions with Johnny.

'Do you remember, sir, when we started on this case, less than a week ago?'

'Yes.'

'Well, when we started we had solid evidence by way of dental information.'

'We did.'

'Then we met Mrs Bantry. And got a lucky break, with her knowing about dialects. Again, solid evidence, and we both knew she was right.'

'Correct.'

'But now, these three men in a boat, it could all be quite innocent, you've given two good reasons why that life raft could be legitimate, and yet you're convinced it contained drugs. You say they're not typical sailing types, they look typical sailing types to me.'

'Well ... go on.'

'The thing is, these three men, they've all got good jobs and seem to be quite wealthy. I don't think they would risk their present lifestyles by doing something seriously corrupt. A bit of tax evasion, yes, but not drugs.'

'What do you think about Mrs Hargreaves?'

'I think she's a lady of leisure, enjoys the good life. You saw her coming from that house in Upridge, but we don't know who the house belongs to. For all we know, the woman with the pram, she could be Mrs Hargreaves' daughter. Couldn't she?'

'She could.'

'And another thing. You say not to interview Mr Hargreaves as you're convinced he's going to go on another drugs run.'

'Have you got to put it that way?'

'Yes. The thing is, sir, Mrs Hargreaves will have told him about our visit and he'll be expecting us. If we don't go to see him, and if he is into drugs, then he'll smell a rat, because we will be acting out of character.'

'Sarah's very lucky to have you, Johnny.'

'She doesn't think so.'

'You see, Johnny, what I thought we would do is to watch the house in Upridge, take photographs of who comes and goes, and generally observe the behaviour of Mr and Mrs Hargreaves.'

'Well, we can do that, sir. But it would be unnatural not to go and see Mr Hargreaves.'

'Detective Constable Johnston. You've convinced me.'

'Thank you, sir.'

They arrived at Mr and Mrs Hargreaves' house, the garage door was open, the Range Rover was there but not the Mercedes. They rang the front doorbell. Jeff noticed the housemartins swooping for and catching insects, giving a spectacular display of their agility, climbing quickly up to the eaves of the house, turning and swooping out again. Mr Hargreaves opened the door. He was about six feet tall, slim but solidly built, with bare sinuous arms. He had a light stubble covering his slightly sunken cheeks and a sun-tanned face. He had a ready smile, slightly uneven, although his teeth were white and healthy, and a good head of brown hair, greying all over. All of which gave him a lived-in, hard-working, dependable look. He was dressed in summer white cotton trousers and a light blue, short-sleeved shirt. He was standing bare footed. He had a comfortable, relaxed, easy going demeanour and a noticeable light cigar aroma about him. Jeff introduced Johnny and himself, they were invited in and sat around a kitchen table.

'Doris said you'd been around. I was sorry to hear about Harry.'

'You see, sir, Mr Taylor was murdered.'

'Bloody hell!'

'So, this is a murder investigation and we are leaving no stone unturned. We know Mr Taylor was to have sailed with you, along with Mr Brown and Mr Baker. We have also seen CCTV footage of the marina on the Wednesday before you sailed. We know Mr Taylor and Mr Brown left Duet before you sailed. Can you explain why?'

'Course I can. Harry said he was feeling bloody awful, said he was on some tablets for his blood pressure and he thought they were having an adverse effect on him. Said he'd have to go to the doctor's on Thursday morning.'

'And Mr Brown?'

'David was having difficulty getting a bloody chemist to stand in for him, for a couple of days, who could do prescriptions while he was away. So he had to get back to Glasgow. But came down to see the boat and to arrange when and where he would join us at the weekend. He went home and got the train to Holyhead on Saturday.'

'So, how did you spend the time from when Mr Brown joined you in Holyhead, and your return to Frampton?'

'We sailed around Anglesey, went across to the Lynn Peninsula, and back to the Menai Straits. With the weather being settled we anchored in coves overnight, and then came back to Frampton.'

'You didn't bother to inform the coastguard of your whereabouts?'

'I don't bother when we're just bloody coastal hopping.'

'How did you get to know Mr Taylor?'

'Harry had sailed Duet for a number of years and when I bought her he came out with me, a number of times, on the river around high water, so I could get used to her.'

'And Mr Brown?'

'I import shoes, and one of my best customers is Charley McAteer. He has a shop in Glasgow near David's chemist, and one in Largs. That's a seaside

138

town on the Clyde. Charley and David are mates. When I go and see Charley in Glasgow, the three of us go out for a pint. David's got a small boat and when he heard I'd bought a bigger boat he said he fancied coming sailing so we agreed to take a couple of weeks off. But he was having trouble getting a bloody chemist to stand in for him, so it cocked us up.'

'And Mr Baker?'

'Me and Doris have been members of the golf club for about twenty years now. We've known Julian and Penny all that time. He's a solicitor, but I suppose you know that?'

'We do, Mr Hargreaves. Tell me, where do you import your shoes from?'

'I used to be a wholesaler for shoes manufactured in Lancashire, but now they come from Spain, Italy, India and more recently from China.'

'Do you visit the manufacturers?'

'Oh, I do. You've got to make sure you get what you're bloody paying for. I buy container loads to keep the price down and I like to see what I'm getting.'

'Do you pay import duty on shoes?'

'I pay bloody everything, import duty, VAT, income tax. I employ about thirty staff and pay their holiday pay, sick pay, national insurance contributions … how I make a living out of it I'll never bloody know. I seem to spend all my time working for the bloody government. But I've always been the same, always been straight and above board, only way in business, wouldn't have it any other way.'

'Is Mrs Hargreaves in the business?'

'She's in the business of spending my bloody money, that's what she's doing now, playing bloody golf, I'm more of a social member myself.'

'Well, thank you, Mr Hargreaves, we may need to speak with you again.'

'Anytime, Inspector, Constable, any bloody time.'

As they were leaving the premises and getting into the car, Johnny remarked, 'That was bloody marvellous, sir. Bloody, bloody marvellous.'

Jeff shook his head from side to side, and gave a wry smile, as they entered the lane to drive back to Blackpool.

Chapter 16

It was about six thirty when Jeff dropped off Johnny at home, saying he'd collect him at about eight in the morning. All the black bins had been removed from the pavements. Jeff had then driven back to Upridge and at seven fifteen he located himself in a position which enabled him to see the house in High Street. Nothing happened around the house. From his position he was able to see three pubs. As the evening progressed, activity around the pubs began to increase. One pub was obviously catering for older people, judging by the age of its clientele. Another seemed to cater for families and advertised its beer garden with swings and a children's play area. The third attracted mostly young people, some of whom sat at wooden tables with umbrellas positioned on the pavement. All the pubs offered food.

It had been a typically pleasant evening in this typically pleasant Lancashire village, with people obviously in good humour. The young people drinking outside were enjoying themselves, laughing and joking, and while in high spirits all had seemed sober and well behaved. Jeff was reminded of his student days at Lancaster when, especially on Friday and Saturday evenings, he'd gone out with his mates and they had always drunk too much and he'd always regretted it the following morning. He reflected on Mr Hargreaves who had seemed more decent than he'd imagined and was beginning to doubt his suspicions. But, after consideration, he still believed his gut feelings to be correct.

Dusk was closing in. The street lights came on. The pubs were brightly lit inside and out. More young men and women had joined the others standing outside what appeared to be the most popular venue, still laughing and joking. A couple of older men had left one of the pubs, individually and smoking. Jeff suspected that this had been their usual evening addiction for many years. And he imagined they'd staggered home to empty cold houses, to crash out between not too clean sheets. They'd need to get up in the night on several occasions to empty their full bladders. Then they'd wake in the morning feeling fit for nothing. Only to repeat the performance the following evening. No matter where you go, similar types of people exist, no matter which village, town or city you visit. At this time in the evening, similar people would be doing similar things, very few of us are absolute individuals. Somewhere, there will be another detective inspector doing the same as Jeff, just watching and hoping something will happen to advance his investigation.

It had passed closing time, the pubs were being vacated. Several older men had staggered home, all were smoking. The young people, although in high spirits, still seemed sober as they made their way home, laughing and joking. It had gone midnight and the street was nearly deserted. Jeff never thought this practice a waste of time, as you always learnt something, even if you only learnt that nothing has happened. He started to feel this was the case. Then a small white van arrived and parked outside the house. A stocky, muscle-bound man got out. He gave the impression of having no neck and was bald with a shiny head. He looked like a bodyguard or bouncer, the type who'd pump iron down at the gym. He opened the van's rear doors and took from it a life raft valise. He walked up the steps, took out a key and opened the door then walked into the house, closing the door behind him. Bingo. Jeff made a note of the van's registration number, went home and slept like a log.

Chapter 17

When Jeff dropped off Johnny at home. Johnny was well aware that Sarah and the boys would be returning tomorrow and he believed this would be his last night of freedom. But he'd started to feel a little guilty as should he drink too much it might undo his feeling of wellbeing and his contracting waistline. However, he decided that one night out wouldn't do any harm and chose to follow the routine he'd planned before ending up in Glasgow. He thought that to compensate for his indulgence he'd eat what remained of the healthy food Sarah had left for him in the fridge. When he had done so, he left the house at eight fifteen, to sample the amber nectar. Johnny was well known in various hostelries where he was considered to have an exceptional capacity for lucid thought and intellectual conversation. Especially when discussing the past, present and future of his beloved Liverpool Football Club, whose talents and abilities on the field of play always improved in direct proportion to the amount of alcohol consumed. The problem was, he normally passed his pearls of wisdom on to dyed-in-the-wool Everton supporters, who'd have nothing of it. Indeed, the Everton fans were just as vociferous in their condemnation of the overpaid and under-talented players and manager of Liverpool Football Club. All of which led to gripping bar room debate and a tendency to lose all track of time. Johnny was shocked when last orders were called, and he ordered a double round.

As he walked home he recalled what Mrs Bantry had said about him becoming anorexic. Bugger this for a game of soldiers, he thought. He called at a chippy and bought a large haddock with chips. He arrived home at midnight then climbed the stairs and got into his unmade bed between creased but clean sheets. He got up three times to empty his full bladder and thought it strange as he normally got up just once. My bladder must be contracting, he thought.

Johnny was up early, and in spite of showering, shaving and having breakfasted, he still looked knackered and red eyed when Jeff arrived to collect him. He got into the car.

'Good morning, Johnny.'

'Good morning, sir.'

'How are you feeling this morning?'

'As rough as a bear's arse.'

'Why's that?'

'I had a good night last night. My mouth feels like the bottom of a budgie cage.'

'It's a long time since I felt like that.'

'You should try it sometime, it does you good.'

'Well, Johnny. After I left you last night, I went to Upridge and watched the house in High Street.'

'You should have taken me with you.'

'I thought you needed an early night.'

'And?'

'Nothing happened.'

'I didn't think it would.'

'Until after midnight, when a white van arrived, driven by a thick-set, burly chap. He got out, opened the

145

van's rear doors, took out a valise, and went in the house with it.'

'Get away.'

'I'm afraid so.'

'What do we do now?'

They discussed events and Johnny agreed it must be drugs, they now had to involve Customs and watch the shops and warehouse belonging to Hargreaves' Discount Shoes. They must also watch the house in Upridge and the Hargreaves' home, and check out the owner of the white van. This was becoming a much larger operation and maybe Customs could help with manpower, especially for surveillance purposes. They had to set up a meeting with Superintendent Hird and Customs officials. Superintendent Hird would enjoy overseeing operations and liaising with Customs, he was good at that, leaving Jeff and Johnny to deal with the main perpetrators of the crimes.

On arriving at Regent Road they checked with the DVLA to establish ownership of the white van. It had been registered to a Blackpool man by the name of Alan Trotter. Once he knew the address, Johnny knew who he was.

'I know who Alan Trotter is, sir, it's Piggy Trotter.'

'Who?'

'Piggy Trotter, he's a bouncer, always roughing someone up, he's well known.'

'I don't know him.'

'That's because you don't go in pubs, everyone knows Piggy. He's got a reputation. He's a small time bruiser. They say he's as thick as pig shit, which he is. I can't imagine Mr Hargreaves dealing with someone as daft as Piggy.'

'Nothing surprises me anymore.'

'He used to work out at the True Grit Gym. Maybe he still does.'

'We're going to have to see Superintendent Hird. I'll see if he's available.'

Superintendent Hird made himself available and they were shown in by Jean.

'Good morning, Detective Inspector. Good morning, Detective Constable.'

'Good morning, sir.'

'How can I help?'

'Detective Constable Johnston and I are now convinced we are dealing with drugs trafficking on a substantial scale, sir, and we need to liaise with Customs and mount a surveillance operation. One of the gang members is known to Detective Constable Johnston.'

'Jean. Would you contact James Ferguson in Customs for me, please?'

'Yes, sir.'

'Good morning, James.'

'Good morning, Charles.'

'James. DI Dewhurst and DC Johnston are working on a case, and they now believe it to be very much drug related, we need to set up a meeting.'

'Very well, Charles. When would you like to meet?'

'As soon as possible.'

'How about four this afternoon?'

'Excuse me. Four this afternoon, is that okay,

gentlemen?'

'Yes, sir.'

'That's fine, James. In my office.'

'Look forward to seeing you, Charles.'

'And you, James. Bye.'

'Right, gentlemen, you'll need to prepare a presentation to acquaint Customs with your findings. I suspect Mr Ferguson will bring along a couple of colleagues. So, let's put on a professional show, you may decide to use the overhead projector or flip chart. Will that be all?'

'Yes, sir.'

'Very well, see you at four.'

Jeff and Johnny returned to their office and decided on the format for the presentation. They agreed that the most successful means of communicating the information would be by typed notes to be handed out at the meeting, and the use of transparencies with headings to be used with the overhead projector. They made a few notes to guide them. Johnny was surprised at the speed with which Jeff could type. He quickly typed ten pages of notes with headings and sub-headings describing the sequence of events to date. He printed one copy out and read it through carefully. Spelling and punctuation were corrected then six finished copies were printed out.

Jeff remembered his college and university days when he always felt better acquainted with a subject when he'd taken typed written notes away from lectures, ones that had been handed out by the tutor. Since then, when making a presentation, he had used the same format. Headings were boldly typed onto transparencies for use with the overhead projector, using a power point program, corresponding with the sequence of the typed notes on the handouts.

He believed the best presentations had a firm focal point; this would be the projection of the headings onto a white board and the subject would then be discussed, rather than reading the prepared notes. The notes would be used by the presenter only as a prompt and taken away so that those present could refer to them should they have the need. He thought presentations that comprised reading from notes when the participants were sitting around a table tended to be boring. If the format was too prescriptive it destroyed spontaneity and the presenter appeared characterless.

By lunchtime the presentation was prepared. Then they had a sandwich before going to the True Grit gym on the off chance that Piggy was around. And if they got lucky and found him there, they decided to dream up some bogus incident and question Piggy about it. It was about one o' clock by the time they arrived at the gym. Piggy's van was in the car park. They parked close to the entrance doors.

Chapter 18

They went inside and were immediately hit by the musty odour of stale perspiration and deodorant pervading the atmosphere. The walls of the entrance foyer had been covered in photographs of unnatural-looking, muscle-bound hulks in various poses. The photographer's lighting had been so arranged as to produce shadows and highlights which enhanced the muscles to their best advantage. A thin partition wall separated the gymnasium from the foyer and sounds of grunting and heavy breathing could be heard coming from the other side. A muscle-bound strong man sat at the reception desk wearing an open-neck, short-sleeved white shirt and blue denim jeans. He had a gold chain and medallion resting on his hairless chest, and various tattoos on his arms. He had a tattoo of a scorpion on his neck and the words love and hate on the backs of his fingers. He'd grown a Mexican-type moustache and had thick black hair. Both moustache and hair appeared to have been dyed. He was smoking a black cigarette.

'Can I help you, lads?'

'Yes, sir. This is Detective Constable Johnston and I'm Detective Inspector Dewhurst. We wondered if the owner of the white van on your car park is one of your members?'

'I don't know which van you mean.'

'And you are?'

'I'm Tony Grimes, the owner. Get it, True Grit,

clever, in'it? Know wha' ar mean?'

'If you say so, Mr Grimes. Would you like to step outside with Detective Constable Johnston? And he'll point out the van to you.'

Johnny and Mr Grimes went to the car park, looked at the van, and returned.

'That van's Piggy's.'

'And who is Piggy, Mr Grimes?'

'He's one of our members.'

'But that's not his real name?'

'No. It's Alan Trotter. But we call him Piggy. Clever, in'it? Know wha' ar mean?'

'It's very clever, Mr Grimes. Would you tell Mr Trotter we'd like a word with him?'

'Come inside, I'll introduce you. There's not many people in at the moment, it's a bit too early. Know wha' ar mean?'

Mr Grimes led them into the gymnasium, which was filled with various torturous contraptions, only three of which were being used, by grunting perspiring individuals, each wearing lycra shorts. There were mats and weights on bars, weights on pulley systems and treadmills lying idle, awaiting the next fitness fanatic.

The person lying on his back on one of the contraptions, with his ankles tucked under restraining hoops to prevent his legs from lifting as he pulled and pushed on various levers, with a round red face and perspiring vigorously, was pointed out as being Piggy. As the three men approached, Piggy sensed danger and stopped pumping iron.

'Got a minute, Piggy?'

'What is it, Tony?'

'These two men want a word with you.'

'What about?'

'I don't know, you'd better ask them.'

'Okay.'

Piggy exhaled noisily and released his grip on the bars, unhooked his ankles from under the restraining hoops, swivelled his body around, placed his feet on the floor and, with a little difficulty, because of slight stiffness, stood up to face the three men.

'Mr Grimes. Is there somewhere we can speak with Mr Trotter in private?'

'Use the lounge through that door, there's no one in there till later.'

Piggy picked up his towel, dried the perspiration from his body, and with the towel resting around his shoulders he walked towards the door offering access to the lounge. They entered and sat at a table.

'Mr Trotter. I'm Detective Inspector Dewhurst and this is Detective Constable Johnston.'

'I've seen you about, haven't I? Usually in uniform …'

'You have, Piggy, lots of times. Normally when there's been a fight and you've been involved.'

'Only doing me job. I'm a bouncer. You can't be a bouncer wivart getting into a few scwapes.'

'The thing is, Mr Trotter, last night there was a robbery in the town, and a witness reported seeing a van, similar to yours, leaving the scene at about twelve thirty. And just by chance Detective Constable Johnston and I noticed your van in the car park.'

'Well, it weren't my van.'

'Where were you last night, Mr Trotter?'

'I don't work Wednesdays, so a came here.'

'And then?'

'Went home and went to bed. And besides, there's lots of vans abaht like mine.'

'Is there anyone who could verify what you say?'

'What do you mean?'

'Did anyone see you? Do you live with anyone who was with you at twelve thirty?'

'No. I live by me sen, and the constable knows I'm not into fings like that. I don't do wobbewies.'

'It's true, sir. Piggy's never been involved with stealing, just beating people up.'

'I don't beat people up, it's uvver people pick on me when they've had a few dwinks, and they start to fink I'm fucking fick or somefink, so a fucking show em.'

'Who employs you, Mr Trotter?'

'Tony. Him you've just met, and his partner … hire out bouncers to pubs and clubs.'

'Don't the pubs and clubs have their own bouncers?'

'Well, some do. But the pwoblem is, when they sack a bouncer it usually causes a fight, and you're better wiv a bouncer on your side. So, Tony and his partner move the bouncers awound. If the club's not happy, they tell Tony and dere's no fights.'

'Do you work six nights per week?'

'In summer, yes, in winter about four nights.'

'So what do you do with the rest of your time?'

'Work out evewy day, a body like dis has to be looked after, it needs lots of exercise and plenty of good food.'

'Very well, Mr Trotter, thank you for your time. We won't bother you again with this matter.'

'That's okay.'

'How many hours per day do you spend here?'

'About six, from ten till two, when it's quiet.'

'That's four.'

'Is it?'

Mr Grimes was still at the desk in the foyer as they were leaving, reading a magazine directed at people who were intent on creating a perfectly toned muscular body.

'Everything okay, lads?'

'Everything's fine, Mr Grimes.'

'No trouble?'

'No trouble at all. You provide bouncers for the clubs, Mr Grimes?'

'I do.'

'How many do you have on your books?'

'About thirty and growing. More and more places prefer to use us rather than deal direct. Know wha' ar mean?'

'Yes, Mr Grimes. Thank you.'

'Okay, lads.'

They returned to the car park, got into the car and slowly drove through the holiday traffic back to Regent Road with the windows wound down.

'Did you notice, Johnny?'

'Notice what?'

'The resemblance.'

'What resemblance?'

'The mouth, nose and eyes.'

'Whose mouth, nose and eyes?'

'The person we've just been speaking with.'

'All I noticed was his bloody stupid moustache.'

'Not him. Your mate, Piggy.'

'He's not my bleeding mate.'

'You know, Johnny, I sometimes think my talents are being wasted in the police.'

'What are you talking about?'

'I'll bet you anything you like. That Mrs Hargreaves' name, before she married, was Doris Trotter.'

'Now you've really flipped.'

James Ferguson arrived for the meeting at three forty-five. He was a tall, well-rounded, broad-shouldered man aged fifty-five. He sported a neatly trimmed grey moustache, with cauliflower ears and a nose that could have been broken on several occasions. He could have been an ex-rugby player. He was wearing a grey, pin-striped suit, white shirt, colourful – though mostly yellow – tie, and shiny black shoes.

He was accompanied by two colleagues. Jim Burton, a tall, thin gormless-looking married man of thirty-five years of age, with a Master's degree in psychology from Leeds University. He was dressed in sports jacket, cavalry twill trousers, a woollen check shirt with woollen tie and brown suede shoes. Polly Peters was a not so gormless-looking; twenty-six-year-old attractive, black-haired, unmarried lady, with a Tyneside accent. She looked as if she'd thrown a few clothes on before leaving the house, and had not bothered to look in the mirror, although she had taken the trouble to put on her simply designed elliptical lens spectacles. Judging by her overall casual appearance she probably hadn't bothered to comb her short hair, which she constantly twisted between the thumb and forefinger of her left hand. She was sitting at the table with her left elbow resting upon it.

James Ferguson introduced his team, and Superintendent Hird introduced his. To Johnny's delight coffee and biscuits were provided. Jeff made a comprehensive and interesting presentation, which pleased Superintendent Hird, who thought he couldn't possibly have done better himself. A discussion followed and it was agreed a surveillance operation would be mounted. Photographs of Mr and Mrs Hargreaves and Piggy, and visitors to the house in Upridge would be taken so the team could become familiar with them. The shops and warehouse belonging to Hargreaves' Discount Shoes would be observed. And hopefully, a pattern would emerge whereby the activities of the parties would become predictable. Jeff said he intended to return to Upridge that evening with a camera. Jim Burton and Polly Peters would join the team in the morning. Johnny agreed to try to get some photographs this evening of Mr and Mrs Hargreaves, Piggy, and the solicitor Julian Baker. Jeff borrowed a camera with a telescopic lens from Jim Burton. But Johnny, being interested in photography, had his own. They disbanded and agreed to meet in the morning at nine.

Jeff dropped Johnny off at home, his escort was

parked outside. Sarah and the boys had returned from her parents. Jeff then went home to have something to eat before going to Upridge.

Chapter 19

Johnny had barely closed the door behind him when Sarah asked, 'Did you enjoy the fresh salad I left in the fridge for you? You know. The one on top of all the rubbish in the bin. You know the bin. That black thing you forgot to put out. Where do you expect me to put the rubbish this week? If the bin lid isn't closed the binmen won't take it. If there's a bin bag at the side of the bin, the binmen won't take it. If the binmen won't take it, what do you expect me to do with all your rubbish? Take it to the tip myself? Well, you can take it. You can't remember a simple thing like putting the bin out. No, but I suppose you remembered to go to the pub at night. And don't you deny it, you lying toad. Mother was right when she said the house would be a tip when I got back. I don't know how you do it. The minute I turn my back, you turn the house upside down … just look at this lounge. And the kitchen, well, it looks as if a bomb's been dropped on it, and God only knows what you were doing in that bed last night, it looks as if you've been pillow fighting.'

'Did you have a nice time, dear?'

'Don't you start getting around me, Jonathan, and yes, we did have a nice time, no thanks to you. Father took the boys fishing and they thoroughly enjoyed it.'

'That's good.'

'And what are your plans for tonight? I'm going to have to clean the house from top to bottom. John and

Jim have gone to see their friends for a couple of hours.'

'I've got to work tonight, love.'

'Well. The sooner you get from under my feet the better. I can't be doing with you hovering around when I've got so much to do.'

'Do you know where my camera is?'

'It'll be where you left it, it always is. Do you know where you left it?'

'No, dear.'

'You never know where anything is. The last time I saw it was on the top shelf of the plate cupboard in the kitchen.'

'What's it doing there?'

'I don't know. Go and see if it's still there. Have you eaten or have I got to make you something?'

'I've not eaten.'

'Then I'll make you a salad, I suppose you've been stuffing yourself with chips for the past few days.'

'Yes, dear.'

'What do you mean, yes, dear? You know it's not healthy for you. What's the point in me buying healthy food when the minute I turn my back you're stuffing yourself with junk?'

Johnny went to the kitchen and got the camera, which happened to have a film in it. Sarah made him a ham salad and a mug of tea. Johnny had a shower and changed into his jeans and casual clothes. Sarah kissed him as he was leaving and told him to be careful.

Chapter 20

Jeff had parked up at about seven fifteen. Upridge was very much the same as it had been the night before. He checked the camera that he'd borrowed from Jim Burton and found the telescopic lens easy to operate. Next he focused it on the door of the house and took several shots of the front elevation. By eight there was more activity on the street than there had been the previous evening. Maybe people got paid on Thursday. By eight thirty the young people's pub was bustling. Jeff decided to have a stroll around the rear of the terrace property and had to count the yard gates along the back alley to establish which house it was. There were no people at the back of the buildings so Jeff took a photograph of the rear elevation, which was neat and tidy, well painted, with clean curtains at the windows. The gate was slightly ajar so he pushed it gently to reveal a motorbike parked in the yard. He noted its number, returned to his car and waited. Somebody was in the house and Jeff hoped they would make an appearance.

At ten fifteen the motorbike came out of the back alley driven by a person in leathers who sped down the hill and away. It was dusk. Jeff walked around the back of the building again. The curtains had been drawn closed, and lights had been put on. In the bedroom some movement could be seen as the light bulb cast feint shadows onto the curtains. The bedroom light went out, so Jeff returned to his car. Five minutes later Mrs

Hargreaves came out. Jeff took a photograph and hoped it would turn out okay. She walked up to the young person's pub and went inside. At ten forty-five a silver Mercedes drop head coupe joined the High Street from the pub car park and cruised down hill, driven by Mrs Hargreaves. She was alone in the car.

Johnny thought Piggy would probably be on the door of one of the six night clubs located centrally within the resort. He parked his car in the municipal car park; armed with camera, and dressed casually, he looked a typical tourist. It didn't take long for him to spot Piggy leaning against a steel balustrade at the top of a shallow staircase. He was dressed in his black dinner suit with dress shirt and bow tie. He looked to be the perfect gentleman, apart from the habit he'd developed of picking his nose every few minutes. Johnny could only observe Piggy from a distance, but his body language spoke volumes, no wonder he ended up fighting. Johnny quite liked photography and took several shots of Piggy in various poses as he greeted the nightclub's clientele for the evening. The formidable-looking doorman frisked some of the men before they went in. This responsibility was one he obviously enjoyed. He asked some of the ladies to open their handbags so he could look inside and smiled at each one as he said, 'That's okay, luv.' Then he would allow them into the building. He was like a lion in a cage, prowling back and forth behind the vertical steel balustrade, guarding his territory from undesirables. Johnny would have liked to have observed Piggy's antics a little longer but decided he had to go to Fairhaven to see if he could spot Mr

Baker.

He went to St. Anne's first and photographed Mr Baker's office, then his house, which he photographed. Then he hung around, a discreet distance away, and waited. Fortunately he didn't have to wait long as Mr Baker came off the sand dunes, and crossed the sand-covered road with his springer spaniel, which he'd taken for a walk. Johnny got several good shots of Mr Baker and his frisky spaniel and wondered if Mr Baker was a hunting man. There were lots of opportunities and places to shoot on the Ribble Estuary. Happy with the results so far, he proceeded to Skidmore.

Johnny had slowly driven past the Hargreaves' house. The garage door had been left open and both vehicles were absent. He decided to drive to the golf club to see if Mr Hargreaves' car was in the car park. The drive took no more than five minutes, and proved worth the effort as Mr Hargreaves' car was there. It was now just after nine, so Johnny took a couple of photographs of the car before losing light and decided he had about an hour of light left, after which photography would be useless. He hoped Mr Hargreaves would return to his vehicle before then. At about nine thirty Mr Hargreaves came out of the golf club, paused at the top of the stone steps leading down to the car park, lit a cigar and strolled across the gravel car park to his car. Johnny got several good shots then decided to go back to Blackpool via Skidmore. When, in the fading light, he passed High View, he could see the garage door still open. None of the vehicles had returned.

Chapter 21

Jeff arrived at his office at eight thirty on Friday morning to find that Polly Peters had already arrived and was seated at the smaller of the two desks, resting her elbow on its surface and twiddling her hair with the thumb and forefinger of her left hand. She was neatly dressed in dark trousers and a light blue blouse, buttoned to the top. Polly was also wearing black casual shoes. Her short, light grey, casual jacket had been draped over the rear of the chair. She was wearing the same spectacles as she had the previous day. But today, they were slightly lopsided across her nose. Jeff noticed all of these things.

Polly had attended a local Catholic primary school and was sufficiently bright to have gained good results in all of her studies. She'd continued at convent school, generally taught by nuns, gaining excellent results. She'd always been something of a tomboy and enjoyed fishing off the North Shields quay, by the fish dock. She'd gone on to Durham University where she'd gained a degree in economics. She'd always wanted to work for Customs or fisheries protection ever since seeing their launches leaving and entering the Tyne while fishing. She'd always been slightly built, and had never been particularly interested in dressing smartly or wearing make-up and had always been more interested in what people thought and said rather than how they looked. Her father was a production engineer for a

Tyne-based engineering company, her mother a photographer. She had a younger sister, now at Durham, studying archaeology.

'Good morning, Miss Peters, lovely morning again.'

'It is, pet. And don't be calling me Miss Peters. The name's Polly.'

'Very well, Polly.'

'And another thing. You're late this morning. Where is everybody?'

'We did say we'd meet at nine, Polly.'

'I know we did, it's half past.'

'It's half past eight, Polly.'

'I'm going to have to get a new watch, pet. I'm bloody sick of this one. It's one my dad gave me. I'm sure he gave it me for a laugh.'

'Would you like a coffee, Polly?'

'You know, I'd love one, pet. I'm spitting feathers.'

'Milk and sugar?'

'Please.'

Jeff left the room, chuckling to himself as he walked along the corridor towards the coffee machine. It had been quite an amusing week working with Johnny and he had the feeling things could become even more amusing with Polly around.

He returned with the coffees and placed a cup in front of Polly. She thanked him as he sat at his desk. Jim Burton arrived followed by Johnny, who'd collected coffees for Jim and himself.

A discussion took place about the case as a whole and the events of yesterday evening in particular. Jim Burton took the films for development and advised Jeff to keep hold of the camera he had loaned him as it may prove to be even more useful. He would take another from his department for his own use.

They agreed to use the morning to visit the various locations of interest. On the way Jim dropped the films off at the Customs office for development, and arranged to collect them on their return, at about lunchtime. The four of them went in Jeff's car and visited the Burnside guest house, followed by Mr Baker's house in Fairhaven, his office in St Annes, and Duet in the marina. They went on to call at the Hargreaves' house in Skidmore, Mrs Taylor's house in Upridge, the terrace house in High Street and the golf club. They returned to Blackpool via Hargreaves' Discount Shoes shop and warehouse in Preston, and the shop in Blackpool, and, finally, they visited the True Grit Gym. Jim Burton made notes as they travelled and prepared a surveillance rota, based on his assessment of the limited manpower and the interest value of each location.

They collected the films showing the various persons involved in the case so far, excluding Mr Brown in Glasgow. They then returned to Jeff's office, where the rota had been finalised. The rota had each of them acting individually for surveillance purposes. It was recognised there may be times when Jeff and Johnny could be called away to do other things. And they may need to meet collectively to discuss events. The terrace house in High Street, Upridge, was to receive maximum attention. The rota had the complete week covered from eight in the morning until half past midnight, including weekends, with changeover times indicated. The six until half past midnight slot this evening had Johnny at the High Street House, Jeff at the Hargreaves' warehouse, Jim Burton at the True Grit Gym and Polly Peters at the Hargreaves' house. The Hargreaves' house was considered a particularly sensitive location as parked vehicles on the quiet lane were to be treated with suspicion. It was decided the pretence of collecting blackberries from the hedgerow may prove a plausible reason to be there, at least for part of the day.

A check on the ownership of the motorcycle in the yard of the house in High Street had shown that Tony Grimes was the registered keeper. The surveillance operation commenced and continued over the weekend, with all parties maintaining contact and reporting back to Jim Burton, who'd produced a log of activities in sequential order. Changeovers had gone smoothly, with additional cars and vans being introduced, as felt necessary, to reduce the possibility of arousing suspicion.

During the week a substantial amount of information had been recorded. The only vehicles to visit the Hargreaves' house, apart from the Range Rover and Mercedes, had been the post office van, which arrived about ten each morning, and the refuse collection vehicle that had arrived on Wednesday morning to collect the rubbish from the black bin that Mrs Hargreaves had put out on Tuesday evening. A second refuse collection vehicle had visited on Friday morning to collect the contents of the blue bin, presumably waste paper, that Mrs Hargreaves had put out on Thursday. Mrs Hargreaves' daily help had arrived on a bicycle on

Tuesday and Friday mornings and had spent four hours in the house. A Ford Transit van had arrived on Wednesday morning with Garden Maintenance Services written on it, and had spent six hours at the house.

Mrs Hargreaves had not visited the shoe shops or warehouse. But she had gone to the High Street house on three occasions during the week and on one occasion on Saturday. The young lady, previously seen at the house, had arrived on each of the occasions Mrs Hargreaves visited. Mrs Hargreaves had played golf on Thursday and Friday afternoons, having spent Monday, Tuesday and Thursday evenings at the golf club, unaccompanied, arriving home after eleven thirty.

Mr Hargreaves left the house at about eight in the morning and travelled to the warehouse, where he stayed until lunch time. He visited a hotel close by for lunch. Then, in the afternoon, he went to the shops in Preston and Blackpool, returning home between five and six in the evening. The only visitors to the shops appeared to have been customers buying shoes. Several commercial vehicles had arrived at the warehouse and delivered large boxes. And many small vans had arrived, probably sole traders buying shoes to sell at various retail outlets in markets, show grounds or shops around the north-west. Mr Hargreaves visited the golf club on Wednesday evening only, but he went out each evening to return a little later than Mrs Hargreaves. Mr and Mrs Hargreaves had never accompanied each other during the week or at the weekend.

All appeared normal around Julian Baker's house. Mr

Baker had taken the dog out onto the dunes at eight thirty each morning, returned home then gone to work in his car just before nine. He stayed in his office for the whole of each day, apart from visiting a sandwich shop at lunchtime before returning to his office. He had a few visitors to his office each day, several of whom were young couples. Mrs Baker would leave the house around lunchtime, take the dog onto the dunes, return, then go to the office, presumably to type up letters. Mr Baker went to the golf club on Wednesday evening, but had spent every other evening at home, apart from going onto the dunes with the dog. Mrs Baker had gone out every evening at eight, apart from Wednesday, smartly dressed in casual attire, and had returned at eleven. Polly thought Mrs Baker was having an affair, possibly with Mr Hargreaves, but this was not important and never pursued.

On the Saturday and Sunday Mr Hargreaves had left his house at about ten in the morning, and Mrs Baker had left her house at a similar time. Both returned to their respective houses at about nine in the evening. This fuelled Polly's imagination even further. On each of the days Mrs Hargreaves had visited the High Street house, either Piggy or Tony arrived, between four and five, and on each occasion had taken away several large brown envelopes. They'd then driven straight to the True Grit Gymnasium.

The operation most certainly involved Piggy, Tony and possibly other bouncers distributing drugs to pushers who frequented the Blackpool nightspots, who would in turn sell to their customers.

The team arranged to meet in Jeff's office at 3.00pm Thursday to discuss events and the next moves which would, hopefully, provide more solid evidence to secure an eventual conviction.

Jim Burton arrived dressed in brown corduroy trousers and a brown sports jacket, carrying his case file which, even now, was beginning to fill; some slots had been allocated for photographic evidence to be inserted later. Polly arrived wearing trainers, jeans and tee shirt, with a tuft of what was otherwise straight hair sticking out above her left ear. Johnny was dressed smart, casual, while Jeff wore a suit and tie.

The team were acquainted with activities at the various premises by Jim Burton, as only he had an overview of the case. Each member had reported back to him so that information could be logged, an area in which he had excelled.

Jeff decided one of the team had to go undercover at a number of nightclubs and let it be known they wished to purchase drugs. He said that Jim just didn't look the type and that he and Johnny were known in the town, which left Polly.

'You can fuck off, pet,' was her reaction.

Chapter 22

After they'd finished arguing with Polly, who had no suitable evening clothes, it was decided they'd buy her a dress. Nor had she any suitable shoes, so they purchased a pair for her. They also had to buy her make-up and a suitable handbag. By the time she'd changed in the ladies at the police station, it was eight thirty. Jeff and Johnny dropped Polly off a block away from the nightclub and parked up, some distance away, but in sight of Piggy strutting back and forth behind the balustrade at the top of the steps by the nightclub entrance. He frisked some of the men and looked in some of the ladies handbags, before allowing them to pass. Polly walked up the steps in a skimpy dress and make-up, blending into the nightclub scene. She looked like a girl who liked a good night out. She had her handbag inspected by Piggy and was allowed to pass into the club.

Once she was inside the club, Polly began to find the atmosphere oppressive and very noisy. People were dancing on the square hardwood dance floor, which had been centrally located and surrounded on three sides by tables and chairs, on its fourth side by a stage. A group was on stage pounding out a loud sound, which Polly suspected must be popular music. She went to the bar to order a drink. Although she wasn't sure what to order, she decided, seeing what other people were drinking, to order a WKD and to lounge around on a barstool for a while as if waiting for someone. Then at an opportune moment she would follow some likely looking girl into the toilets and enquire about buying drugs. She didn't have to wait long, as three half-drunk giggling girls made their way towards the toilets and disappeared inside. Polly followed and was looking in the mirror over a vanity unit, pretending to adjust her make-up, when the still giggling girls emerged from the toilet cubicles and gathered around the second vanity unit and wash hand basin at the side of Polly.

'Excuse me asking, girls, but is there anywhere I can buy drugs around here?'

'Where's that accent from, love, you're not from round here, are you?' said the most mature looking of the three.

'No, pet, 'am from up north, we're on a hen night and me and me mates are meeting back up here later. But ar was wondering if ar could get something for afters.'

'You're not a copper, are you?'

'Do I look like a bloody copper?'

'No, love, you don't. You're far too skinny. Go to the ladies cloakroom, just by the front entrance and ask for Frances. She'll sort you out.'

'I'm very grateful, pet, I'm getting desperate at the moment. I could do with an ounce just to keep me going.'

'Tell Frances Stella sent you.'

'Thanks, Stella, I'll do that.'

Polly made her way to the ladies cloakroom and met Frances. She simply and discreetly, under the palm of her hand, passed Polly a sachet and took sixty pounds in return. It had been as simple as buying an ice cream, or drink, or cigarettes; no problems, no questions, happens all the time.

'You've saved me life, pet.'

Polly walked out of the building, observed by Jeff and Johnny. She passed Piggy who was still strutting up and down, and walked down the steps to the next block. Jeff and Johnny drove around the block, stopped by the side of Polly and she got in the car. She handed the sachet to Johnny who placed it in an evidence bag and wrote details upon it.

The second nightclub chosen appeared to be guarded by one of Tony Grimes' bouncers. He was dressed immaculately in dress suit and shirt with black bow tie. Polly was dropped off around the corner from the nightclub and she walked up to the entrance. The bouncer had taken no notice of her so she entered. Inside, the lights were dimmed, loud music was playing, and some of the people were dancing on a central raised dance floor, lit from above and underneath by coloured flashing lights. The furnishings were plush and expensive looking. She walked to a corner of the bar and waited to be served. Then she ordered a WKD and turned around to face the dance floor. Men were dancing with men and women were dancing with women. This nightclub was part of Blackpool's active gay scene. Most of the men had either shaved heads or very short hair, most had tattoos, and they were nearly all dressed in white tee shirts and tight blue jeans. The bodies of those on the dance floor were gyrating sensuously to the throbbing music. Most of the women in the room were dressed in clothes similar to the men's, and had short hair, tattoos, and a considerable amount of body piercing. Some of the girls were dressed in skirts, so Polly didn't feel out of place. She was standing at the corner of the bar, wondering who she could ask about drugs, when a clean-shaven, short-haired young man came and stood alongside her, clearly waiting to be served, dressed in the ubiquitous all white tee shirt and blue jean uniform, with bright new tattoos adorning his bare upper arms. Polly thought he looked nice.

'Excuse me asking, pet. But do you know where I can buy some drugs?'

'I'm not your pet. Petal.'

'It's just the way we talk up north. It's like when you say love and don't really mean it. Or when you call me petal and you know I'm not a flower.'

'I've never been called pet before.'

'You should go to Newcastle. Everyone will call you pet.'

'I've missed me bloody turn now with you talking.'

'I'm sorry, pet, but do you know where I can buy some drugs? You'll save me life if you do.'

'Bloody hell. Go to the fucking cloakroom and see Frances.'

Again, not a problem. A small sachet was handed over, sixty pounds was handed to Frances. Polly walked out of the nightclub, down the steps, around the corner to where Jeff and Johnny had been waiting, and got into the car. Johnny placed the sachet in an evidence bag and recorded the details.

'Guess what, boys?'

'What?'

'Frances is a password.'

Polly explained.

They decided on one more hit and selected another nightclub guarded by what looked like a Tony Grimes' bouncer. Polly went in, found the ladies cloakroom and asked for Frances. Ten minutes later she left the third nightclub, walked to the next block, the car came alongside, and she got in. Johnny put the drugs in an evidence bag and recorded the details.

'The thing I want to know,' Johnny said, 'is what if you were a bloke, what would the password be?'

'The same, it's got to be the same. Frances can be a boy or girl's name.'

'Of course.'

'Well,' said Jeff, 'I think we should meet at my office at nine in the morning and bring Jim up to date. But in the meantime, I think I can just about manage to buy you a couple of drinks.'

'Not before time, sir, I've not had a bleeding drink all week.'

'I thought you'd never ask, pet. I'm feeling right parched.'

They visited a pub on the outskirts of central Blackpool, not far from Johnny's home. As Johnny and Polly had left their cars in the police station car park, Jeff said he'd drop them off at their homes and collect them in the morning on his way in.

They each decided to have a pint of the guest bitter. Jeff ordered, as Polly and Johnny sat on the bench seating at a corner table. Jeff joined them and sat on a stool on the opposite side of the table, facing them.

When Jeff looked up, Polly had white froth from the head of her pint, covering her top lip. He noticed that Johnny hadn't and was sure that he too had a froth-free top lip. He decided Polly was not normally a beer drinker. Unlike Johnny who'd only half a pint left and was gagging for a second.

'What do you mean, pet? You'll drop me off at home, and collect me in the morning. I could live in bloody Timbuktu for all you know.'

'My dear Miss Peters, I know exactly where Detective Constable Johnston lives and I know, within a few metres, where you live.'

'How do you know?'

'I've seen you around, on several occasions, in your Custom officers' uniform and also walking from your car to one of those modern flats by the marina.'

'Are you some kind of pervert, or something?'

'No. I park my car on the marina car park and from there I can see the Customs office on the dock, the Customs launch and the flats where you live.'

'Well that's settled, pet. Get me another pint, Johnny.'

'Sure will, you have one, sir?'

'Just a half while I'm driving.'

Having had his second drink, Jeff dropped off Polly and Johnny at their homes. He arrived at his house pleased with the week's surveillance activities. He was impressed by the way Jim Burton had quietly controlled the rota and recorded their findings. And he was particularly satisfied with the evening's outcome.

Chapter 23

On Friday morning when Jeff set off from his home to collect Polly, there was a different feel to the weather, with a noticeable westerly breeze, and low stratus cloud in all directions for as far as the eye could see. White horses topped the waves, and seagulls hovered on the breeze, not needing to flap their wings to remain airborne. Dogs being walked along the promenade were having their hair groomed by the wind, and people were protecting their eyes from the sand-laden breeze. The forecast was for a couple of days of fresh winds before settling again on Sunday.

When she noticed Jeff's car enter the quadrangle, which was for residents parking only, Polly came down from her flat and walked outside wearing jeans, trainers and floppy jumper, before he'd been able to ring the bell.

'Good morning, Polly.'

'Good morning, pet.'

'Sleep well?'

'I would have, had ar not been up all night peeing.'

'That's your own fault, drinking so much before going to bed.'

'You sound just like my dad.'

They returned along the promenade and into Bispham to collect Johnny, who felt bright eyed, having slept well, and feeling ready for the day ahead. They arrived at Jeff's office at eight forty-five. Jim Burton was there, drinking coffee, and volunteered to get three more coffees before discussions commenced.

Jim was brought up to date with the events of last night. And the evidence bags were passed to him for processing.

They now knew that drugs were transported from the High Street house to the True Grit Gym as Piggy and Tony had been seen and timed doing this. They had not, as yet, recorded anybody leaving the True Grit Gym and seen them making a delivery to a Frances, at their homes, or in the clubs. This was missing evidence which would help to close the circle. They decided to concentrate their efforts on proving deliveries were made to the clubs from the True Grit Gym. So they mounted a further surveillance operation concentrating wholly on those who left the gym, and tracking their destinations.

Jeff was convinced that Duet would be leaving shortly to collect more drugs and he advised of his intention to follow her, if possible, to find out exactly where she went and who she met. The drugs could be transferred at sea or on land, or distributed in other ports along the coast. As this was obviously a sophisticated operation no one could guess how wide the net would spread.

Johnny was horrified when Jeff said they would have to go to the chandlers to buy some heavy weather clothing to fit Johnny. But he had sufficient lifejackets and safety harnesses on board.

'Can I come, pet?'

'No.'

'My dad's got a sailboat in North Shields and we used to sail to the Farne Isles and Holy Island.'

'No.'

'We used to stop overnight at Seahouses. I always liked sailing. That's how I came to join the Customs, 'cos ar used to see the Customs launch on the Tyne and I fancied it.'

'It's only a small boat, Polly.'

'You won't notice me, pet. I don't take up much space.'

'No.'

'I've got all the weather gear, and I can navigate, I've got the qualifications.'

'No.'

'And besides, I leave all my inhibitions ashore, you can treat me just like one of the lads as far as I'm concerned.'

'Very well, Polly. The marina will let us know when Duet arranges to leave. Jim will need to continue to co-ordinate the operation.'

'I'll base myself at the Customs office on the docks,' said Jim.

Jeff rang Frampton marina and spoke with Chris Jones. Nothing had been heard from Duet's owner but he would let them know immediately he made arrangements to leave.

The remainder of Friday and Saturday was spent observing the True Grit Gym, the three night clubs they knew to have drug dealings and other nightclubs in the resort, where Tony would arrive during the day. It appeared that Tony was the main courier for the area and also probably dropped quantities of drugs at houses where a Frances lived.

Jeff prepared Marie for passage making by filling with fresh water, diesel, food and drink. He took Johnny to the chandlers where he'd bought some heavy weather clothing to fit him. All gear had been stowed on board, including Polly's weather clothing. He advised there were sufficient sleeping bags on board but if they required pillows they'd have to bring their own, and suggested they should pack a holdall for a two-week passage, and keep it at home ready for a quick getaway should the need arise.

By Sunday evening they felt well acquainted with the operation, apart from how the drugs got onto Duet. Jeff had a meeting with Superintendent Hird to bring him up to date with developments. He was quite pleased with progress and didn't think he could add anything, just reminding Jeff to 'be bloody careful in that boat.' And they waited.

Given what they perceived to be the number of drug outlets and the amount of drugs that would fit into a life raft valise, they decided there must be a need to top up the supply on a regular basis – unless there was more than one valise on Duet. But more than one valise would create immediate suspicion from a knowledgeable observer. No, they would be leaving soon. Monday had been a day for twiddling thumbs, anything else they did would be simply going over old ground. They could do nothing to further the investigation. Not a word from the marina. Could they have other ways of bringing the drugs in? No, John

Hargreaves would run a tight ship. The fewer people involved at the top of the chain the better. It would be more controllable.

Monday turned into Tuesday. The four of them had gathered in Jeff's office for another day of thumb twiddling. It was ten fifteen when Jeff's phone rang.

'Dewhurst.'

'Inspector Dewhurst, it's Chris Jones from the marina.'

'Good morning, Mr Jones. Good news I hope.'

'Duet has booked to lock out of the marina at 1300 hours today.'

'Thank you, Mr Jones, excellent news.'

'Will that be all, Inspector?'

'Unless you know her destination?'

'Afraid not.'

'Thanks, Mr Jones, you've been a great help.'

'No probs.'

Jeff placed down the receiver. 'Bingo!'

Jim Burton agreed with Jeff that if he called Marie on VHF, he'd use the name Pluto, so that anyone listening to the conversation would think that Pluto was another yacht making contact. He then returned to his office at the docks. Polly took her car home. Johnny dropped off his car at home. Jeff went to Johnny's house and waited for him to change into some older clothes and to collect his holdall. They then went to Jeff's house so that he could change and collect his already packed holdall. And at eleven thirty they arrived at the marina and found Polly waiting at the marina entrance, ready to go.

Chapter 24

Jeff tapped the access code into the keypad. The automatic gate swung open and they walked down the ramp to the floating pontoons. Jeff and Polly felt invigorated walking along the pontoon, as they had already experienced the freedom they were about to feel when entering open water. Johnny experienced feelings of trepidation at having to undergo a new and possibly frightening experience. But he was no wimp when the chips were down, and was determined to rise to the occasion.

All boats were moored bows to the main pontoon, and tied alongside finger pontoons at right angles to the main pontoon. Marie was about halfway along the main pontoon. Jeff climbed on board, opened up and stowed the washboards below. Polly and Johnny passed their holdalls to Jeff and climbed on board. Below, the accommodation was cramped for someone not used to boats, but more than adequate, with standing headroom for people used to sailboats. Jeff pointed out the berth he normally used and told them to decide which berths they wished to use and to stow their gear in a nearby locker, or to leave their holdalls resting on the spare berth.

Jeff made sure they each had a sleeping bag, lifejacket and safety harness adjusted to their individual size and showed Johnny how to put on both lifejacket and harness. Polly was familiar with procedures. He showed them how to operate the spirit cooker, how to flush the marine toilet, even though there were written instructions by its side, and told them not to put anything down the toilet that had not been eaten, as it would become blocked, and whoever blocked it could clear the crap out of the pump. He told Johnny never to call him sir on board and to call him Jeff, and if he ever called him sir, he'd throw him overboard. He explained the reefing system on the foresail and mainsail to them. Polly was familiar with such systems. He explained the whereabouts of the fire extinguishers, fire blanket and emergency flares and told them to read the instructions for operation, so that should an emergency arise they'd at least be partially familiar with their operation. A chart of the East Irish Sea lay on the chart table. He briefly explained the operation of the depth sounder, VHF and GPS. He explained the fuseboard and light switches, and showed them how to operate the sea cocks. He pointed out the life raft, which was located in a canister on the coach roof, and showed them how to start the engine.

With the diesel engine throbbing and water discharging from the exhaust Polly released the mooring lines. Jeff motored astern as Polly coiled the lines and stowed them in a cockpit locker. She then removed each of the four fenders and stowed these in a different cockpit locker. By the time they were leaving the marina, everything was shipshape.

They passed between the stone walls forming the marina entrance and began to punch the flood tide which was making against them. As they motored along the River Wyre heading towards the open sea, a couple of other yachts were heading in the same direction ahead of them, and several were heading from seaward towards the marina. There were several small fishing boats anchored outside the navigable channel with their occupants rod fishing for mackerel, salmon, or any other meal that may come along. Several heron were standing in the shallows seeking an opportune moment to strike, and cormorants were ducking and diving, filling their stomachs, with four of them standing on the wreck of a small timber vessel, in the shallows, their wings outstretched drying in the sun. On this bright sunny day, the water appeared to be bluey green, fresh and clean, as nature intended. The estuary opened up as they approached the open sea. As the wave height increased over the sand bar, Marie came alive rising over the waves and dipping into the troughs. Jeff and Polly felt at ease. Johnny was apprehensive but knew Jeff was competent and wouldn't do anything daft, so he was beginning to feel more relaxed. They left the sand bar astern and entered open water where there were small wavelets on the sea's surface. It was 1300 hours, about the time Duet would be leaving Frampton marina.

'I hope you don't think I'm going to spend all my time sweating over a hot kitchen stove, but do any of you intrepid explorers fancy a cuppa? 'Cos I'm right parched.'

'Yes please, Polly.'

'And you, Johnny?'

'Please, Polly.'

'Milk and sugar?'

'Just milk, Polly.'

'Johnny?'

'Just milk, Polly.'

'Well that's simple enough. I suppose you've remembered to bring some milk, pet?'

'In the locker under the sink, where it's cool.'

Ten minutes later, as they were gently motoring away from the Wyre entrance, Polly emerged with three mugs of tea. They decided to finish the tea before setting sail to take them along the coast to the Ribble buoyed channel where they should see Duet emerging at about 1530 hours.

They headed to windward, hoisted the mainsail, set the auto helm and course to the Ribble channel, unfurled the genoa, switched off the engine, and quietly watched the coastline slipping by. The only sound was the gentle lapping of water on Marie's bow. Jeff explained the need to have a watch system, to enable one of them to be resting at all times with two of them sailing Marie. It's quite easy to arrange with three people on board, he further revealed, and decided to commence at 1600 hours, with one of them resting until 2000, and then from 2000 until midnight, and so on throughout the night until they reached port. In port, two could be resting and one would need to keep a look out for activities around Duet. Jeff explained that it was usually difficult to start the system as the first two people to go below to rest are not tired and tend to lie there listening, but eventually, when the crew become tired, it works quite well. The worst situation is when all the crew stay awake together until they are tired. This is when mistakes are most likely to be made.

They continued along the coast with Marie increasing her speed over the ground as high water approached and the tide began to slacken. They were getting close to the Ribble channel and began to see vessels emerging, first a couple of powerful motor cruisers then four yachts, one of which was unmistakably Duet. As Duet cleared the channel she unfurled her sails and begun to steer a course for the Isle of Man. Jeff followed, about two miles astern and in transit, with a fair weather cumulus cloud developing over the island. It was agreed that Johnny would make sandwiches and tea before going below to rest until 2000 hours.

Jeff and Polly remained in the cockpit as Johnny rested; they simply relaxed with nothing to do, other than to follow Duet and enjoy the sail. Johnny emerged at 2000 hours and Jeff went below, leaving Polly and Johnny on watch. When Jeff returned to the cockpit at midnight it was a clear, cold night with Duet still a few miles ahead and Johnny and Polly fully kitted out in heavy weather clothing to keep them warm in the cold air. The lights of many other vessels could be seen. These vessels would not have been seen without lights during the day. And lighthouses and navigation buoys could easily be identified by their distinctive light sequences.

Polly went below. As darkness descended even further they found themselves sailing under a canopy of bright stars against a black sky. Jeff loved nights like this, those which you don't often see over light polluted land. It made him feel no more than a grain of sand in a

185

desert, privileged to be alive and to do the things he was able to do. He was mesmerised by the awesome beauty. The only light was the navigation lights and the compass light, the remainder of Marie in total darkness. Johnny's eyes were constantly looking upwards. On quiet nights like this Jeff often thought of poetry:

'Continuous as the stars that shine
and twinkle in the Milky Way,
They stood in never ending line
along the margin of a bay.'

'Are you not feeling very well, pet?' Polly couldn't stay below until 0400 hours, as she knew they were closing on the island and didn't want to miss anything. She was up before 0300 hours and made them hot soup with bread and butter, which Johnny thought was the best meal he'd had in years. Jeff wondered whether Duet would enter Douglas, as that was the way she was heading, or whether she would change course and head for Port St. Mary. If she were to enter Douglas, permission would have to be obtained from the Harbourmaster by VHF. But this was probably a risk worth taking. At 0415 hours Duet contacted the Harbourmaster and was given permission to enter. At 0445 hours Marie made contact with the Harbourmaster and permission was granted for her to enter. Marie entered at 0500 hours. Duet was tied alongside a pontoon. Marie picked up a mooring as far from Duet as possible.

Chapter 25

Johnny collected his holdall while on his way to the marina with Jeff. He left a note for Sarah, saying he'd gone and could be away for up to two weeks, and that he'd ring if he could. Sarah breathed a sigh of relief when she read the note, pleased with having the house for just her and the boys for a whole fortnight. She made a cup of tea and sat in the living room, listening to the quietness, which suddenly became ear splitting. And she wondered if she really wanted Johnny to be away for so long. After all, when she'd left Johnny and gone to her parents' house, it had only been for a couple of days; she'd always had the boys with her, and her parents to fill the gap vacated by Johnny. And she'd always phoned Johnny in the evenings. The fact that they'd never been away from each other for so long during the past twenty years began to play on her mind. The quietness became louder and the tick of a small clock on the mantelpiece, that she'd never heard before, became thunderous.

She thought about how she and Johnny had met for the first time. It had been the week after he'd completed his police training. He'd been out with his mate for a few pints and was finishing the evening consuming a double cheeseburger outside a burger bar. She remembered how funny he was. He asked for her telephone number, which she'd given him, not expecting him to ring. But he had. And he'd been funny ever since. She recalled the first car they'd bought and how they'd always been short of money. Then they were married, with his two sisters, Carole and Mary, being bridesmaids, with his best mate as best man. Then they bought a house, with a big mortgage. He was shocked to find she'd become pregnant with twins and would have to give up work. Johnny took her to the hospital for the birth, desperately hoping the car wouldn't break down. He remained more anxious and nervous than her. And when the twins had been born, and she'd had to stay in hospital for a few days, he went to tell his parents, then went to the pub to get drunk with his friends and arrived at the hospital the following day, knackered. Nothing much had changed. She thought of how she'd not worked for many years, when the boys were young, before studying as a mature student at the local college to become a teacher.

Johnny had told her about Mr Taylor and that his wife had lived in Upridge. She wondered how Mrs Taylor had felt, if she'd been sitting in her living room, knowing that her husband had been snatched away, never to return. How would she have been able to cope? What with his forever empty chair; his forever cold side of the bed; his never to be used again shaving tackle and tooth brush; his socks, shirts and underwear, never to be washed by her again; his coats, trousers and shoes, and thoughts of charity shops. The funeral. The dreadful quietness and the forever empty void. Then there'd be his boat, which he'd enjoyed. It would have to be sold, or given away. Sarah started to feel morose and began to wonder about the things she would miss if Johnny failed to return.

He seldom made a meal. Seldom washed a dish. Seldom made a pot of tea. Never did the ironing. Never did the washing. Never cleaned the windows. Never did the hoovering. Never did the gardening. Never did the shopping. Never put the bins out. Never serviced the car, but paid someone else to do it. Never did the decorating, but paid someone else to do it. In fact, she was hard pressed to find anything Johnny did. He'd sit in the chair, eating, and leave crumbs under the cushions and on the floor. He'd have a can of beer and leave the empty can on the kitchen work surface. He'd have chips and steak pudding, and have the house smelling of food, with the chip papers in the bin and the bin lid not properly closed. He'd leave belly button fluff on the bedroom carpet. And sometimes his language was so foul it would make your toes curl. He always wanted his own way when watching television and the boys would fall out with him. But he'd always been kind hearted. He'd always been cheerful. He'd always been generous and honest. He was always thoughtful about important things. He always spoke well of people. He was reliable and funny. And he had been the best pal anyone could wish for.

When the boys came in the thundering clock suddenly stopped ticking. Sarah told them their dad had gone away. They said simultaneously, 'When will he be back?'

Since Johnny had been away the days had been spent fishing, with Sarah making packed lunches and taking the boys to one of their favourite places. They would go to a cinema during the evening or to a friend's house, or stay in. One day Sarah took them to Liverpool, where they visited the cathedrals, art galleries, and impressive buildings, especially those near the pier head. The boys hadn't particularly enjoyed this excursion, but had happily accompanied their mother.

Chapter 26

Jeff and Johnny went below. Polly positioned herself in the cockpit, wearing gloves, dressed head to toe in her sailing clothes and fully zipped up to a position above her nose to keep out the cold night air. With Jeff's binoculars to hand she would be able to record any movement aboard Duet. The warm air rising from the lower part of her hood, above her nose, was condensing on the inside of her spectacles making it difficult to see. She had to remove them periodically, to enable cold air to pass over the surface of the lenses to clear them so she was able to see again. Other yachts, fishing vessels and Ro-Ro ferries entered and left the harbour. Vehicles were queuing to take advantage of the less expensive early morning sailings to Liverpool and Heysham.

Polly had seen the sun's reflection on the clouds to the east prior to it becoming visible over the horizon. By the time it was fully visible the sky was light with a corresponding temperature increase. Polly's spectacles no longer steamed up and she was able to un-velcro the lower face protection from the bottom of her hood and breathe in the morning air, which was fresh and tinged with the smell of seaweed. It felt like Heaven.

By 0700 hours the inner and outer harbours had become quite busy. Trawlers were leaving for a day's mackerel fishing. Parties of rod fishermen were waiting on the quay for chartered vessels to collect them and take them out to a wreck, where they hoped the day's fishing would be memorable, and become a good conversation piece in the pub tonight, and for weeks to come. Crews of yachts intent on more civilised and socially timed passages were preparing to leave, but those on board Duet had shown no sign of activity at this early hour.

Jeff rose at about 0800, made three mugs of tea, prepared three halves of grapefruit and three bowls of cereal. Johnny was in the cockpit with Polly by the time the tea had brewed, with the smell of bacon wafting across from another yacht. Polly and Jeff seemed not to notice the aroma and were tucking into their breakfasts. But Johnny could have easily devoured a full English, followed by two rounds of toast, smeared with his favourite thick cut marmalade.

There was still no activity around Duet. So all they could do was relax and watch the world go by. They rang Jim Burton after 0900 hours and advised him of their whereabouts. Just as the day was warming up nicely Polly went below to sleep for a few hours, while Jeff and Johnny relaxed on deck.

As Duet had been tied alongside a pontoon, her crew, should they wish, would be able to walk ashore. Marie, on the other hand, had been secured to a swinging mooring and they would not be able to walk ashore but would need to row ashore in the tender. Jeff inflated the rubber dinghy and tied it astern.

Polly was up and about before midday. She washed, cleaned her teeth, combed her hair, changed her clothes, washed her used clothes and pegged them around the side of the boat to dry. When she arrived, with three mugs of tea, she was looking clean and fresh, with a tuft of hair sticking out over her left temple.

'You know, pet, I've never known anyone sleep so long, I hope they're not dead.'

'I don't think so, Polly. We'd have had a lie-in had we not needed to keep an eye on them.'

Johnny was getting used to using the binoculars, setting each individual eyepiece to perfect vision, then turning them upside-down to check if the vision of both eyes was the same, and being surprised to find he couldn't see through them very well in the upside-down position. He then proceeded to look through the large lens to view everything in miniature and was looking at Duet in this position when he noticed some movement in the cockpit; he turned the binoculars the correct way around to perfect vision. The three crew having breakfast in the cockpit were John Hargreaves, David Brown and Julian Baker.

David Brown and Julian Baker were walking along the pontoon and up the stone steps leading to the road. Then they walked towards the town. Jeff and Polly climbed in the tender, leaving Johnny aboard. Jeff rowed quickly to a set of stone steps closer to the town, and tied the tender to a mooring ring. He and Polly climbed the steps and were about fifty metres behind Brown and Baker when they reached pavement level. They walked up to and over a bridge that opened to allow vessels into the upper part of the harbour. Then they turned right and continued to walk along the fish quay. At the end of the fish quay, where the pubs and guest houses began, they knocked on the door of a small terrace house and were allowed in. Polly sat on a mooring bollard on the harbour wall from where she could see the front door of the house, and made a note of its address. Jeff walked around the rear of the premises. The rear of the house faced a narrow road with an up-and-over garage door offering access to the yard. He heard some conversation in the yard then the up-and-over door was raised to reveal a blue Saab convertible. He made a mental note of its Manx number plate and feigned walking by. When the engine started he turned around and walked in the opposite direction, and was sufficiently close as the vehicle passed to see that Messrs Brown and Baker were passengers, with a large man driving. The vehicle quickly sped out of sight.

Jeff joined Polly and explained what had happened. They decided to return to Marie. As they were walking along the fish quay towards the bridge the blue Saab convertible slowly crossed the bridge. Then headed towards Duet, avoiding pedestrians who were walking in the road.

They quickly crossed the bridge, walked along the road opposite the fish quay to the stone steps and climbed aboard the tender. Jeff rowed to Marie, but no activity could be seen around Duet. Johnny had been observing and had seen the blue Saab arrive; the three men got out, the large man opened the boot and took out a blue life raft valise. Messrs Brown and Baker walked down the steps along the pontoon and placed the valise on Duet.

194

Polly spoke to Jim Burton and passed on the Douglas address and the Saab's registration number. They waited, soaking up the sun, having light snacks and gentle conversation, wondering whether Duet would be sailing back to the Ribble or going elsewhere. Each of them went below to rest while the others kept an eye on Duet. Vessels continued to enter and leave the harbour. Rod fishermen began to return from their day's offshore fishing, and local sailors returned following a days sailing, going home for the evening.

At 1750 hours Messrs Hargreaves, Brown and Baker emerged and strolled along the quay towards the town. Jeff, Johnny and Polly took to the tender, tied alongside the steps and followed discreetly a good distance behind. They took the same route as before, over the road bridge, along the fish quay, past the small house, finally entering a restaurant where they selected a table by the window. The window was a bay with small glass panes, some of which were of the bull's eye type, offering privacy to the diners within. There was sufficient clarity, from the outside, to be able to identify the diners by the window.

They hadn't been able to enter the restaurant as Jeff and Johnny were known to Mr Hargreaves. They decided to hang around and see what happened. To Johnny's delight Jeff volunteered to bring fish and chips from a takeaway he knew around the corner, which they consumed while sitting on a bench overlooking the harbour.

Fellow diners could have been forgiven for thinking the three men occupying the window table were friends.

These men had forgotten what it was like to have a fellow human being care for their well being. Nor could they remember how it felt to care for the well being of a fellow human being. They were friendly towards each other. Laughing, talking and smiling together. But the bond that joined them was one of common greed. They each only befriended those who could help them financially, as greed was all they knew. They occupied a world where money and wealth were king, where deceit reigned supreme. Their natural instincts, over many years, had become so twisted and distorted that these men were now representative of only a minor percentage of the human race. But they thought they were just like everyone else – only a little more successful. Theirs was a world of material wealth. Of daily helps to clean their large, mostly unoccupied, houses. Of gardeners to tend their large, seldom-used gardens. Of wives who were ladies of leisure. They were people who had expensive meals in restaurants, and took exotic holidays, and delighted in telling others of their expensive, extravagant lifestyles.

They never noticed the seasons rolling by. They took no delight in seeing the changing shades of greens and browns of trees passing through the seasons from spring to winter. They had left simplicity behind. Theirs was a world filled with envy of others who possessed more material wealth than themselves. Especially if the wealth had been handed down, or acquired through honest and talented means.

They never stopped to consider the effects their actions had upon others. Their only concern was whether or not things affected themselves. They felt no guilt in becoming involved in any activity, providing it was not detrimental to their own well being. And certainly not when money had become plentiful. The waiter came to take their order.

At about 1900 hours Messrs Hargreaves, Brown and Baker left the restaurant. Mr Baker was staggering noticeably as they returned along the fish quay. They then walked over the road bridge and Mr Baker seemed to struggle when, fifteen minutes later, they climbed aboard Duet. Jeff, Johnny and Polly returned to Marie, deflated the dinghy and stored it in a cockpit locker. They instigated the watch system, with Johnny in the cockpit and two resting below, agreeing to change watches at midnight.

Johnny felt the cold intensifying as the evening progressed and by 2200 hours he was fully clothed in his heavy weather gear to retain heat. Ferries, trawlers and pleasure vessels were still entering and leaving the harbour. Jeff relieved him with a welcome mug of tea and a chocolate bar at midnight. Johnny went below leaving Jeff on watch.

It was 0230 hours when one of Duet's internal cabin lights came on. Jeff had left Marie's VHF switched on to pick up any message transmitted from Duet. At 0300 hours Duet's navigation lights were switched on, and Marie's VHF came to life with Duet requesting permission to leave. She slipped away from her berth at 0315 hours.

Chapter 27

Fifteen minutes later Marie had been authorised to leave the harbour and motored through the harbour entrance, about a mile astern of Duet. Jeff had to increase the distance between them so as not to arouse suspicion. He motored gently, deciding on her next destination, which appeared not to be the Ribble. She headed along the coast, in a north-easterly direction, keeping about four miles offshore.

Polly poked her head out of the companionway. She felt the cold night air on her face and quickly retreated, returning fully kitted out in weather gear and harness, which she hooked onto one of Marie's four harness points, then sat high on the cockpit coaming, watching the coastal lights slipping by.

It was another beautiful night to be at sea. The lights of many vessels were visible and lighthouses flashed to the north and south. Another starry night with the moon casting a long reflection on the water and Marie's wake sparkling with phosphorescence. Not a night for conversation, but a night for absorbing beauty along with quiet contemplation.

'I suppose you'd like a cup of tea, Jeff?'

'That would be lovely, Polly.'

They passed the north-east of the island. The sun rose over a cloudless sky and a flat calm sea. They adjusted their course to port, and were heading for the North Channel. Polly was acquainted with the charts, GPS and auto helm. All was serene. Johnny rose about 0800 hours and made breakfast including toast. Jeff went below leaving Polly and Johnny to look after things. With the island several miles astern, they came across a shoal of basking sharks, probably around thirty to fifty, which they carefully motored through. Though had they become too close, the sharks would have taken avoiding action. Johnny had never seen these magnificent animals before and had not known they could be found in such numbers around those shores. Polly had seen basking sharks before but not so many together. They were on the surface with their gaping mouths sucking in plankton. The smaller ones had vertical dorsal fins, but the larger of the group, each weighing between three and four tons, had dorsal fins bent over at the top. With the sharks and the island receding astern the shape of the Mull of Galloway had come into view, providing them with a focal point for the rest of the day.

The distance between the two vessels had increased to four miles. A course had been set to leave the Mull of Galloway about five miles to starboard, avoiding the turbulent water close inshore. Mr Hargreaves was probably planning to enter Portpatrick before high water thereby avoiding the need to punch a foul tide by arriving late. Like all good sailors, Polly took her responsibilities seriously and recorded their position on a paper chart every hour, checking her navigational skills against the GPS. She was always a little out, but should the GPS fail they'd have an estimated position on the chart that they'd be able to refer to.

By 1100 hours the wind had begun to freshen from

the west. Polly hoisted the mainsail, unfurled the genoa and turned off the engine. They were now creaming along, much more comfortable, quieter and faster than under engine, with spray occasionally saturating the foredeck.

The outline of the Mull of Galloway had become distinct. Its white lighthouse, clearly visible, perched precariously at the top of the headland. They were enjoying sailing in a moderate breeze with white horses topping some of the waves, and the warmth of the day permeating their bodies. Johnny no longer felt embarrassed urinating over the stern, with Polly in the cockpit. Inhibitions had fallen away as they became a more cohesive team.

Jeff got up at midday and made a simple lunch of tinned potatoes, beans, cold meat with bread and butter, followed by fresh fruit and a mug of tea. Even basic food tasted good in these fresh conditions. Polly, who'd really enjoyed this warm daytime sail, reluctantly went below at 1300 hours. The wind continued to freshen from the west. Jeff put a reef in the mainsail and slightly furled the genoa as they continued to make a fast passage into the North Channel. The tide against them slackened and the speed over the ground increased. When the tide turned in their favour, or, as Uncle Harry would have said, all those years ago, 'We caught the young flood and it carried us all the way to Portpatrick,' they made good time and were able to see Duet turn to starboard and enter the harbour about three miles ahead. Other yachts could be seen heading towards Portpatrick. A couple were heading south from the Clyde punching the tide, some were sailing across from Northern Ireland, and two a few miles astern of Marie following her track.

They entered Portpatrick to find the harbour filled with fishing vessels and yachts. Duet had moored alongside the harbour wall and two other yachts had moored alongside her, pinning her against the wall. Marie tied alongside a French yacht at the opposite end of the harbour wall. Mr Hargreaves probably would not recognise Jeff and Johnny, dressed in sailing gear with an unkempt appearance, not having shaved since leaving home. But they felt it best to maintain a low profile. Polly must have been feeling tired as at 1800 hours when they tied alongside she was still below sleeping. They decided to leave her alone and enjoy a couple of cans of beer in the cockpit and the peace and tranquillity of the evening.

Polly rose at 1930 shocked to find she'd slept so long.

'Why didn't you wake me up, you pair of tossers?'

'We thought you must have needed your beauty sleep,' said Jeff.

'You must have known I'd want to be on deck coming into harbour.'

'Well you can be on deck when we leave, you won't miss anything.'

'Have you two been drinking?'

'Just a couple of cans,' said Johnny.

'Well you can get me one. 'Cos I'm parched.'

Peace and tranquillity returned as they continued to observe Duet.

At about 2100 hours a Land Rover arrived on the quay and parked at the top of the wall by Duet. Mr Hargreaves climbed the vertical steel wall ladder carrying a rope, and greeted a young lady who'd got out of the vehicle. Polly dashed up the wall ladder to take a look at the registration number. The tail gate was opened and a life raft valise was taken out. Mr Hargreaves tied the valise to the rope and lowered it down the wall to Mr Brown who stowed it below. The young lady got back into the Land Rover and drove away. Mr Hargreaves climbed down the steel ladder and stepped back onto Duet.

All was observed from Marie. Polly rang Jim Burton with the latest information.

Polly wasn't feeling tired and said she'd stay up until 0400 hours to return the watch system to good order. By 2300 hours Jeff and Johnny were below, sleeping. Polly was in the cockpit, fully kitted out with her hood up and condensation forming on the surface of her spectacles. Polly had never visited Portpatrick before, but it was so busy; it seemed that all the west coast inhabitants had descended on this tiny village. People were noisy and shouting as they strolled home, having left the many pubs around the harbour. Polly thought there may have been caravan sites in the vicinity to accommodate so many people. Sailors returning to their yachts from pubs precariously climbed down the steel wall ladders and, as yachts were tied alongside each other, carefully stepped from one to the other before arriving at their own. Some people had been drinking in the cockpits of their yachts, but the cold air had forced them below. Lights on boats

202

had been extinguished within the confines of the harbour, but the streetlights on the quay remained lit. By 0100 hours all was peaceful, not a soul stirred, the only sound to be heard was fish rising.

Johnny was up at 0400 hours to relieve Polly. She and Johnny each had a mug of tea then she went below. All was quiet until dawn, when rod fishermen began to gather on the harbour wall and vessels began to leave. Several yachts had already left when, at 0730 hours, he saw activity on Duet suggesting it was preparing to leave. Johnny woke Jeff and they watched as Duet's crew, assisted by crew from one of the other yachts, adjusted the mooring lines so that Duet could slip away from the wall. Jeff climbed the wall ladder, walked to the breakwater and saw her turn to starboard and continued north.

Chapter 28

Jeff returned to Marie and prepared to leave. After they'd passed through the harbour entrance and entered open water it was noticeable that this was a different type of day, although it was bright and sunny. Small cumulus clouds were scudding across the sky from the west and the coastguard had issued a strong wind forecast on the VHF. Jeff put two reefs in the mainsail and half unfurled the genoa. The auto helm was set and Marie began making good way with spray washing her foredeck and side decks. Jeff and Johnny, who were sitting in the cockpit, clipped on with their harnesses, having received several good soakings, were able to taste the salt water in their mouths. Johnny now knew the value of the heavy weather clothing Jeff had bought. Duet could be seen only when both yachts were on the top of a wave at the same time, otherwise, when one yacht was in a trough, waves obscured the view. It was now obvious they were heading up the Clyde. Polly came to the companionway.

'Can you keep this boat still, pet?'

'Get to sleep, Polly, you're not supposed to wake before twelve.'

'Sleep? With all this bloody racket? You must be joking.'

'Don't cock the watch system up again, Polly.'

'Cock it up? I was up all night in the bloody cold while you two were snoring and farting.'

'Get to sleep, Polly.'

Ten minutes later Polly had joined them in the cockpit, fully kitted out and harnessed on, with the three of them drinking mugs of tea, slightly laced with salt from the stinging spray.

They continued along the Galloway Peninsula and followed Duet into the outer reaches of the Firth of Clyde. If boats had been able to enjoy sailing then Marie would have been in her element, climbing over the peak of one wave and dropping into the trough of the next. Johnny was feeling safe and confident in her and was impressed by the way she responded to each different wave formation. It reminded him of a horse jumping over fences, and then the owner patting the horse's neck in appreciation. He wondered how Jeff had felt, a man who loved the sea, sailing his own boat in these rock and roll conditions, and wondered whether he'd felt like patting Marie, in appreciation, at the end of it.

They headed to starboard, into the Clyde, the outline of Ailsa Craig becoming visible in the distance. The wind was from astern. Jeff dropped the mainsail, lashed it to the boom and they continued under reefed genoa only, surfing down the back of one wave then riding over the crest of the next. Polly elected to be the galley slave and rustled up very welcome hot soup with bread and butter, which was a little soggy. This was followed by chocolate bars, apples and mugs of tea. Johnny had found his sea legs and was beginning to enjoy the experience almost as much as Jeff and Polly.

The day progressed and the Christmas pudding shape

of Ailsa Craig had become more distinct. The outline of massive Arran could be seen rising vertically from the sea. When Jeff got to this position on a passage to Scotland he realised why the Clyde was such a popular cruising ground for north-west yachtsmen, being magnificently beautiful and protected from the full force of the Atlantic by the Kintyre Peninsula. It was, however, open to winds from the present direction.

By mid-afternoon the wind had begun to moderate. Duet was just about visible in the distance passing between Arran and the mainland. Jeff fully unfurled the genoa. With calmer conditions, less wave height and more sail, Marie began to increase her speed, and slowly but surely began to close the distance between her and Duet.

The coastguard had stopped issuing strong wind forecasts on VHF, but radio traffic had increased as they continued up the Clyde towards the areas of intense yachting activity. Yachts were reporting their arrivals and departures to the coastguard, and requesting permission to enter the many marinas in the area.

At 1850 hours Duet requested a berth for the night at Largs marina, and was told to tie alongside the visitors' pontoon, and report to the marina office on arrival. By 1940 hours Marie had contacted Largs Marina, just one of the many yachts to do so, with the same request, and received the same instructions. Marie tied alongside the seaward end of the visitors' pontoon. Duet was by the clubhouse.

Jeff looked wholly unkempt and felt relaxed as he walked along the pontoon, passing Duet. He was wearing his sailing jacket, Guernsey sweater, jeans, blue bob hat and salt-stained brown leather sailing shoes, to pay for the night's berth. They'd all taken advantage of the marina's shower and its laundry and drying facilities. By 2130 hours they were spic and span, although they were still unshaven when they entered the clubhouse for a few pints of the local beer.

They returned to Marie and as some bacon needed to be used up, they had bacon sandwiches in the cockpit under a cloudy sky while enjoying the warmth of the night. Jeff said he'd stay on watch until 0400 hours, and Johnny agreed that he'd take over until 0800. Polly was told not to cock up the watch system again. She just ignored the comment, before retiring.

Nothing happened overnight. Apart from the occasional yacht entering the marina, all was quiet, pleasant and warm. At 0400 hours Jeff and Johnny had a mug of tea. At dawn, yachts had begun moving out to their next destinations. Jeff was up at 0900 hours. From their present position they could see if Duet left the marina, but they could not see people joining or leaving her. Jeff went to the marina office to have a quiet word with the manager, explaining that they were carrying out an investigation and needed to relocate to a more advantageous position. He was given the choice of several berths, one of which he chose. They motored alongside and were able to see Duet more clearly. Polly was now up and about and by 1000 hours they'd breakfasted, washed the dishes and tidied Marie.

At about 1100 hours a visitor arrived at Duet, a stocky man about fifty years of age. He climbed aboard.

Ten minutes later the stocky man and Duet's crew climbed onto the pontoon and headed towards the marina exit. Jeff, Johnny and Polly followed. They walked across the marina car park. Jeff noticed a shiny black Range Rover with the letters CMA prominently displayed within the personalised number plate. Though they'd not walked towards the vehicle, Jeff suspected it belonged to Mr Hargreaves' good customer, Charley McAteer.

They took the paved coastal path leading from the marina to the town. As quite a lot of people were using the path walking in both directions there seemed no reason to appear inconspicuous, so they just remained well behind. The four men walked into the centre of Largs and paused, looking across the main street at what appeared to be a new stainless steel and glazed shop front. The stocky man and Mr Hargreaves seemed to be discussing its design. The name over the shop front was *McAteer Quality Footwear*. This must be Charley McAteer. The four men then walked into a hotel for lunch. As it was approaching lunchtime the pubs and hotels were becoming quite crowded.

Jeff and Johnny sat on a bench by the seafront from where they were able to see the hotel. Polly went to one of the many food outlets and returned with three soups in polystyrene cups, and three baguettes with meat and salad fillings. They consumed the food while sitting on the bench, looking at the hotel, and watching gannets, in the sound, diving for fish. Polly then returned to the shops and purchased fresh provisions for the next few days.

The four men left the hotel and strolled back to the marina. Charley McAteer drove off in his Range Rover. The remaining three returned to Duet.

Polly rang Jim Burton, and passed on the latest information. Jeff returned to the marina office and paid for a second night. This looked like being another evening and night of little activity, but it couldn't be helped. Duet's final destination had to be close by and they must be vigilant.

The remainder of the day was uneventful; they simply relaxed in the cockpit, as many others were doing, drinking tea and chatting about nothing in particular. Johnny made cheese omelettes from the ingredients in the galley and later they had a couple of cans of beer. They started the watch system again with Jeff and Johnny going below, leaving Polly to it. Johnny relieved Polly at midnight, and Jeff took over at 0400 hours. At 0800, when Polly was beginning to think of rising, activity on Duet commenced. The three men took breakfast in the cockpit. By 0900 hours Duet was slipping away from her pontoon berth, discreetly followed by Marie. Many vessels had been leaving the marina, some setting off for the day, to return later, others heading to new overnight destinations. Duet headed in the direction of the East Kyle of Bute, along with many other vessels whose crews were intent on seeing this most beautiful of cruising grounds.

Chapter 29

It had developed into a hot sunny day, with little wind and a flat calm sea. The Kyle had seemed a most civilised place to be. Many houses on the mainland and on Bute faced the tidal water, with shore frontages. Some had small boat houses as outbuildings to the main house.

Where the East and West Kyles meet there are several small islands called the Burnt Isles, which are used by cruising yachts to anchor overnight or to shelter from foul weather. At the Burnt Isles, Duet turned to starboard and entered Loch Riddon. This was an area Jeff had cruised before, he'd sailed into this loch, which held no real interest for cruising yachtsmen – unless they were seeking an anchorage – as it was very short, becomes shallow and leads nowhere, although it would be of interest to those wishing to simply take in the beautiful scenery. The surrounding forests extend to the water's edge and the branches of the thick vegetation dip into the water. A salmon farm had been developed in the loch's deep water. In the shallows, at the loch head, multitudes of heron feast on the loch's richness.

A timber landing stage had been built close to the loch head, which dried out at low water. Vessels sometimes pulled alongside. Duet headed towards the landing stage, and with Marie still pottering about at the loch entrance, she could be seen tying alongside.

This posed a dilemma for Jeff. It would be unlikely

that another yacht had tied alongside this landing stage while Duet had been there before, and to do so now could arouse sufficient suspicion for Mr Hargreaves to change his plans. To anchor at the Burnt Isles could result in them losing Duet and her crew, as they would have to trek through the forest back to the landing stage and this could take several hours. They could anchor at the Burnt Isles, and take the rubber dinghy with the outboard. Small boats around the salmon farm would not be thought suspicious, and at some point between the salmon farm and landing stage they'd be able to take the dinghy ashore and trek a short distance only, through the forest, by the water's edge. They decided upon this course of action.

It was about half tide. With the tide ebbing, Jeff anchored, ensuring there was sufficient chain to enable Marie to rise safely to the top of high water, with the anchor remaining firm in the kelp-covered bottom. The dinghy and outboard were prepared. Johnny made sandwiches and some provisions were put into a small bag and placed in the dinghy. Marie was secure. They set off wearing sailing jackets and lifejackets, and carefully picked their way along the shoreline, sometimes under a canopy of trees, avoiding branches overhead and in the water. Fifteen minutes later they'd passed between the shore and the salmon farm. Duet could be seen in the distance alongside the landing stage, and from the water level against her hull, Jeff could tell she was grounding out, and would have to stay in that position for at least six hours.

They turned off the engine, which was fixed to the

transom, and lifted the propeller out of the water then rowed the dinghy between a number of exposed rocks before bringing it onto a shingle shore beneath the tree line. They carried it up above the high water mark, clearly indicated by a line of dry seaweed, and tied it to a tree. They removed their lifejackets, and stowed them in the dinghy. Then they shared the provisions, storing them in their pockets, before commencing the trek through the virgin forest, hitherto untouched by man. Most people walked through a forest on a well-trodden path, but in the absence of a path each metre of travel seemed like fifty, with branches and roots interlocking. What appeared to be rhododendron bushes filled the gaps between the trees. The sun had never broken through the dense forest canopy. From the beginning of time water had gushed from the hills down frequent deep, narrow gorges to the loch, which they had to traverse. They came across many ant hills, which, Johnny was warned, were not to be sat upon. After about thirty minutes they came across a clearing, beyond which was a path leading along the periphery of the forest, by the shore, to the road and the landing stage which had become clearly visible.

Duet's propeller had become wholly exposed above the ebbing water level. They re-entered the tree line and continued to progress in a clockwise direction until they'd reached a position by the side of the road, which led to the landing stage where they were able to look at Duet's stern. To have gone any closer could have resulted in possible exposure, so they remained in the forest and watched, not sure if any or all of the three men were still aboard.

'You know, pet, I'm bursting for a pee.'

'There's no shortage of trees to hide behind, Polly.'

'It's okay for you and Johnny, it's easy for you to have a pee, it's more complicated for me, and them ant hills frighten the life out of me.'

'There's no ant hills around here, it's too close to the road, you can see how people have trodden the ground down.'

'Are you sure?'

'Course I'm sure.'

'I'll just go behind that big tree then.'

'Isn't it funny, Jeff, when someone says they want a pee, everyone else starts to want one?'

'It is, Johnny, suddenly I'm bursting.'

After having had a pee they decided to have the sandwiches and cold drinks they'd brought, using dirty hands, while waiting and watching until something happened.

This was not one of the usual tourist routes as it had been so quiet. Only occasionally had a vehicle driven along the road to the landing stage, when people got out, walked to the end of the structure, looked up and down the loch, returned to their cars then drove away. This was a dead end lane, a road to nowhere.

Although it was still early evening, the sun had set below the tops of the steep forest-covered hills. Dusk came early to this loch and the drop in temperature could be felt. Hands and feet were beginning to feel cold; lightweight sailing shoes didn't offer much protection to feet on evenings like this. Noses felt cold and breath could be seen. This was an evening for the rubbing of hands and the stamping of feet, when bodies needed to move to keep warm. Darkness had descended, and though it would probably be a moonlit night, they'd resigned themselves to being up and in the area until at least dawn. It would be too dangerous trekking through a virgin forest in the dark, with the possibility of falling and breaking limbs.

Suddenly, in the distance, the lights of a vehicle heading down the lane could be seen shining through the trees. It would dip into a hollow and be hidden, then the lights would shine high into the sky as it was climbing before eventually lighting the trees as it became level. From behind the tree cover the engine could be heard, then a black Range Rover arrived at the landing stage with the letters CMA contained in the registration. Charlie McAteer got out, accompanied by a large, broad-shouldered man, and walked to Duet. They climbed down from the landing stage and entered the cabin. Ten minutes passed then the five men climbed onto the landing stage with three valises, carrying them to the car, opening the tailgate and putting them inside. The men got into the car. The driver executed a three-point turn and drove up the road, but only for a short distance; then the brake lights came on. Jeff, Johnny and Polly came out of the forest and walked along the road, not feeling a bit cold. The vehicle had turned right and was heading along a track. Its lights could be seen between the trees, slowly threading through the forest, disappearing into the blackness.

Charley McAteer had been the youngest of six children, brought up by his parents in a rough area of Glasgow. His father had worked on the docks and was a drunk and a bully. On pay day, after spending half his wages in the pub and on the horses, he went home, gave his wife a small amount to spend on food for the family and a good hiding. This was Charley McAteer's world. A world of ne'er-do-wells, of bullies and thugs, of parents who had no care for their children's education. A man whose mother hadn't bothered to give him breakfast before he'd left for school in the morning. 'Light me a fag', she'd say, and at the age of six he'd become adept at lighting a woodbine from a match or a lighted taper from the fire.

But young Charley had a cruel streak. More cruel than most. It became noticeable when he was six or seven and could light a fag and play with fire without burning his fingers. It started gently, no different than any other boy really. He'd catch a spider or fly in a cleaned out jam jar, and screw the lid back on, then he'd watch it to see what happened. Sometimes he'd leave them to die quietly, other times he'd put them out in the sun so that the jam jar acted as a non-ventilated greenhouse and watch the contents suffer in the slowly increasing temperature. Then he started to turn the jam jars upside down and heat the lid with a lighted stick from the fire, and watch the suffering. This amused Charley. He then progressed to catching moths and butterflies, and would light one of his mother's cigarettes, slowly burning holes through their wings, with the glowing end, then delight in watching them try to fly.

The cruelty then extended to catching mice and birds. Mice would have their tails cut off, and birds some feathers plucked out, before being forced to suffer a slow and painful burning death at the hands of Charley McAteer.

His friends hadn't done these things. It was at this time that other boys started to fear him; they knew he was different. They didn't mind so much that he tortured spiders, moths and butterflies. As the contents of jam jars and moths and butterflies could be dropped on the ground and trodden into the earth with a shoe, any signs of the pain suffered mixed with the earth. But when he started to torture mice and birds, the pain suffered was visible for all to see, as Charley would carry the small, burnt and mutilated bodies around in his pocket for a few days and frighten his friends with them, until the creatures became rancid and were thrown in the bin or the river. It was at this time Charley began to enjoy putting fear into people. Then something happened that made his friends truly terrified of Charley. He had reached the age of twelve and was becoming muscular and strong. A black and white cat was minding its own business, sitting on a wall, and Charley caught it. He took it by the tail, swung it around several times and smashed its head against the wall, killing it instantly. Any bravado within the group of boys immediately disappeared, and they became quiet and subdued. Charley was the only boy not to wince. The other boys slowly deserted him. After all, this was serious. This had been someone's pet cat, just like their own. Like the pussy cats they had at home who'd sit on their laps purring. Like the pussy cats that rubbed against their legs with a vertical tail when wanting to be fed. This was the time when the boys in the neighbourhood gave Charley a new name: Killer.

Throughout his childhood he'd been able to skive off from school whenever he'd chosen, nobody cared. As he grew older, and became a teenager, he developed muscles and was thick set and tough, like his dad. He belonged to gangs who made life hell for the more respectable people in the neighbourhood. Woe-be-tide anyone who crossed Charley McAteer. He'd been no pushover, he became a ruthless adversary, no quarter was given. If an opponent went down, the boot went in, in the mouth, in the head, in the groin. When you went down you stayed down, well and truly bloodied. Charley was one who'd really been educated at the school of hard knocks. Some boys latched onto Charley. Boys who felt good and protected, mixing with someone with a cruel and tough reputation. But these acquaintances didn't last long. There'd be no sincerity. They would soon get on the wrong side of Charley and the relationships often ended violently. When he became old enough to go into pubs and visit dance halls, where the latest pop music was played, some girls found his reputation as a hard man strangely attractive. He had no difficulty in finding girls to end the night with, girls who'd allow him to have his way with them. While he liked sex with his women – or girls as they usually were – he had no respect for them. If a woman were to cross him he'd hit her in the face with his fist as he would

217

with any man. Many a woman still bore the scars of her brief encounter with Charley.

At the age of eighteen, in an effort to earn money legitimately, he became a street trader, and started to specialise in boots, shoes and slippers. Other traders selling similar goods at street markets where Charley traded were soon intimidated and frightened off. It was said that he killed a man in a frenzied attack while walking home from the pub, but this was only hearsay. It was said the body had looked as if a truck had hit it. Nobody dared grass on Charley; after all, he may have got seven years. Then you'd be a corpse. He then moved into a covered market and used the same bully boy tactics to frighten off other footwear traders, until eventually, at the age of thirty, he leased a shop and never looked back. He'd buy high volume at low prices and sell at top rates to nice, middle-class ladies and gentlemen.

As Charley matured he mellowed a little. He always felt a sense of loathing when he looked in the mirror first thing in the morning, in an unshaven dishevelled state, and saw his hated dad looking back at him. This was one of the reasons he always made sure he was clean shaven and wore smart clothes. Something his dad never did. He tried to be as unlike his dad as possible. But Charley knew the similarities. He became a pillar of society with a wife he'd married twenty five years ago, a wife he'd never beaten, and a son and daughter who had little respect for him. He lived in a fine, spacious, detached house in a leafy Glasgow suburb and owned several flats, which he leased out. He had a villa in

Spain and a holiday home by the loch. He'd become a member of the golf club and had taken up helicopter flying lessons.

The Range Rover arrived at a house. The five men got out with the three valises, entered, and made their way to the dining room. Charley poured four tumblers of whisky. The fifth man, Jimmy Tay, Charley's full time minder and occasional chauffeur, being teetotal. They sat around the dining table, unlaced the valises, carefully removed and placed their contents in the middle of the table. The used bank notes had been counted and bundled into wads of five thousand pounds. Charley had the means to turn this into legitimate gains and deposit it into offshore accounts belonging to individual syndicate members.

Jeff, Johnny and Polly walked along the road to the bottom of the track. There was no gate. But a small weathered sign said *Private*. They began to walk along the concrete covered track, which had been cast with furrows in its surface to aid traction. There was thick vegetation to both sides, ideal for shelter should headlights be seen. The trees either side of the track sometimes joined together, overhead, to form a tunnel. When this happened the dark beneath the canopy became as black as the hobs of hell, making it impossible to see the ground being walked upon. The track dipped and curved. At its end they came across a clearing of level ground, a lawn and stoned drive leading to a substantial three-storey house, built from local stone, with dormers, and a slate roof. The corners of the front elevation comprised circular bay windows with conical turret roofs. The Range Rover was parked by the centrally located front entrance. The house was in darkness apart from the ground floor right-hand bay window.

They moved in an anti-clockwise direction, keeping to the edge of the forest which joined the lawn under the overhanging canopy, until they had positioned themselves where they were slightly behind the lighted bay window. A chink of light could be seen through the drawn curtains.

It was agreed that Johnny and Polly would remain in the shadow of the trees, and Jeff would stealthily approach the lighted window. He removed his conspicuous sailing jacket and proceeded to silently walk across the lawn in his dark blue Guernsey sweater, jeans and dark blue woollen bob hat, blending nicely into the darkness. Fortunately, the gravel surface to the drive finished at the front of the bay window, enabling him to walk wholly on the grass. Jeff was out in the open, walking across the middle of the lawn, when he heard a sound. He stopped. He was immediately hit on the back of his shoulders. When he turned around Polly was standing there holding her nose that she'd hurt when she'd walked into his shoulder blade.

'What are you doing? You stupid woman!'

'Don't you call me stupid.'

'What the bloody hell are you doing? You're supposed to be in the bushes with Johnny. Can't you understand instructions?'

'What gives you the right to go around issuing

instructions? I don't work for you.'

'Will you keep your voice down? You daft bat.'

'You're the one making all the noise. I just thought I'd come along and keep you company. Can you see my glasses?'

'What glasses?'

'I dropped them when you bumped into me. Don't stand on them.'

'Bloody hell, Polly.'

From the bushes Johnny had seen the commotion on the lawn with both Jeff and Polly on their hands and knees, carefully caressing the surface of the grass. They were taking ages so he decided to take off his jacket. He hung the three waterproof jackets over a tree and, in his dark attire, set out to join them in the middle of the lawn. When he arrived, Jeff noticed his shoes and looked up.

'God give me strength. What are you doing?'

'I wondered what all the fuss was about. I thought you may need some help.'

'This daft bat has dropped her glasses.'

'No she's not.'

'What are you talking about?'

'They're stuck to the wool on the back of your jumper.'

'Don't move, pet. I'll get them off.'

'Now. Will you both go back?'

'I'm coming with you. So you can like it or lump it.'

'Bloody hell, Polly. Don't walk into me again.'

'It wasn't my fault you stopped walking.'

'Polly. Shut up.'

Johnny returned to the cover of the bushes. Jeff and Polly continued across the lawn and arrived at the lighted window, beneath the gap in the curtains. As there had been several steps between the ground level and floor level, the sill height was above Jeff's head and higher than he thought, with nothing to grip on, to lift his body up and peer in.

'You'll just have to lift me up, pet.'

Polly put her finger tips on the sill and Jeff lifted her.

She was able to focus one eye through the slit between the curtains. The men were sitting around a large dining room table and drinking whisky. Hargreaves and McAteer were smoking cigars. The opened valises rested at the end of the table, their contents having been piled in the middle. There were stacks of what appeared to be twenty and fifty pound notes. The five men looked content and relaxed with their bounty. Jeff lowered Polly down and she described the scene.

'Are you going to arrest them?'

'No, Polly. If they knew we were here they'd kill us and throw us to the fish.'

'Bloody hell, pet. I think we should be going.'

They carefully and silently made their way back across the lawn to where Johnny was waiting with the jackets. They put on their jackets then returned along the forest track to the safety of the dense forest by the landing stage.

Having had a couple more drinks and cigars, Charley and Jimmy Tay went to the cellar, where the drugs were kept cool and fresh. They then returned with three more pre-packed valises. Apart from doing business with John Hargreaves, Charley used various suppliers of footwear from around the world and was able to include discreet amounts of drugs among his imports. Not too much, not too greedy, just enough to keep the wolf from the door. He'd always been able to trust the syndicate members, as they were aware of his reputation, and would not dare cheat on him.

At about 0300 hours the Range Rover lights could be seen through the trees, descending upon the forest track, and arriving at Duet. Lights were turned off, the five men got out, and took the three valises onto Duet. Charley and friend got back into the vehicle, turned around, and drove off. They passed the track leading to the house and continued straight up the road, presumably to Glasgow with the money. Duet's cabin lights went on then off.

'Do you think they've got central heating in that boat, pet?'

'They most certainly will have,' said Jeff.

'Do you think they'd mind if I asked them for a little warm?'

'Can I come, Polly?' said Johnny.

'I wish you two would stop acting stupid.'

At 0500 hours it had become sufficiently light for them to carefully pick their way back through the forest. The dinghy was a welcome sight. Jeff untied the painter from the tree. They carried it to the water's edge and launched. Polly climbed in then Johnny, each of them getting their feet wet, followed by Jeff. The engine was started and they returned beneath the tree line, between the shore and the salmon farm and eventually arrived at Marie.

Polly made tea and toast while Jeff and Johnny stowed the outboard and dinghy. From the chart Jeff was able to give Polly the approximate co-ordinates of the house that she could pass onto Jim Burton later. Polly said she felt wide awake so she'd stay on watch while the men got their beauty sleep.

Chapter 30

Polly still felt wide awake when Jeff got up at eleven. She'd been watching the comings and goings of various yachts sailing in and out of the anchorage. No yachts had sailed in or out of Loch Riddon while she'd been on watch. Using her mobile phone she'd been able to pass on the latest information to Jim Burton, who'd been communicating with his colleagues on the Isle of Man and in Scotland. They'd been able to establish ownership of the vehicles delivering the valises and had mounted surveillance operations, which Jim Burton had co-ordinated. Polly went below. Johnny was up at about twelve.

The day had been relaxed and warm, with hardly a ripple on the water. Many yachts had passed the Burnt Isles, all under engine power. A few ventured into Loch Riddon, completing their exploration of the area. They'd probably anchored at the head of the loch, taken lunch in the cockpit, surrounded by nature's beauty, before continuing on their way.

It was about 1500 hours when Duet slowly emerged under engine and proceeded along the West Kyle. Jeff and Johnny waited awhile and followed about two miles behind. There was much activity in the Kyle, with people water skiing and jet skiing. In spite of the lack of wind others were dinghy sailing and sail boarding. Many small boats contained rod fishermen, and the ever-hungry gannets were out in flocks, hunting.

They motored along the full length of the Kyle and crossed over to Arran. Duet turned to port and entered Lochranza, before anchoring in deep water, along with many other vessels. Then Marie arrived. As Marie had a shallow draft she was able to motor into shallow water by the ruins of the castle and anchor. The noise of the anchor chain running over the steel stem head fitting woke Polly, who again reprimanded them for not waking her. She was ignored.

Jeff had seen Mr Hargreaves and friends, in the distance, preparing the dinghy to go ashore. Probably to sample some of the array of single malt whiskies displayed in their optics behind the bar of the pub overlooking the anchorage. Jeff prepared the dinghy. Johnny was transfixed by seagulls picking up shellfish and dropping them onto rocks to split them open and devour their contents.

Polly had been in the galley complaining about sailing with a shower of selfish tosspots who only think of themselves. She arrived with three mugs of tea and digestive biscuits. The dinghy was launched and tied astern. They sat in the cockpit drinking tea and eating biscuits. Johnny had been surprised at how quickly seagulls took over. Within a few seconds several were perched on the inflation tubes of the dinghy, squawking and watching them eat their biscuits. Jeff said not to encourage them, so Polly threw them a couple of biscuits. More arrived and landed on Marie. Jeff called her a dopey get. So she threw them a couple more.

They decided not to go to the pub, but to go ashore and take a walk along the road by the water's edge through the village, up to the small car ferry that came from the Kintyre Peninsula. They took the dinghy and rowed ashore. Other yachts entered Lochranza, intent on an overnight stay. The anchorage was becoming crowded. While returning along the water's edge Polly noticed the pub did meals.

'Do you think that pub will do a takeaway, pet?'

'I would imagine they will if you ask,' said Jeff.

'What do you want?'

'Anything will do me, Polly.'

'How about you, Johnny?'

'Fish and chips for me, Polly.'

Twenty minutes later, with Jeff and Johnny sitting on boulders by the dinghy, Polly emerged from the pub surrounded by an aroma that made Johnny's mouth water.

'Them three tossers are well on the way to getting pissed,' said Polly. 'They won't be sailing tonight.'

They returned to Marie and sat in the cockpit, eating the best fish and chips Johnny had ever tasted. Surrounded by seagulls.

Even though they knew Duet would not be sailing until morning they decided to organise a watch system; Polly took the eight till midnight watch. She sat in the cockpit, surrounded by silence, which was occasionally broken by the occupants of dinghies returning to their yachts from the pub. Some had forgotten to take a torch and arrived at the wrong yacht. As sound travels well over water, the comments were hilarious. By 2300 hours the quietness was broken only by a single distant bagpipe. Polly was in heaven.

Jeff completed his watch from midnight until 0400 hours when Johnny took over. It was still dark. When dawn came something caught Johnny's eye. The dinghy had been tied astern of Marie overnight and in it was a young seal sleeping. Johnny thought he was seeing things at first, but remained perfectly still so as not to disturb it. He'd seen more of nature in the past few days than he'd seen in thirty-nine years on the planet. He'd found it agreeable. When Polly entered the cockpit, at about 0730 hours, the seal was still there. She thought it happened all the time but when she started talking it left with a plop. When it bobbed up again, out of the water, Johnny was sure it winked at him before leaving. Just wait till he told Jim and John!

By 0830 hours Jeff was up and they had breakfast in the cockpit. Jeff brought the dinghy aboard and stowed it in its locker. They noticed movement on Duet as they were bringing their dinghy aboard, preparing to leave. Duet left at about 0930 hours.

Along with other vessels which had been leaving the anchorage at that time, Marie motored out with Duet about two miles ahead. They would be returning to Portpatrick.

They continued under engine with the dramatic mountains of Arran, shrouded in mist, to port and the Kintyre Peninsula to starboard. Ailsa Craig came into view. With Arran astern there were fewer vessels to be seen. A few were heading towards the North Channel and a couple heading up the Clyde. It had turned out to be another hot, wind-free day with a smooth surface to the sea. Many seals popped up to watch them passing and lots of jellyfish were spotted. Numerous birds sat on the water and dived collectively, as if on command, as they approached.

'Have you got any fishing tackle, Jeff?'

'In the locker under your berth, Johnny. I'll get it.'

'My dad says fishing hooks are dangerous on yachts,' said Polly. 'You never know what might get hooked.'

'I've not been fishing since I was a boy,' said Johnny. 'And even then I never seemed to catch any.'

'I think it's cruel. How would you like a hook through your top lip?' said Polly.

'Fish don't feel pain,' said Jeff.

'If they don't feel pain, why do they fight to get off the hook?'

'They don't fight to get off the hook,' said Jeff, 'they just don't want to go in the direction you're pulling them.'

'Well don't come anywhere near me with those hooks.'

'Shut up, Polly.'

'Shall I get the first aid kit ready, pet?'

'Just ignore her, Johnny, we're going a bit too fast for fishing, we need to slow down.'

Jeff prepared a short boat rod, with a fixed spool reel and line, with a spinner at the end, to lure an unsuspecting mackerel. He slowed Marie to two knots and gave the tackle to Johnny who trailed it astern.

'You won't catch anything,' said Polly. 'I've seen it so often. The only thing you'll hook is yourselves.'

'Don't be a spoilsport,' said Jeff.

After about half an hour nothing had happened, other

than the fact that Duet was further away, so Jeff gave the engine a few more revs. Johnny's initial enthusiasm and concentration had begun to wane. He'd been spending more time looking forward than astern. They heard a plop in the water behind, and looked around to find the sky filled with a flock of gannets, one of which had Johnny's hook in its beak and was being towed behind Marie.

'Bloody hell, Jeff. It's taken the bleeding hook.'

'Reel in, quick. Don't let it fly off.'

The rod had bent double, the gannet seemed miles away, and was so strong. Johnny thought Marie was being towed backwards by the bird. Slowly but surely he managed to bring the bird closer to the stern and was amazed at the size of its wingspan and how vicious the beak seemed. Its eyes were sparkling, surrounded by beautiful spectacles of feathered markings. Jeff felt sorry for this proud hunter. It was fortunate the line had wrapped around the bird's wing and prevented it from taking off. It appeared that all the gannets in the area had come to see what was happening to one of their own, as the sky over Marie was black with them. Johnny brought it to the stern. Jeff grabbed its neck, which was so thick his hand would not close around it, and took out his sailor's knife. Johnny wondered if he was going to cut its head off. But he cut the line near the hook then carefully extracted the hook from its beak. Then he released the bird. The bird settled on the water, exhausted by its ordeal. Then it took off and headed towards the North Channel, to continue hunting, with its friends.

'I can't wait to see what you two tossers are going to do for an encore,' said Polly. 'You could have killed that bird.'

'Sorry, Polly.'

'I used to think that when I die, I'd like to come back as a gannet, but with tossers like you around I've changed my mind.'

'Don't change your mind, Polly, you'd love the freedom.'

'Aye, ar would, pet, and do you know that gannets have binocular vision and can see for miles?'

'Yes, Polly.'

'Do they close their eyes when they hit the water?' said Johnny.

'You know, pet, surprising as it seems, that's something I've never noticed.'

Johnny lost all interest in catching fish, so Jeff put the tackle away.

The distance between Duet and Marie had increased to about four miles. Jeff gave Marie full revs and began to make a steady six knots. Duet entered the North Channel. Arran had disappeared astern and Ailsa Craig would soon be hidden from view. Jeff had noticed before, when leaving the Clyde and entering the North Channel, a quietness descended upon a yacht. It was as if the crew knew they were leaving behind a place so stunningly beautiful, they would love to remain. But on entering the North Channel, feelings of disappointment were soon erased. When the sea state changes, the wind freshens, you find yourself able to unfurl the genoa, switch off the engine, and run before a fresh breeze down to Portpatrick and enter the harbour. This was what they had done, and they saw a valise being transferred from Duet to the Land Rover they'd seen before. They tied alongside a fishing vessel.

They had been unable to get signals for their mobile phones low down against the harbour wall, so Johnny and Polly climbed to the top of the quay. Polly reported to Jim Burton. Johnny reported to Sarah. Jeff made three mugs of tea and awaited their return.

'You know what I think, pet?'

'What do you think, Polly?'

'I think we should go out tonight and get sloshed.'

'We can't do that, Polly, we've got a job to finish.'

'The job's finished. According to Jim Burton it's done and dusted.'

'Well, we can go out for a drink. But we need to finish what we started out to do, which is to keep an eye on Mr Hargreaves and pals.'

This conversation had become music to Johnny's ears, who'd been quick to wash the dishes and put them away. They climbed the steel wall ladder and walked along the quay to the nearest pub, which had tables at the front, overlooking the harbour. They ordered three pints of the guest beer and sat outside. It wasn't long before Mr Hargreaves and friends decided to spend the evening in a similar manner, as they too entered the same pub and sat outside, just a few tables away. Mr Hargreaves smiled at Polly, who had looked at him, thinking he looked like a nice man. Mr Hargreaves and friends began drinking and were doing so at a fair rate. They were on their second pint before Johnny had finished his first. They seemed relaxed and jovial. Jeff noticed the more they drank, the noisier they became. But not in an offensive manner. Johnny arrived with the second round just before Mr Hargreaves ordered their third, and by the time Johnny had finished his second, they were on their fourth, and obviously feeling pleased with themselves. Mr Hargreaves began smoking a cigar. Jeff brought the third round of beers, and bumped into Mr Brown who was going for their fifth. By the time Jeff, Johnny and Polly had nearly finished their third pints, Mr Hargreaves and friends had consumed six and Julian Baker appeared quite drunk. Mr Hargreaves went back in the pub and returned with six large whiskies, two each, which they heartily consumed. When they got up to go it was evident that Mr Hargreaves and Mr Brown were unsteady on their feet. But Julian Baker could hardly stand. Jeff said it was going to be a pantomime watching them go down that ladder. So they watched the three men staggering to the ladder, with Julian Baker supported in the middle. Sometimes he'd scratched the toes of his shoes on the paving stones. At the ladder their problems began to multiply. Mr Brown got onto the ladder first and, with the top rung at about his eye level, he helped Julian to locate his foot on the first rung, while Mr Hargreaves held and guided Julian's shoulders to steady him. Julian appeared not to have a care in the world and stood on Mr Brown's head on several occasions, and on his fingers, while Mr Brown held on to Julian's ankles, doing his best to guide him. Slowly but not so surely the three men, all laughing and swearing, climbed down the ladder and landed on Duet. They sat at a table in the cockpit. Mr Hargreaves brought out a bottle of whisky and three tumblers.

'You know, pet, I don't think I want to get sloshed after all.'

Johnny bought another pint for Jeff and himself, Polly had a half, before they too negotiated the steel wall ladder, climbing across the fish-smelling vessel they'd tied against, and landed on Marie. Jeff set his alarm for six in the morning and they crashed out.

Chapter 31

Jeff's watch alarm sounded at 0600 hours. He got up, opened the main hatch and looked over to Duet. She was still there, berthed against the wall. Given the state they'd been in last night, he couldn't see her moving for quite a while. But he was up, and vessels had started entering and leaving, so he brewed a mug of tea and sat in the cockpit watching the activities developing around the quay. He stripped to the waist, took the bucket, which was always kept in the cockpit, and usually used for washing dishes, filled it with water from the harbour and had a wash. Washing in salt water, even though he'd used ordinary soap, which hadn't lathered well, made him feel as one with nature. He dried himself, cleaned his teeth, applied roll on under-arm deodorant, put on a clean rugby shirt and his old and comfortable Guernsey sweater. He was ready for the day.

While Jeff enjoyed sailing, it could also be very pleasant lying in a harbour, on a nice day, reading a book, drinking tea, having occasional meals and watching the world go by. Days like this could be very relaxing indeed and were just one of the many delights of cruising around the coasts.

Johnny and Polly were up at about 0800 hours. They brewed the tea and made the usual simple breakfast between them, then sat in the cockpit, with the sunny day warming their bodies.

Jeff checked the provisions and made a list of

additional requirements. Polly said she'd go to the shops as she wanted to send her mum and dad a postcard showing the harbour and tell them where she'd been, so off she went. Half an hour later she returned, stowed the provisions below and sat in the cockpit. Johnny washed and was happy to sit around all day.

'You know, pet, I feel like a right mucky pup. Are there any showers around here?'

'There's a pub over there, Polly. They have a couple of showers, and let sailors use them for a small fee.'

Polly set off again, up the wall ladder, with her bag of tricks, and disappeared into the pub.

Half an hour later she returned, looking as bright as a button, and changed into fresh clothes.

'That nice lady in the pub said I could wash my clothes in her sink.'

Polly went below, obtained the plastic peg bag and pegged her washing and towel around the boat to dry.

'Did you send a postcard to your parents?' said Jeff.

'I did. I told them I was spending a few days with a couple of tosspots.'

'Where do they live, Polly?'

'They live in North Shields.'

'That's bloody miles away,' said Johnny.

'Aye, it is. And another thing, if you thought them fish and chips were good on Arran, you want to try them in North Shields.'

'They can't be better than them, Polly,' said Johnny.

'I'll tell you. They travel for miles to sample North Shields fish and chips. And you know why? Because the best chippies are by the fish dock and everything's dead fresh. They as good as jump straight out of the water and into the frying pan.'

'Are you exaggerating?' said Jeff.

'No, ahm not, pet. And if you want to eat in, at a table, you'll have to queue. Every day's like the first of January outside Harrods.'

'Polly,' said Jeff. 'I think you're getting carried away.'

'No, ahm not. Go and see for yourselves. Are those three tossers still sleeping?'

'Looks like it, Polly.'

'I'll make us a cuppa.'

Polly returned with three mugs of tea and sat in the cockpit next to Jeff, with their backs to the quay. Johnny was on the other side facing the quay.

Polly looked at her toes, thinking she should have cut her nails, when a dog barked on the quay behind. She looked around to see a man holding a lead with a black and white border collie, tugging at it as it barked at them.

'Did you do something to that dog, Johnny?'

'Of course not.'

'You must have done something. 'Cos they don't normally do that for no reason.'

The man on the quay said, 'Sorry. He doesn't usually do this.' He pulled the dog away.

Jeff said, 'Johnny was bitten by a dog recently.'

'Were you, Johnny. Whereabouts?'

'In the dentist's.'

'No, Johnny. Where on your body?'

'It snapped at my finger and drew blood.'

'What sort of dog was it?'

'A labrador.'

'And what did you do to cause that?'

'Nothing.'

'Johnny. Labradors don't bite unless they're seriously provoked.'

'Well this one did.'

'You know, Johnny. We've had dogs and cats in our house since I was born, and never had any trouble.'

'Don't mention cats,' said Jeff.

'Why not?'

'Johnny was scratched by one.'

'Whereabouts?'

'On the leg,' said Johnny.

'No. Where were you when it happened?'

'Are you taking the piss, Polly?'

'Of course not. You know, our animals are teenagers now, that's very old in animal years, and they've been as good as gold.'

'What animals do you have?' said Jeff.

'They're my mum and dad's now. 'Cos I don't live at home. But we have a dog and two cats.'

'What are the cats called?' said Johnny.

'Andy and Pandy.'

'Andy and Pandy. Who thought of daft names like that?' said Johnny.

'I did.'

'Bloody hell. What's the dog called?' said Johnny.

'Jerome.'

'The poor bastard.'

'I think they're lovely names,' said Polly.

'Have you got any brothers or sisters?'

'I've got one sister.'

'What's her name?'

'Thecla.'

'Thecla? Bloody hell. Thecla, Andy, Pandy, Jerome and Polly. Your parents must have a bloody good sense of humour.'

'I don't know why you're so smug with a bloody stupid name like Johnny Johnston. Whoever gave you that name should have been put away for child abuse.'

'Do you realise,' said Jeff, 'Duet is preparing to leave.'

Julian Baker couldn't be seen. He'd remained below and was probably nursing a thundering great hangover. Mr Hargreaves and Mr Brown were releasing the mooring lines and were coiling them. The engine was ticking over with water pouring from the exhaust.

They quickly moved away from the quay and motored through the harbour entrance into the North Channel. Jeff checked the tide tables. It was not the best time to be leaving, as they'd have to punch the flood tide where it was strongest.

Polly released the mooring lines from the fishing vessel they'd tied alongside, they then motored out of the harbour. When they entered the channel and turned to port they experienced a moderate breeze from the starboard side. Ideal for a fast comfortable sail south. They motored well away from the harbour and set sail with Duet a few miles ahead.

Jeff suggested it was about time Johnny learnt how to be a helmsman, and sat him down on the starboard side, tiller in hand, and went through the rudimentary steps of maintaining a course, and setting sail to suit varying wind conditions. The compass confused Johnny, but Jeff said to just point the stem of Marie at Duet and everything would be fine, and he proceeded to do so. The stem seemed to swing from side to side as Johnny had a tendency to over correct with the tiller, making the situation worse. But when this over correcting had been pointed out to Johnny he developed a lighter touch on the tiller and was able to maintain a course. Jeff explained what a gybe was and said that should he involuntarily gybe Marie it could prove to be a disaster. This sharpened Johnny's concentration. Jeff said he or Polly would sit in the cockpit with Johnny until he'd got the hang of things. Johnny began to enjoy this new experience, looking at Duet, looking away, then counting seconds, before looking back again to see if he was still on course then correcting as necessary, finally repeating the process. As time went by the tiller became lighter in his hand, and eventually it seemed like a natural extension of himself. He was able to maintain a course for five, then ten, then twenty and thirty seconds, without looking. But he knew he must not get over confident, so he maintained his concentration.

Jeff and Polly had attended to the navigation and provided adequate food and refreshments. Johnny was amazed to find he'd been helming for over two hours, he'd become so content in doing what he was doing, it only seemed like minutes.

'Do you think, Jeff,' said Johnny, 'that if we put the auto helm on for a few hours I'd forget how to helm?'

'No, Johnny. It's just like riding a bike. Once you stop falling off, your technique improves along with experience, but you still have to concentrate and look where you're going, especially when other vessels are around.'

'I think I might buy a boat one day,' said Johnny.

'I wouldn't if I were you, pet. My dad says it's a mug's game, and he should know. He's had a boat for over thirty years. He says it's more expensive and time consuming than having kids. He says he'd have been able to retire by now had it not been for having had a boat all these years.'

'Why doesn't he sell it?' said Johnny.

'He's thought about it. Lots of times. He used to say he'd find it easier to put me up for adoption. So he just keeps paying the bills.'

They continued along the Galloway Peninsula. It was early evening by the time they passed the lighthouse perched on the headland, having kept about five miles offshore to avoid the turbulent inshore waters by the Mull. They changed course to take them towards Douglas, then introduced the watch system with Polly going below at 2000 hours. All was serene. As dusk closed in, the wind became light and eventually dropped off completely. The engine was started, the mainsail lowered and the genoa furled. Polly got up at midnight and Johnny went below. Duet contacted Douglas Harbour and entered. Marie had been motoring along on a flat calm sea and entered Douglas about an hour later. They picked up the same mooring they'd used before.

Duet had tied alongside the pontoon; her silhouette could be seen against the darkness of the harbour wall. It was a little before dawn. They went below and slept.

Chapter 32

Johnny was first up at about 0800 hours. He brewed a mug of tea and was sitting in the cockpit when Jeff popped his head through the companionway. Jeff noticed that Johnny had sat in a position towards the stern, with one hand on the tiller while drinking his tea. He had the impression that Johnny had quite enjoyed his stint on the helm, and was looking forward to having another go. Polly got up at about 0900 hours. They sat in the cockpit having the usual simple breakfast. Polly had spoken to Jim Burton who told her that their colleagues in Douglas had already advised him of Duet's arrival and they would contact him when Duet departed. Johnny had spoken to Sarah, letting her know all was well.

Jeff said he expected Duet would leave at about five in the evening or six in the morning, and it would be more likely to be in the morning, enabling them to take full advantage of the daylight hours. There was no activity on Duet. It turned out to be another pleasant warm day, with a few high clouds in an otherwise cloudless sky.

At about 1100 hours the blue Saab arrived. The man who'd been seen driving before got out, walked down the steps along the pontoon and climbed aboard Duet. Mr Hargreaves entered the cockpit, transferred a valise to the man who'd returned to the car, placed it in the boot and drove off.

Jeff inflated the dinghy and tied it astern. It would be available should they decide to go ashore. The afternoon was spent lounging around, sometimes resting below or sitting in the cockpit. Others were doing similar things, waiting to leave on the next leg of a passage, their bodies bathed in warm sunshine, able to easily drift in and out of sleep.

Mr Hargreaves and friends went ashore at about 1700 hours. Jeff, Johnny and Polly decided to follow, though they knew they were probably only going for a meal. They entered the same restaurant they'd visited a few days previous and sat at the same window table. Jeff, Johnny and Polly walked along the promenade, had fish and chips from polystyrene trays, returned to Marie and stowed the dinghy.

Polly took the first watch. Jeff and Johnny had gone below when Mr Hargreaves and friends returned. Johnny's watch was from midnight until 0400 hours. At 0400 Jeff arrived in the cockpit. Johnny went below.

Several yachts had requested permission to leave harbour, and at 0615 hours Marie's VHF came alive with Duet wanting to leave. Duet slipped away from her pontoon berth and disappeared behind the stone breakwater wall to complete the final leg of her passage. Jeff waited twenty minutes, obtained permission to leave, started the engine, released the mooring buoy and motored around the breakwater to see Duet in the distance. Her course was set to take her back to the Ribble. They were motoring at about four knots with no wind and a flat, calm sea. Polly was up at 0730 hours, and made breakfast for her and Jeff. With the auto helm doing the work, they were able to sit and relax in the warmth of the early morning sun. Johnny was up at about 0900. He made his breakfast and more tea for Jeff and Polly. The wind had freshened enabling Jeff to unfurl the genoa and turn off the engine. They were maintaining four knots. Jeff suggested that Johnny may like another stint on the helm. Johnny agreed and was happy and content with his new role pointing the bow in the direction of Duet. The only sounds to be heard were of water squishing along the hull and a ripple behind the rudder.

'You know, when I said I wanted to come back as a gannet,' said Polly, 'it got me thinking about death.'

'We all hope it will be later rather than sooner,' said Jeff.

'I know, pet. But you see, as my dad gets older he thinks more about his own funeral, in fact, he's become obsessed with it.'

'We're all going to die, Polly,' said Jeff. 'And I've not noticed death having any respect for youth. Is your dad unwell?'

'No. He's as fit as a fiddle. He just likes talking about his funeral.'

'What does your mum say?' said Johnny.

'She won't listen to him. She tells him not to be so stupid. And she'll decide what happens when he's gone.'

'If she won't listen, who does he mention it to?' said Jeff.

'Me and Thecla. He's always ringing us. Says he likes to keep in touch, and likes to know what we're doing, and likes to be helpful if possible. But we always end up talking about his funeral.'

'So what does Thecla say?' said Jeff.

'She says the sooner he snuffs it the better. We'll all have a holiday.'

'So why is he so concerned about his own funeral?' said Jeff.

'Well, the thing is this. He says that as a boy he was indoctrinated into religion, and no one gave him a choice. And as he's got older he's decided that he's not a religious person, in fact, he's become a non-believer. So he doesn't want to have a church service, as it would be like having lived a lie.'

'So what's the problem?' said Johnny.

'It's my mum. She comes from a very religious family, and she won't listen to him. 'Cos she's concerned at what relatives and friends will think if he doesn't have a church service.'

'So what do you think, Polly?' said Jeff.

'I agree with my dad. It's up to him. It's his funeral.'

'And what does Thecla think?' said Johnny.

'She doesn't give a toss. Well, she does really. But she says that as far as she's concerned we can throw him in the Tyne when he's gone.'

'So what does your dad want to happen?' said Jeff.

'Well, he says he's going to arrange his own funeral. Apparently, there's a place in North Shields that takes advance bookings, and he wants an environmentally friendly exit, with no fuss. And certainly no church service.'

'What does he mean by environmentally friendly?'

said Johnny.

'It's bizarre really. He doesn't want burying as he says land's too precious, and he doesn't think we should bury diseases underground. He would prefer cremation, but says what's the point in polluting the atmosphere with unnecessary smoke? He's found out that a company are going to introduce a deep freezing process. So cold that the body becomes brittle, and all diseases are killed off, then it can be crushed into dust and scattered on the earth to nourish it and help plant growth.'

'Bloody hell,' said Johnny. 'When it thaws won't it go all mushy?'

'I don't know. I don't think my dad's thought it through properly, and besides, he's only fifty-five.'

'Well,' said Jeff, 'I think that's a very commendable way for your dad to feel. He's obviously a man with high ideals, and they should be respected.'

'I know, pet. That's what I think. But mother says she hopes she goes first. 'Cos she couldn't stand the shame.'

'They could have another thirty years of life ahead of them,' said Jeff.

'I know they could. But he's started to say he thinks of death as a friend.'

'Bloody hell,' said Johnny. 'What does he mean?'

'Well. He says that only a friend would release a person from all their problems.'

'Polly,' said Jeff. 'Are you sure he's not just winding you up?'

'Well if he is he's doing a really good job. 'Cos mother's absolutely livid with him.'

'Marie, Marie, this is Pluto, Pluto, over.'

'Pluto, Pluto, this is Marie, Channel 77, over.'

'Channel 77.'

Jim Burton requested Marie's position and course.

Jeff provided the information in latitude and longitude and course in degrees true.

'Many thanks, Pluto out.'

From this information Jim Burton could locate them and intercept their track.

The wind backed to the south, continued backing and freshened further. Jeff hoisted the mainsail and slightly reefed the genoa. Marie was now heeled at between fifteen and twenty degrees and going like a train. As was Duet, four miles ahead. Johnny was still on the helm, feeling in control, and enjoying it.

At about 1500 hours, as the onshore breeze set in, and fair weather cumulus clouds were developing over Lancashire, two dots could be seen on the horizon. Jeff took a bearing with his hand-bearing compass. Two minutes later he took another and noted the same bearing. On a collision course. It was Jim Burton. The dots grew larger and developed shape. As they became closer white bow waves could be seen. Then, growing even larger, there was a deep throbbing of the powerful twin diesels. They went astern of Marie, their white wakes confusing the wave pattern on the sea's surface, and turned to port, banking over as they turned until they were on the same heading. As they slowed they settled lower in the water and motored towards Marie's starboard side. Jim Burton gave the thumbs up sign. With Marie heeled at twenty degrees and riding over waves, the launches were given full throttle and sped towards Duet.

Jeff altered course, trimmed the sails and headed towards the River Wyre. As the effects of the onshore breeze were felt, their speed increased to a steady six knots. Jeff thought Johnny had been stuck to the tiller with superglue, the only time he'd let it go was when he'd wanted a pee. About five miles offshore they were joined by a school of dolphins. They'd suddenly arrived, about twenty of them, made up of five or six families, with the male, female and youngsters of each family rising out of the water together as if holding flippers. Then they dived under Marie and rose with a swish of water on the other side. Johnny noticed how they looked at him with their left eyes then went under the boat and out again and looked at him with their right eyes, and they were so close. They'd probably taken time off from chasing salmon towards the Lune and Wyre, to have a bit of fun with humans. Two miles offshore the dolphins lost interest and left.

'My dad always said that when you are at sea, looking at cloud formations, you are uniquely privileged.'

'Bloody hell, Polly,' said Johnny.

'No, it's true. The thing is, no one else can see those clouds from the angle we can see them. It's not like being in a city when everyone can see the clouds from the same perspective.'

'Well. Go on, Polly,' said Jeff.

'Well. Because there's nobody else around for miles, apart from the dolphins. We are the only people on the planet able to see those clouds from this angle, so, we are uniquely privileged.'

'I completely agree with your dad,' said Jeff.

'When did your dad tell you this?' said Johnny.

'When I started to go sailing with him. When I was about nine. He told me that clouds are nature's moving sculptures in the sky.'

'Did Thecla go with you?' said Jeff.

'Sometimes, but she wasn't really interested. She liked doing things with mum. My favourite clouds have always been cumulus. I can look at them all day and not get bored. I like standing on hills overlooking farmland and watching them casting moving shadows over the land. And I like seeing them at sunset. 'Cos every sunset's different with clouds in the sky.'

Marie entered the River Wyre when it was getting close to high water. Johnny telephoned Sarah who said she would collect him at the marina. They sailed upriver. The herons and cormorants were in their usual locations. They furled the genoa, and lowered the mainsail, then motored into the marina and tied Marie alongside her pontoon berth.

Polly was quick to clean and tidy Marie, she'd packed her bags and was ready to leave.

'Well, I'll be seeing you then,' said Polly.

'What are you doing tomorrow?' said Jeff.

'I'll have to report to Jim Burton and find out what's happening.'

'Okay, Polly. Take care.'

'Will do. Bye. See you, Johnny.'

'Bye, Polly.'

Polly walked along the pontoon with her holdall slung from her shoulder. She walked up the ramp, out of the marina and across the car park to her flat.

Sarah rang Johnny to say she'd arrived at the marina entrance with the boys.

'Can the boys come and see your boat, Jeff?'

'Of course they can, Johnny.'

Johnny walked up to the marina security gate and pressed the button activating the gate-opening mechanism. They walked along the pontoons and arrived at Marie. Jeff noticed immediately that no one could have been more unlike Johnny than Sarah, who was small and petite. The boys towered above their mother and seemed to have inherited Johnny's height but their mother's slenderness, as they were both tall and thin. Though they were twins they were not identical as they had noticeably different facial features, but even a stranger would think they were brothers.

Johnny introduced Jeff to Sarah, and to Jim and John he introduced Jeff as Inspector Dewhurst. They were polite and said, 'Hello, sir.' Jeff invited Johnny to bring Sarah and the boys on board, and show them below while Jeff sat in the cockpit.

Jeff could hear Johnny telling Sarah and the boys where he'd slept, where he'd cooked, where he'd been to the toilet, where the fire extinguishers were, where the chart table was. He told them about the basking sharks, the seal in the dinghy, that he'd caught a gannet and seen dolphins. Sarah and the boys looked shocked when they returned to the cockpit. Johnny told them about the tiller and helming the boat for hours on end. Jeff decided that Johnny was able tell a good tale.

Jeff and Johnny agreed to meet at the station in the morning. Johnny took his holdall and pillow. The family said goodbye and walked along the pontoon, up the ramp and out of sight. Jeff brewed himself a mug of tea and sat in the cockpit in quiet contemplation. The ever present seagulls were floating astern waiting for scraps. He checked over his boat, removed some food that may go off, closed the sea cocks, isolated the battery, locked up and went home.

Chapter 33

Jeff had slept well, and risen early. He showered, shaved, and arrived at his office before eight o' clock. He took a coffee from the machine then went to see Superintendent Hird, who'd arrived early as usual, and was at his desk. Superintendent Hird advised Jeff of the progress made in rounding up the known members of the drugs syndicate in Scotland, on the Isle of Man and at sea. Duet had been escorted into the docks complex and thoroughly searched. Mr Hargreaves and friends had been detained in custody.

Charley McAteer had been apprehended at the airport while on his way to his holiday home in Spain and had turned violent. Superintendent Hird told Jeff that the drugs operation would be dealt with by Customs and uniformed police officers, and he could now concentrate his efforts on solving the murder of Harry Taylor. It had been agreed with Customs that the apprehension of Mrs Hargreaves, Tony Grimes and Alan Trotter would be left to Jeff because at the moment the murder investigation in Blackpool was of prime importance and they may be implicated.

When Jeff returned to his office Johnny had arrived. He was clean shaven and drinking coffee.

'Good morning, Johnny.'

'Good morning, Jeff.'

Jeff described his meeting with Superintendent Hird and told Johnny they now had to resume their efforts in solving Harry Taylor's murder.

'We need to consider events very carefully, Johnny. You see, I thought it was obvious the murderer was David Brown, the chemist. That fitted in neatly with the poisoning.'

'Have you changed your mind?'

'Well, I'm not certain anymore, we now have more players in the frame, several of whom could be the murderer.'

'So. What do we do?'

'When we spoke with Piggy he said Tony Grimes had a partner. We never asked who that partner was. Also, I said I thought Piggy and Mrs Hargreaves were brother and sister. We never established whether that assumption was correct.'

'Why would it matter?'

'Because, Johnny, I think a brother would do anything for a sister, and possibly her husband. Do you have a sister, Johnny?'

'I have two.'

'So?'

'I wouldn't commit murder for them.'

'No. But if your values were different. Say you had the mindset of Charley McAteer, or Piggy, or Doris, or Tony Grimes. And let's be fair, Piggy and Tony aren't the sharpest tools in the box.'

'I know they're not. But Piggy and Tony would never commit murder.'

'Who do you think Tony's partner is?'

'It'll be one of those muscle bound hulks.'

'You see, Johnny, the more I think of this, the more I

believe Doris Hargreaves to be a very greedy, very persuasive and very manipulative woman.'

'Jeff, I can't see any of them taking the life of another person. None of them are so evil.'

'I think, Johnny, from the little I know, Charley McAteer is the boss. And having seen him and his rotweiller minder, I think they are men for whom violence is second nature. I don't think any of the other players are violent by nature. But if Charley says it's Sunday, it's Sunday. And they dare not question his instructions.'

'I agree with that.'

'We also need to get one of our colleagues in Glasgow to track down the chemist who stood in for Mr Brown. Mr Brown's shop assistant will be able to help. And find out if what Mr Hargreaves said about Brown having to return to prepare prescriptions was correct. There will be records, prescriptions and signatures that can be checked.'

'So. What would you like me to do?'

'Johnny, we know the face of Harry Taylor's murderer. The trouble is, it's one of five or six. In a few days we'll have our man. I'm feeling good about this. I'll ring Glasgow, you get the coffees.'

'Coming up.'

When Johnny returned with the coffees, Jeff was on the telephone to Glasgow CID. The reputation of Charley McAteer was known to his colleague who thought he'd now gone straight. Jeff explained the drug involvement, the possible connection with the Blackpool murder, the need to investigate David Brown and particularly to seek out information about his relief chemist from the first to the fifteenth of July. His colleague said he would treat Jeff's request as urgent and get back to him as soon as possible. Jeff finished the conversation and put down the telephone.

'Right, Johnny. Your mate Piggy said he works out between ten and two at the True Grit Gym. We'll go to see him, and ask a couple more questions.'

Piggy's van, along with other vehicles, including Tony Grimes' motorbike, were in the True Grit Gym car park. It was about ten thirty when they entered the foyer. The smell of stale perspiration still pervaded the atmosphere. The reception desk was unmanned so they rang the push down brass bell perched on its surface. Tony popped his head around the door of a small office to the rear of reception. His moustache seemed longer and darker than before. He was dressed in a tight white tee shirt, enhancing the muscles of his upper body, and blue denim jeans.

'Good morning, Mr Grimes. You remember us? I'm Detective Inspector Dewhurst and this is my colleague Detective Constable Johnston.'

'Course I remember you.'

'Would you let Mr Trotter know we'd like another word with him?'

'I've not seen him today.'

'Well, his van's in your car park.'

'He must be here somewhere then. Know wha' ar mean?'

'We know what you mean, Mr Grimes. May we go through to the gymnasium?'

'Course you can, it's a bit quiet at the moment. Know wha' ar mean?'

'Thank you, Mr Grimes.'

They walked through the double swing doors leading into the gymnasium. Three men were manipulating the various contraptions. Piggy was on a treadmill with his back to them. His stocky, short, slightly bandy legs were walking at a pace a man of his stature should never walk at.

Jeff observed Piggy's thighs and thought he would be unable to bring his knees together unless he sat down. His neck and ears were red, his tee shirt perspiration stained and riding up his body above his lycra shorts, revealing fleshy protrusions above the sides of the waistband, and the bottom of a tattoo at the base of his spine.

'Good morning, Mr Trotter.'

Piggy couldn't look round with the treadmill operating for fear of falling off. He switched the off button and the machine slowly came to a stop, enabling him to turn his body and look at them. He looked slightly stunned at seeing them and took a moment before recognising them.

'Hello.'

'Hello, Mr Trotter. Do you think we could have another word with you?'

'If you like.'

'We like, Mr Trotter. Could we go into the lounge?'

They walked towards the lounge. Piggy had his towel wrapped around his shoulders, wiping his face and neck as they went. They sat at a circular table designed for four persons, with Jeff facing Piggy. Johnny sat at the side.

'Tell me, Mr Trotter. Does the name Harry Taylor mean anything to you?'

'I don't fink so. Why, should it?'

'Well. It either does or it doesn't. Have you heard the name before?'

Jeff noticed a thick vein on Piggy's temple beginning to pulsate more quickly, and the thick flesh covering his Adam's apple could not hide the fact he was gulping as his mouth became dry through nervousness.

'No.'

'Never?'

'Never,' said Piggy.

When we last met, you said Mr Grimes had a partner. Who's his partner?'

'My sister.'

'And who's your sister, Mr Trotter?'

'Our Doris.'

'Doris who, Mr Trotter?'

'Doris Hargreaves.'

'Are you able to remember what you did on the second and third of July?'

'Just the usual.'

'And what's the usual?'

'Working out in the day, and being a bouncer at night.'

'You didn't do anything out of the ordinary?'

'I don't fink so.'

'Thank you, Mr Trotter. That will be all.'

Piggy looked relieved. When he got up to go, Jeff

noticed his shoulders were a little slumped as he walked back to the gymnasium.

Jeff and Johnny walked back to the foyer. Tony was sitting behind the reception desk.

'Could we have a word in private, Mr Grimes?'

'Come in the office.'

They entered the office behind reception. It had a desk, a computer, two filing cabinets and three chairs, one behind the desk and two in the opposite corners of the room. Tony sat behind the desk, Jeff and Johnny brought the other chairs and sat facing Tony.

'Mr Grimes, it seems unusual that Mrs Hargreaves should be your partner. How did you become associated?'

'Two years ago I didn't do any bouncing and the bank were on to me for money. Know wha' ar mean? So. 'Cos Piggy's me mate, Doris helped me out. She said she'd help me as long as we hired out bouncers.'

'So, how did you advertise your services?'

'Doris had some cards printed, and she went round to all the big clubs and pubs, and saw the owners. And in no time at all, I was in the black at the bank.'

'Who prepares your accounts for submission to the Inland Revenue?'

'Doris does that and deals with the accountants. I deal with the day to day running of the business. Know wha' ar mean?'

'Does the name Harry Taylor mean anything to you?'

Tony's moustache seemed to droop at the corners and his previously taut stomach seemed to expand behind the desk. He now looked more beaten than upbeat.

'Is he one of our clients?'

'No, he's dead.'

'I've never heard of him.'

'Are you able to cast your mind back to Thursday the second and Friday the third of July? And tell me if you did anything out of the ordinary on those days?'

'Such as?'

'You have a motorbike?'

'Yes.'

'Did you follow a taxi from Frampton Marina to Upridge, then from Upridge to Blackpool?'

Tony's hand took on a slight shake, his moustache seemed to droop further and he started to blink his right eye.

'No.'

'Thank you, Mr Grimes. That will be all.'

They left the gymnasium and crossed the car park to Jeff's car.

'Well, Johnny. Those two certainly had some involvement in Harry Taylor's death. I've never seen two people become so dejected so quickly.'

'I still think the chemist is our man.'

'You could be right, Johnny. They could have followed Harry Taylor to the Bantrys and passed on the information to David Brown.'

'But David Brown met Mr Hargreaves in Holyhead.'

'We only have Mr Hargreaves' word, and besides, he could have easily travelled from Blackpool. Or, he could be lying, they could have met at Douglas or Portpatrick.'

'Why did they go to Holyhead?'

'I suppose that trip was the first they'd made to collect the drugs, so they'd chosen to introduce confusion and provide an alibi should they be questioned later.'

'Unless they had business in Holyhead?'

'You mean a fourth valise, Johnny?'

'Could be.'

'Interesting. We'll mention that to Jim Burton. I think it's time we visited Doris Hargreaves.'

Chapter 34

It was getting close to lunchtime when they arrived at Skidmore. The double garage door had been left open revealing the silver Mercedes and Range Rover. Jeff parked his car, they walked up to the oak front entrance door and pressed the brass doorbell several times before deciding to walk around the rear towards the log cabin and hot tub from where music could be heard. Mrs Hargreaves was sunning herself, sitting on a reclining seat which, along with a table, had been sited on the paved patio between the house and log cabin. She was eating a sandwich and drinking a glass of white wine.

'It's you two, is it? If you want John, he's not here.'

'We know, Mrs Hargreaves.'

'Well, what do you want then?'

'It's you we'd like to speak with, Mrs Hargreaves, about your business dealings.'

'I know nothing about business. It's John you'll have to talk to, he should be back in a couple of days.'

'He won't be coming back for a while, Mrs Hargreaves.'

'What are you talking about, you stupid man?'

'He's in custody, Mrs Hargreaves, for drugs trafficking.'

'John! Drugs trafficking? Never.'

'You know all about drugs trafficking, Mrs Hargreaves, and the house in Upridge. Which, incidentally, is being searched.'

'I know nothing about John's business dealings. Never have, never will.'

'The thing is, Mrs Hargreaves, we've been watching you, along with Customs, and we've recorded your activities.'

'Rubbish.'

'We know how the drugs get to Upridge. And we know you distribute them to various Blackpool nightclubs, using your brother Alan and Tony Grimes as couriers. We also know drugs are passed on to the public by people using the name Frances as a password.'

Doris became quiet and withdrawn and didn't respond, realising her back was against the wall, not knowing which direction to take. But her mind was racing. She had to prove she was an innocent party, afraid to disobey orders for fear of her life and had to do exactly as she was told. She could do this, after all she was an expert at deception. She and John had deceived all their lives and two retarded coppers weren't going to get the better of her.

'I'm afraid I don't know what you're talking about.'

'But Mrs Hargreaves. Detective Constable Johnston and I aren't here to discuss the drug operation. We are investigating the murder of Harry Taylor.'

'I told you before. I don't know any Harry Taylor.'

'Yes, you did. But Mr Hargreaves knew him, as did Mr Brown and Mr Baker. And Tony Grimes and your brother Alan knew of him.'

'You've spoken to Alan?'

'Of course we have. He's our prime suspect.'

'How can you be so stupid? Alan would never do anything like that.'

'I beg to differ, Mrs Hargreaves. If you allow me to read between the lines, Harry Taylor was to sail Duet to Scotland, but when the purpose of the mission was explained to him, he pulled out. The syndicate then decided that Harry knew too much and if he were to remain alive could prove to be a liability. It was decided he had to be snuffed out and Alan was told to do the dirty deed. How am I doing, Mrs Hargreaves?'

'I don't think, Inspector, you have any evidence to connect Alan to Harry Taylor's death. In fact, I think you're grasping at straws.'

'Very well, Mrs Hargreaves. I shouldn't bother leaving the house today. Customs will be along shortly and you'll notice a police presence in the lane.'

Jeff and Johnny returned to the car and headed back towards Blackpool.

'You know, Jeff, Harry Taylor must have known there was a serious risk of being killed to have booked into Mrs Bantry's using a different name.'

'He most certainly did.'

'Why didn't he just go to the police?'

'We don't know what was said on Duet. He could have been told he would be killed if he went to the police.'

'But he was killed anyway.'

'I know. But when he went home to change his clothes, he wouldn't have known of any connection between Hargreaves, Piggy, Tony and Blackpool. It was unfortunate so many cards were stacked against him, otherwise, he could have paled into the background and become just another holidaymaker.'

'You know my boys were talking about your boat all last night, Jeff?'

'Tell them I'll take them sailing, Johnny.'

'Would you?'

'Course I will. All boys of that age love sailing, especially if they happen to see some wildlife, and get a few dollops of salt water in the face.'

'I'll tell them. They'll be dead chuffed.'

'I think we'll have our man tomorrow, Johnny. Tony and Piggy are worried. Doris is hard, but she's worried, 'cos she won't have her little brother going down for murder. And she knows more than she's letting on.'

'And now, Jeff, you're going to tell me we're going to worry Julian Baker?'

'Somehow, I don't think Julian Baker has murder on his mind.'

They dropped into the Frampton Marina cafe on their way to interview Julian Baker and had soup and rolls for lunch. They then continued through Blackpool along the coast road and on to Fleetwood Police Station where Messrs Hargreaves, Brown and Baker had been provided with accommodation for the night.

Jim Burton was interviewing David Brown. Jeff interrupted the interview for a quick word with Jim who had interviewed Julian Baker earlier in the morning and had found him to be an honest interviewee, resigned to the fact that he'd be facing a term in prison for his activities, whereas Mr Brown was proving difficult, as had been expected. Jim was planning to commence interviewing John Hargreaves at about 3.00pm.

A room was prepared and Julian Baker was brought in. Jeff instructed the officer accompanying Julian to wait outside.

Julian was clean shaven and, in spite of his problems, looked to have slept well. His eyes were bright and clear, his face and arms were tanned.

'Mr Baker. I'm Detective Inspector Dewhurst and this is my colleague, Detective Constable Johnston.'

'Inspector. I've told Mr Burton all I know about this matter.'

'I believe so, Mr Baker. But we're conducting a different investigation. We're interested in the murder of Harry Taylor.'

'I heard about that, such a tragedy, but how can I possibly help?'

'What we would like to know is what happened on Duet the night before you left for Holyhead and before Harry Taylor returned to his boat?'

'Well, I can't help you with that.'

'Why not?'

'Because, Inspector, my mind was numbed with whisky and I was sleeping it off.'

'How did you become involved with this business?'

'If I told you, you wouldn't believe how stupid a so-called intelligent man can be.'

'Try me, Mr Baker.'

'I suppose, Inspector, it started just after Penny and I were married. Being married to a solicitor, Penny became an aggressive social climber. She wanted us to be seen to be successful. But her idea of success was to flaunt material wealth. I would have liked us to have had children, but she wouldn't have her good looks and slim body bloated by pregnancy. She became envious of others and always wanted the best. The best house, best cars, best holidays, and always socialised with people wealthier than ourselves.'

'Why didn't you do something about it?'

'I should have done, but I never did. This put a great deal of financial pressure on me as my salary couldn't cope with constant expenditure. It was Penny's idea to start our own practice, which proved to be a good move as many of my previous clients stayed with me, and I was able to charge fees instead of receiving a salary. But there was no way of satisfying her greed. No sooner were we feeling a little more financially secure, then we had to have a larger house in a more prestigious area, which we couldn't afford. Then I started to drink. Just a little at first, but I soon became a regular drinker, every evening, then it was a quick vodka in the morning before leaving for the office. Then I began to lose a few clients. The cars aren't paid for, and the house is mortgaged to the hilt.'

'Did Mrs Baker have a career?'

'She was a solicitor's clerk. That's how we met. Anyway, money was getting very tight, so one night at the golf club I was telling John Hargreaves how I was experiencing a few cash flow problems. He said he could help, providing I was discreet and prepared to take a few chances. He had a word with Charley McAteer. You see, it was all to do with having various methods of transporting the drugs. John thought that if we used several people, which by now included me, and different modes of transportation, then no one would be any the wiser.'

'What other methods did you use, Mr Baker?'

'We used cars and vans, but we thought no one would suspect a yacht in the middle of summer, doing what yachts normally do. But we were wrong.'

'You were, Mr Baker.'

'But you know, Inspector, I was awake last night, just thinking. And I'm glad we've been caught. No more deception. I've always found it difficult to deal with deception. Penny will certainly divorce me and I won't be able to practise as a solicitor again. But I'll have what I've always wanted, a simple life, free from greed. There's lots of ways I'll be able to earn enough money to satisfy my simple needs. And you know, even now I feel as if a load has been lifted from my shoulders and I can breathe more easily. Suddenly the future looks happier and brighter than it's looked for years.'

'I hope you're right, Mr Baker.'

'Getting back to your original question, Inspector, I only met Harry Taylor a couple of times. He showed John and me how to sail a ketch, as neither of us had done so before. Harry was a perfectionist, very exacting in all he did. When I climbed aboard Duet, the day before leaving for Holyhead, I'd already had a couple of vodkas and I remember Harry coming aboard. Harry didn't drink much, but John had the whisky bottle out, and as we weren't leaving until morning, I made the most of it, and to my shame, became completely drunk. By mid-afternoon I had to go below and sleep it off and never heard a thing until John woke me saying to get prepared as we were leaving in an hour.'

'Very well, Mr Baker, I'll have the constable return you to your cell.'

'You know, Inspector, my father was a very honest man. He only ever wanted what he himself had worked for, and always did what he knew to be correct. He wouldn't cheat a soul, not even the Inland Revenue. His tax returns would always stand scrutiny. It's a good thing he died when he did, because had he known what I'd become, the disappointment would have killed him.'

'Thank you, Mr Baker.'

As Mr Baker was explaining how he'd become involved with greed and drugs, and remained childless, Johnny was making a mental comparison between Mr Baker and his wife and Sarah and himself. While more money would always have been welcome in the Johnston household, lack of material wealth, having to budget, and only buying what they could afford, had never seemed a problem. Sarah had controlled expenditure, and money was always available for holidays. Johnny had always been able to afford to go out for a few pints. The boys were well looked after and had an interesting, active life. They'd always been encouraged to participate in sports, swimming and fishing, and anything else they wanted to do, though not much encouragement was needed, and they'd always done well at school.

Johnny could not understand this presumption that material wealth can buy happiness. In fact, he was thinking that material acquisitions at the expense of common sense seemed to buy misery. And this business of social climbing, what a load of bollocks, and envying the possessions of others, what a load of crap. And yet, to have a lifestyle that couldn't be afforded seemed to make the Bakers feel superior. Mr Baker's father seemed to have possessed sound values and, probably, Mr Baker could have been the same and remained a respected solicitor with moderate desires. It didn't wash with Johnny that Mr Baker's wife's greed was the problem. He could have been more firm had he wished, he'd probably allowed himself to be manipulated by his wife, but only because he wanted to, and he felt good about having a grand house and driving a top of the range car.

'So, what do you think, Jeff?'

'You know, Johnny, I've seen it so often, when people start to envy others, there's just no end to it. They envy the possessions and lifestyle. They don't envy the other person's limp, or bald head, or dandruff, or acne, or false teeth, or bad breath, they ignore these things and just envy the bits they choose, instead of just being themselves. It's a load of crap.'

'That's what I was thinking.'

'And another thing, Johnny. These people who envy others, think you and I envy them. It's the same with people who are dishonest, they think everyone else is dishonest.'

They returned along the coast to Regent Road, collected a message to contact their colleagues in Glasgow, and were informed that Mr Brown's shop assistant and locum had been contacted. The locum had relieved Mr Brown for two weeks from the last day in June, and was serving a further two weeks at present.

'So that's it then, Jeff. Do we question him?'

'I'm not so sure, Johnny.'

'Why the doubt?'

'Harry Taylor would not have quietly climbed those stairs at Mrs Bantry's with David Brown behind him. Nor could David Brown have carried Harry up the stairs as he wouldn't have had the strength.'

'So?'

'Tony Grimes or Piggy would have had the strength to easily carry Harry up the stairs, with him drugged, undress him, put him into bed, then inject him to finish the job.'

'Bloody hell.'

'Let's call it a day, Johnny, and sleep on it. We'll meet in the morning and decide who to bring in.'

'Jim and John said the tide will be right to go fishing from the sea wall tonight. I said I'd go with them if I got home in time.'

'The tide will be right, enjoy yourself, see you in the morning.'

Jeff decided to make a phone call.

'Polly, it's Jeff.'

'Hello, pet.'

'What are you doing tonight?'

'I'm probably going to get soaked through on that boat of yours.'

'It looks like a good evening for a sail. What time can you be ready?'

'About an hour.'

'See you at the boat.'

'Bye.'

Chapter 35

Jeff went home and changed into his old sailing clothes. This always made him feel as if he had an extra spring in his step, especially when he put his sailing shoes onto his sockless feet. He had a quick sandwich and a cup of tea before heading to the marina. Polly had arrived early and was sitting in Marie's cockpit when Jeff arrived.

The tide was flooding upriver, many yachts were being prepared for an evening sail. People had finished work early to take advantage of these near perfect sailing conditions. The blue sky over the sea was cloudless. Small cumulus clouds had developed over the land and were being driven by a fresh onshore breeze.

They quickly slipped away from their pontoon berth and entered the river, punching the tide under engine only. The usual herons, cormorants, and fishermen were concentrating on the next meal. They passed over the sand bar, Polly hoisting the mainsail then unfurled the genoa. They were close hauled on a starboard tack, heeled at an angle of thirty degrees, heading into the sun, with the sunlit sails looking whiter than white and sunlit sparkling spray washing over the foredeck and occasionally across the coach roof, saturating their faces.

Many other yachts were out, their crews luxuriating in the fresh evening warmth. They continued for about an hour then went about onto a port tack. After about another hour, and with the shore line about seven miles astern, they came about, and ran before the fresh breeze back into the Wyre, entering the marina and tied alongside their pontoon berth.

They decided to have a pint in the sailing club before leaving. Jeff brought the drinks to the table and told Polly he'd agreed to take Johnny's sons sailing. Polly invited herself along, asking what would happen if someone fell overboard. It would be wiser and safer to have two people aboard who could sail.

Polly knew quite a lot about the relationship between Messrs McAteer, Hargreaves, Brown and Baker. Jeff explained to her about the relationship between Doris Hargreaves, Piggy and Tony Grimes. He advised Polly that David Brown could not have been the murderer, as he thought he was not physically able, and it was either muscle-bound Piggy or Tony, carrying out orders.

Polly sat back in her seat, sipped from her pint and paused awhile, looking at Jeff.

'You know, Jeff. You're a living, breathing example of what I think most men are.'

'And what's that?'

'Blind to reality.'

'How do you mean?'

'You've no idea, have you?'

'About what?'

'About the relationship between men and women.'

'Enlighten me.'

'You're engrossed in your work, and when you're not thinking about that, you're engrossed in boats and sailing, and don't think much about anything else.'

'I'm happy that way.'

'I know you are. But that's why you're blind to reality. And Johnny's just as blind 'cos he's engrossed in his own life. Men are just that way. My dad's the same, he doesn't even know the names of his neighbours.'

'Well go on, clever clogs.'

'Do you think Doris Hargreaves is an attractive woman?'

'I suppose she is.'

'And you'd say she's manipulative?'

'In my opinion, yes.'

'The thing is, Jeff, you and Johnny, and my dad, and other men, only see things from the male perspective.'

'We're men, for Heaven's sake. What do you expect?'

'Precisely. And you're also easy going and gentlemanly. You would never force anyone to act against their will, because you would not know how to be manipulative.'

'So? I don't want to be manipulative.'

'But if you were able to look at it from the female perspective you would consider that Harry Taylor climbed those stairs quietly because he thought he was going to bed with Doris Hargreaves.'

'That is not what happened. Harry Taylor was a happily married man, Polly. He wasn't the type to go with other women.'

'See what I mean by being blind to reality? Think about it, Jeff. Wife away, no one knows him, seduced by an attractive woman, resistance weakened by a little drug and a little alcohol. He wouldn't stand a chance, and Doris Hargreaves being what she is, she would know. Because Doris has been manipulating her husband for years. Just as Julian Baker has been manipulated by his wife. Once Doris made contact, Harry would be putty in her hands and she would make sure he acted against his natural inclinations, because Doris is naturally manipulative.'

'Bloody hell, Polly.'

'Another pint, Jeff?'

'Please, Polly.'

Polly returned with the drinks and sat down.

'You could be right, Polly.'

'There's no could about it, pet. If Jim Burton were here he'd agree with me and explain, graphically, why Doris would do this, then you'd be convinced. You know Jim's a psychologist?'

'I do, Polly.'

'Well, cheer up, you miserable old sod. You'd have got there eventually. But, tonight, you've solved the murder of Harry Taylor.'

'It's one thing me thinking I know. It's another thing proving it.'

'Let me tell you something else, Jeff, which you blind to reality men never think of.'

'Bloody hell, Polly. There's no stopping you when you get the bit between your teeth.'

'It doesn't seem to matter to a man that he shared the same womb as his sister, but it matters to the sister. You ask your sister. You say Piggy is the prime suspect, Doris would not allow him to go down for a crime she'd committed.'

Chapter 36

Johnny arrived home earlier than Sarah and the boys had expected. Sarah had planned to take the boys fishing from the sea wall between Blackpool and Fleetwood and was surprised that Johnny was so early. She prepared something for Johnny to eat, and sandwiches and coffee for the evening. They set off as a family unit, including fishing tackle and a picnic, in the Ford Escort. Julian Baker's comments earlier in the day had made Johnny realise what a truly fortunate man he'd become, having Sarah and the boys in this closely knit family. His mother and father and sisters lived close by and were always in contact. Johnny was feeling particularly secure and cheerful this evening. In fact, he thought he may have a few pints later. Besides, they would be arresting someone tomorrow: Piggy, Tony, or whoever, for Harry Taylor's murder.

They parked close to the sea wall and began to prepare the fishing tackle. Jim and John were capable of preparing their own rods, reels, hooks and bait, and were more than able to tie knots, including the fisherman's bend. But Johnny, who was totally incapable of tying any knot, had to interfere and participate fully, even though he hadn't a clue when it came to anything of a practical nature. Jim and John were used to their dad's interference and Sarah, in an effort to avoid any form of confrontation, and wishing to ensure the boys had a satisfying time, suggested to

Johnny that as it was such a pleasant evening it would be nice to take a walk along the promenade.

The boys were pleased to see their mum and dad leaving them in peace. Johnny and Sarah decided to walk towards Fleetwood for a while, then return, giving the boys and themselves a little space and time to enjoy themselves. Sarah was linking Johnny as they walked along the promenade by the sea wall. There was a continuous line of rod fishermen for as far as the eye could see, each pursuing his chosen pastime, each hoping for a first class fish supper tonight, or lunch tomorrow. Several small open boats were either anchored or drifting a little offshore, filled with rod fishermen. It being the mackerel season, anything could happen, from catching nothing to a boatload.

Yachts were sailing out of the River Wyre. From this distance they all looked the same, but Johnny thought one in particular looked like Marie, and he pointed her out to Sarah. She was beating hard on a starboard tack, but Johnny didn't know this.

They eventually strolled back to the boys, who'd had about three hours' fishing and caught a dozen mackerel, which Sarah would prepare and cook over the next few days. Johnny remembered Julian Baker and his wife again and thought about the poor bastards and their shite priorities.

The loving lovely family unit returned home, not thinking they were any different from any other family unit, and, of course, they were not. The boys and Sarah filleted the mackerel, while Johnny, in a loving, tranquil state of mind, at peace with himself and the rest of the world, pleased with his relationship with Jeff and Polly, and delighted he hadn't noticed his fear of deep water, went to his local for a pleasant pint or four, and a good lashing of bar room banter, where he had every intention of putting the world to rights.

Chapter 37

Jeff drove into work hardly believing this good weather had held for so long. He arrived at his office to find Johnny ready and waiting to go. Johnny went to the machine and returned with two coffees. They sat down to discuss the case.

'I saw Polly last night, Johnny.'

'Oh?'

'She said that when I take Jim and John sailing she'll come along, just in case I fall overboard, then she'll be able to sail the boat.'

'That's the first sensible thing that girl's ever said.'

'We also discussed the case, Johnny.'

'And did she start talking about her dad's funeral?'

'No. She was very serious for once.'

'Did she not make any daft suggestions?'

'I'm not sure her understanding of events is implausible. In fact, she may be right.'

'So. What did she have to say?'

'Well. First of all she says that you and I are wrong to look at the case from a solely male perspective.'

'What the bloody hell does she expect?'

'I explained about Doris and Piggy being brother and sister and about Tony being Doris's business partner. And after a few minutes Polly concluded that Doris was the murderer.'

'She's a right dopey get.'

'Well. The more I think about it, the more I think it's

Doris.'

'It can't be Doris. How would she get Harry up the stairs?'

'Polly reckons that Harry quietly climbed the stairs with Doris behind him, because Doris had seduced him into thinking she was going to spend the night with him.'

'Harry wasn't the type.'

'That's what I said. But if you're slightly drugged, slightly drunk, and an attractive, sexy Doris is throwing herself at you, what man could resist?'

'I know one man who couldn't.'

'Precisely.'

'So?'

'Polly suggested that Doris would not let Piggy go down for something she'd done. And we've already told Doris that Piggy is our prime suspect.'

'I'm suddenly thinking Polly's not so dopey after all.'

'You'd be right to think that way. I think we should bring Piggy in. Tony's bound to let Doris know, then we'll pop around and see Doris later.'

'Piggy should be at the gym at about ten.'

'That's what I thought. Another coffee, Johnny?'

'Why not?'

They arrived at the True Grit Gym at about ten thirty. Piggy's white van, along with other vehicles and Tony's motorbike, were in the car park. They were greeted on entering the building by the usual aroma of stale perspiration and deodorant. Tony was not so cheerful on greeting them, and seemed to cast his eyes downwards when asked where they could find Mr Trotter. He said that Piggy was in the gym, exercising on the treadmill. So Detective Inspector Dewhurst and Detective Constable Johnston went to speak with Piggy.

Piggy was getting into his stride and walking at a good pace, his chubby thighs rubbing together. DC Johnston, to Piggy's surprise, switched the machine off.

'What the fuck?'

'Good morning, Mr Trotter.'

'It's you again, can't you leave me alone?'

'We don't intend to leave you alone for a long time, Mr Trotter. Would you kindly get dressed and come down to the station with us?'

'What for?'

'We want to talk with you about the murder of Harry Taylor.'

'I hope you don't fink I did that?'

'We have our suspicions, Mr Trotter, which we'll discuss at the station.'

'Alwight. But I'll be a few minutes.'

'We can wait, Mr Trotter.'

Tony was hovering around, watching what was happening, but generally keeping his eyes cast downwards. When Piggy came out of the changing rooms, they handcuffed his hands behind him. He didn't say a word, and offered no resistance. With Tony looking on they escorted Piggy to the car and helped him into the back seat. Johnny sat next to Piggy and Jeff drove off, back to Regent Road. On arriving at the station Piggy was shown to a cell and his handcuffs released.

'Mr Trotter. Would you like a cup of tea?' said Jeff.

'I've not had any bwekfast this morning.'

'Would you like us to bring you a bacon and egg roll and a mug of tea?'

'Yes, please.'

'Would you like brown sauce?'

'Please.'

Jeff gave Johnny a ten pound note.

'Constable Johnston, would you kindly go out and purchase a large bacon and egg roll with brown sauce for Mr Trotter? And I'll brew him a nice strong mug of tea.'

'Nothing would delight me more, sir.'

'Fank you, you're vewy kind.'

'Our pleasure, Mr Trotter. Do you take sugar?'

'Two, please.'

They returned with the bacon roll and mug of tea, telling Piggy to make himself at home and relax as it would be a few hours before they could interview him.

Chapter 38

They took their time driving to Skidmore and arrived about one thirty. The garage door was closed. They parked on the drive, walked up to the front door and pressed the brass doorbell. The door was answered immediately by Doris who was clean and tidy, though without make-up, and not having taken trouble with her hair, looked older than they had seen her. She was first to speak.

'Come in.'

'Thank you, Mrs Hargreaves.'

'You know it's not Alan, don't you?'

'It could be, Mrs Hargreaves.'

'It could be, but it's not, and you know it.'

'Enlighten us, Mrs Hargreaves. Constable Johnston will take notes as we speak.'

'It was the first Friday of the month.'

'Hang on, Mrs Hargreaves. I have my suspicions. But, could you start the day before Duet was to leave the marina?'

'Well, John always liked to be up early, so I dropped him at the marina at about eight in the morning, not expecting to hear from him for about ten days or so. I don't know how Julian got there, I expect Penny dropped him off. David Brown would have come down by train, he's not keen on flying, but I don't know what time he arrived. Sometime in the early hours of the following morning, John rang to say he'd spoken to

Charley McAteer. And Charley was furious that this fella Harry had pulled out, and we had to do something about it quickly. John wanted Harry there to make sure the boat and everything was alright and offered him five grand, but Harry refused when he found out what John was doing.

'I then got another phone call to tell me what had been decided between Charley and John. John had rung Alan and Tony, and told them to keep an eye on Harry and find out where he went and what he did. David Brown had left the boat and was going to sort Harry out. So, I thought that was that.

'David Brown kept in touch with Alan and Tony and they reported back to him. When it was found he'd booked into a guest house in Blackpool, Charley rang to say that David Brown was coming to see me at my house, bringing with him a tablet and syringe. He was going to show me what to do. Charley said I had the charm to succeed, and if I didn't succeed, he'd make sure the charm was removed. I didn't ask him what he meant, but I knew better than to refuse one of Charley's requests.

'David brought the tablet and syringe on the Friday morning, and showed me what to do, saying the tablet would make Harry compliant. Alan and Tony had been keeping an eye on Harry, and he'd gone to this quiet pub for a few drinks on Thursday night. They thought he may do the same on Friday. So, I prepared myself to be charming, but I knew he wouldn't be impressed with too much jewellery and make-up so I toned it down a bit. I was driving into Blackpool when Tony rang to say that Harry had gone out to the same pub again. Tony met me at the pub and pointed Harry out.

'He was sat on a barstool having a pint. I stood close by him and ordered a drink. I told him I was waiting for a friend and couldn't understand why she was so late, saying I hoped she wouldn't be delayed too long. He wasn't talkative, I asked him if he was local or down here on holiday. He said he was here for a few days only. So, I chatted to him. I'm good at getting people talking.

'I offered to buy him a drink, but I knew he'd refuse and insist on buying me one. Gentlemen always do. We had a few more drinks. Then I dropped the tablet in his drink. He suddenly became agreeable and smiling, and as David Brown said, he became compliant ...

'It was getting late, so I suggested we go to his place. He didn't object, nor did he appear drunk. We went to this guest house, the place was in darkness, but the staircase was lit with dim lights. We quietly climbed the stairs, and entered his room. I told him to undress and get into bed, which he did. As soon as his head hit the pillow, he forgot all about me. I took the syringe from my handbag and did exactly what David Brown said, Harry didn't even flinch. I put the syringe back into my bag and removed his personal belongings, as Charley had told me to. I turned off the light and left the room, went down the stairs, out into the street, back to my car and home.'

'What did you do with Mr Taylor's possessions?'

'I cut his wallet and cards into small pieces, smashed his watch with a hammer and put them in the bin, for collection. They'll be well and truly buried in a landfill site by now.'

'Okay, Mrs Hargreaves, we'll need to go to the police station, prepare a statement and ask you to sign it.'

'Will you release Alan?'

'Of course we will, Mrs Hargreaves, but he will face other charges later.'

'He's my only living blood relative, he's not very bright but I love him to pieces.'

'I'm sure he feels the same way about you, Mrs Hargreaves.'

'He does, poor thing.'

They returned to the station with Mrs Hargreaves. They then charged her with the murder of Harry Taylor, cautioned her and prepared the statement, which she signed. Then they released Piggy.

'Well, Johnny, that's that. I think we should take the weekend off and take statements from Hargreaves and friends next week. They won't be going anywhere. And we'll need to go and see Mrs Taylor.'

'Suits me, Jeff.'

'What about Jim and John? Would they like to come sailing tomorrow?'

'They'd love to.'

'Okay. Bring them to the marina about nine in the morning. As a matter of fact, if they like, they can sleep over on the boat. All boys love sleeping on boats, it's a little adventure.'

'I know it is, I've just had one.'

'If they want to sleep over, tell them to bring pillows. I'll let Polly know.'

287

'See you in the morning, Jeff.'

'Okay, Johnny. I hope they don't snore as much as you.'

'They're worse.'

Chapter 39

Jeff rang Polly to say he'd be going home to get changed then to the marina to spend the weekend on the boat. He said he'd be going to the sailing club later for a few pints, and that Jim and John would be arriving in the morning. Polly invited herself along, as he knew she would, and they met at the boat at 1900 hours. Jeff had bought provisions on the way, which he stowed aboard. Seagulls always seemed to know when food was being placed onboard.

They walked up the pontoon ramp and entered the sailing club. Jeff ordered a couple of pints and sandwiches. Then he explained the day's events to Polly, and said he never thought the bond between Doris and Piggy would be so strong given that intellectually they were like chalk and cheese.

Jeff no longer noticed the tuft of hair sticking out above Polly's left ear. They had a couple more pints and returned to Marie. As it was a warm night they decided to leave the washboards out for ventilation. Polly took the quarter berth under the cockpit seating, and Jeff his usual settee berth.

'Did I tell you, pet? My dad's just bought himself a second hand tandem.'

'No, Polly, you didn't. Goodnight.'

'He's bought it from this man he knows, whose wife's just died.'

'Goodnight, Polly.'

'He's going to her funeral next week.'

'Goodnight, Polly.'

'I'll tell you all about it tomorrow.'

'Goodnight, Polly.'

'Goodnight, pet.'

Jeff and Polly were up early, they showered at the sailing club then breakfasted on the usual grapefruit and cereal, followed by mugs of tea. Just before nine, the Johnston family walked along the pontoon and arrived at Marie. Johnny was carrying two pillows, Sarah had two waterproof jackets draped over her left forearm, Jim and John were each carrying a small holdall and dressed in tee shirts, jeans and trainers. They greeted each other and Sarah was introduced to Polly.

'Hello, I'm Polly, boys. Which one of you is Jim?'

'Hello, Pollyboys,' they said simultaneously. 'I'm Jim.'

'You can stop that now,' snarled Sarah, 'otherwise we go straight home.'

'I'm Jim,' said Jim.

'I'm John,' said John.

'Well, that's sorted that out. I'm Jeff, and this is Polly. Are you two going to climb aboard, or shall we go without you?'

Jim and John climbed aboard. Jeff showed them their bunks in the forecabin, showed them how to operate the toilet, and fitted them with lifejackets and harnesses, showing them how to clip onto the harness points in the cockpit. Polly was talking to Johnny and Sarah when they returned to the cockpit. Sarah kissed the boys, telling them to behave themselves. Johnny and Sarah waited on the pontoon while Polly released the mooring lines and brought in the fenders. They continued to stand there watching Marie leave the marina.

Jeff was well aware that introducing someone to sailing had to be done sensitively. To simply dash out into a seaway, with the boat heeled and surrounded by waves can be off-putting and frightening, especially on the first occasion, and they may never want to go again.

So, instead of heading for open water, he turned and headed upriver, with the young flood, as Uncle Harry would have said. It is reassuring, in people's early days of sailing, to be close to land, to be able to see people fishing from the banks or walking dogs. It enables the first time sailor to become accustomed to the boat's motion, the sound of the hull passing through the water, the sound of the engine and the noise made by sails and winches when coming about.

Jeff quickly had the boys helming under engine only, then under sail, and kept them fully occupied throughout. They were obviously enjoying the experience. Polly spoilt them with drinks and biscuits. Time passed quickly. At a little before high water Jeff said they'd go out to sea and sail along the coast, keeping a few miles offshore. They crossed the sand bar and set a course for the Ribble Estuary, with Jim and John taking turns on the helm. They passed familiar landmarks along the coast they'd never before seen from seaward. Jim and John remained interested throughout and seemed more mature than when they'd arrived at the marina a few hours earlier.

Marie was gently heeled at about ten degrees, the

only sound being the lapping of water against her hull. Jim and John were quick to pick up the techniques of helming, and though Blackpool would have been bustling at this time of day, not a sound could be heard from this distance. The trams could be seen, and the Pleasure Beach rides were in full flow, the screams of people enjoying the rides could only be imagined.

Jeff asked the boys if they'd like to fish for a while and they said they would. They anchored about two hours before low water. Polly told them to be careful with those hooks. They caught a few mackerel, which were returned to the water. As the tide turned, the fishing tackle was put away. They had a meal, which Polly had prepared, then began sailing back to the Wyre.

The onshore breeze had set in and they were able to sail close hauled on a port tack, taking them further from the coast. Marie had become alive, and was heeled at an angle of thirty degrees, with spray washing the foredeck and coach roof, and sometimes saturating Jim and John, which they relished. Jeff was keeping an eye on the boys to make sure they were still enjoying the experience, and they obviously were. They continued for several hours. Then, with the Wyre about eight miles off the starboard quarter, they went about and ran for home.

Many other vessels were out. Most were sailboats astern of Marie, with their multi-coloured spinnakers aglow in the light of the setting sun. They entered the Wyre and tied alongside the pontoon berth at about 2100 hours.

Jeff suggested they should finish the evening at the sailing club. They walked along the pontoon and entered the club. When asked what they would like to drink the boys said, simultaneously, 'a pint of bitter.' Jeff looked at them sternly; they both said, 'a lemonade, please, Jeff.' As it was Saturday evening the sailing club was crowded, so they sat on the balcony overlooking the marina. The boys noticed how Jeff kept glancing at Marie. Many of Jeff's friends came to join the company and have a chat. The boys were introduced to Jeff's friends as Jim and John, and Jeff's friends were introduced by their Christian names, even though some of them were ancient. Some wore sailing smocks, some wore blue Guernsey sweaters, some had bare arms with tattoos, some had beards, some were smoking pipes, and all had red faces. They were all cheerful and laughing. Polly was enjoying the conversations and seemed to know lots of people. Jim and John felt comfortable surrounded by these happy, laughing, talkative people.

The boys returned to Marie with their new found friends, Jeff and Polly. Jeff and Polly took their usual bunks, the boys bedded down in the forecabin. Their faces felt as red as those of Jeff's friends. As they closed their eyes, they each saw the multi-coloured spinnakers aglow in the light of the setting sun. And eventually they fell asleep.